RIPPA!

P.J. LAVERTY

RIPPA!

A FOOTBALL NOVEL

P.J. LAVERTY

First published in 2024 by Popcorn Press,
an imprint of Fair Play Publishing
PO Box 4101, Balgowlah Heights, NSW 2093, Australia
www.popcornpress.com.au

ISBN: 978-1-925914-33-7
ISBN: 978-1-925914-34-4 (ePub)
© P.J. Laverty 2024

Cover design and typesetting by Ana Sečivanović

All inquiries should be made to the Publisher via sales@fairplaypublishing.com.au

Chapter 1

ENGLISH GLAMOUR SIDE HEAD FOR THE LAND DOWN UNDER

By George Kostas

Soccer Week

November 9, 1988

Soccer stars Liam Brady, Alvin Martin, and Frank McAvennie will fly to Australia this January as West Ham United take on a Western Australia XI as part of a mid-season break.

With the East Londoners languishing in the Division One relegation zone, long-serving manager Bobby Noll has opted to take advantage of a two-week fixture gap and fly his struggling side overseas to recharge and regroup. However, he insists it's not a holiday.

'The boys will be working hard, never you mind,' Noll told reporters. 'The weather is predictably turgid that time of year in the deepest East End. We'll get far more graft done in the sand and the sun. Honest.'

The announcement has raised eyebrows from some Hammers' fans who have questioned the worth of a 24,000-mile round-trip at this stage of what has been a disappointing season, but Noll defended the decision.

'Airborne for two whole days with a disgruntled bunch of lads in a cramped, confined space? I can't think of anything better to bring us together as a unit. Nothing at all. And as for jet lag, I've heard it's an exaggerated thing that scientists have found no proof of. Though maybe I'm confusing that with the hole in the ozone layer.'

This will be the first time West Ham has visited Australia in their 93-year history and with their array of international stars set to appear, it is a fixture which will capture the imagination of the local sporting public.

Chairman of the Australian Soccer Federation, Tony Lanzarote, welcomed the showpiece.

'We've played host to some great clubs throughout the years, and they don't come much greater than West Ham United. I mean, of course they do, they're 19th in the table for God's sake, but to get someone — to get anyone *— down here when the Euro leagues are in full swing is a coup-and-a-half, and I should be congratulated. Particularly as my contract is up for renewal,' he said unsmilingly.*

'It's also going to provide our local players with some valuable experience to give their careers the boot up the jacksie which every one of them needs. Mamma mia, if the likes of Craig Johnston can swindle their way into a Liverpool shirt and win a European Cup then there's even hope for my nonna, and she's 93 next month.'

Asked if he would be on the lookout for local talent, West Ham boss Bobby Noll was less enthused.

'Dunno about that, guv. Apart from that permed ponce Johnston I don't know any Aussie players who could cut it in Old Blighty without a racquet or a nine-iron. Or a dish rag. Wait a minute, I quite like the cut of the jib of that big fella with the 'tache and the beer belly. Huh, you mean he's a cricketer? Scrub that then. Nope, you got nothing for us. But I've heard your pub gardens — sorry, your training facilities *— are second to none.'*

The friendly will be played on Saturday, January 7, under the lights at the WACA, and the criminally overpriced tickets are on sale now.

Chapter 2

Joey Rippa gazed up at the navy blue and white chequered Tottenham Hotspur flag adorning his wall. It was the one he'd bought with his holiday money when his mother took him to White Hart Lane. Back when he saw Spurs play in that FA Cup tie against minnows Exeter City on their way to winning the thing back in '81. Rippa remembered the stars on show that day. Ossie Ardiles with his lightning flicks and turns. The silky, effortless movement of Glenn Hoddle pulling strings in the middle of the park. And the touch and tenacity of Steve Archibald leading the line.

Now no longer a kid at 19, Rippa thought hard about that trip. He remembered Buckingham Palace and those big red buses where you could sit up top, and how hot chips came with every meal, sometimes even breakfast. You didn't get much news about football this far away, here in Australia, though. Not in Perth, the most isolated city on the planet, and certainly not where he resided, 300 kilometres north of it. He wondered what happened to all those players and if Spurs had won anything since. And he also wondered, as he did nearly every morning when he woke, what had happened to his mother.

Rippa felt the pleasant sea breeze waft through the flyscreen and caress his lightly stubbled jawline. Awake as he'd ever be, he noticed his surfboard next to the flag and smiled. Then he heard a dull groan, followed by a foot brushing his and he smiled wider as he turned and realised just how magical his beach life really was.

Sabrina Byrne was there.

He lifted the light sheet and admired her peach-tinted torso and those fawn-like legs that seemed to keep going forever. She was the best-looking girl in Merri Bay, which in a town of bronzed beach babes was really saying something. She smelled of a lavish mix of sunscreen and coconut oil and was naked except for her sea-blue bikini bottoms, flecked with white sand from the couple's swim the night before.

Rippa edged over on the futon and lazily cuddled up against her, snuggling his chin into the nape of her neck and breathing her in.

And then, quick as a shot, he drew back.

'GET-THA-FARK-AWWF-AH-ME,' she grumbled from somewhere deep inside, as the heel of her foot bucked back like a donkey's hoof and, narrowly avoiding his groin, struck Rippa hard on his inner-thigh.

For all that was beautiful about Sabrina, and there was a lot of it, she had a voice like a foghorn, and the temper of a street drunk. Mornings with her were often trepidatious affairs, where he had to watch his every step for fear of setting her off.

His phone rang. Sabrina, half-asleep, reached out on her side and grappled with the banana-shaped receiver.

'WHA-THA-FARK-DYOO-WANT?!'

As she waited for the caller's reply, she reached over with her other hand for a three-day-old bottle of Mount Franklin on the bedside table and took a glug, making her somewhat lucid.

'It's too early for this shit,' she told whoever it was on the phone. 'It's the weekend. Call back at a reasonable farkin hour, ya cockhead.'

She hung up so hard that the banana receiver bounced and flew up, catching on the blinds behind and dangling there like some self-harming canary that had decided life was all too much.

'Who was that?' Rippa asked, cowering like he did when he asked her anything before one p.m., sometimes even two, depending on whether she'd had her third cup of coffee and her fourth or fifth cig. It was a justified question given that this was his shack, the one he'd converted from a shed out the back of his old man's place. And she had answered *his* phone. But still.

'How the fark would I know?' She replaced the bottle on the stand more carefully and settled back down to resume her slumber. 'They were calling yesterday too.'

'Well, um … it could be important.' Rippa couldn't think of why, though. His only job was a few hours a week behind the bar of the surf club his dad ran, and he'd never gotten any bills, never mind owed anyone any money in his life.

'You farkin answer it then. I need my beauty sleep.' Then she wheeled her heel backwards and gave him another kick, this time striking him dead centre in the nuts as though all this was somehow his fault.

Rippa clenched his manhood and, as he waited for the shooting pain firing up his abdomen to subside, he took the hint that this would not be a *get laid* morning. In fact, he couldn't remember a morning that had been. Not that there had been many *get laid* evenings of late either now he thought of it. Four months they'd been a couple. It was longer than Rippa had been with anyone by a good three-and-a-half, and he was realising that, just like all those magazines said about every relationship, the physical side of their theirs was tapering off.

But what exactly was taking its place, Rippa wasn't sure.

Chapter 3

Rippa cradled his board and leapt over the back sandstone wall in his golden Billabong boardies. He got a new pair each Christmas and they were virtually painted onto his skin for most of the year. These ones were barely two weeks old and were still clean and bright, yet to fray and fade like they inevitably would over the next twelve months.

He cut over the baking hot track and skipped up and over the rocks and down the dunes, a trail he could follow in his sleep. And there it was that she lay. His one true love. The sand and the surf of Merri Bay, framing that gleaming Indian Ocean.

Rippa didn't know how Sabrina could be tired and grumpy when this beach — the best in the entire west, and one of the best in the whole southern hemisphere — lay on their doorstep. Before she moved herself in, Rippa would be up and out here every morning at first light, no matter how late they'd been up, or how many tinnies they'd drank or cones they'd smoked the night before. And all day they'd stay and surf until sunset, stopping only to eat or get higher. This time of the day, when the sun was approaching its strongest point, was usually the time they'd break and seek shelter up by the scrub, the carpark, or the surf club.

But Sabrina making the shack practically hers had changed everything. Even if that did bring its own occasional perks.

'How would you rather die? Stabbed, shot or burned?'

Rippa heard them before he saw them — Voodoo, Jacko and Muggs lazing around a burnt-out fire dug into the dunes, crushed Emu Export cans littering the blackened sand by their bare feet. They hadn't gotten here early. Nope. They hadn't made it to bed.

A stray football bobbled over to Rippa from the direction of a young kid of about seven or eight. He was having a kickabout with his dad on the sand and wearing a singlet with 'Socceroos' across it. Rippa flicked the size five up with his toes, knocked it up higher with his thighs and onto his chest. Then left shoulder, right shoulder, and up to his head, before side-volleying it perfectly back to the kid. He liked the feel of the ball and how he hadn't lost his touch. And he enjoyed watching the boy's face light up at the deft manoeuvre.

'Here he is,' slurred Voodoo, black servo sunnies camouflaging his sunken eyes. 'Diego What's-his-farken-name. Where were you last night?'

'Sabrina wanted an early one.'

Jacko sniggered while Muggs made a whipping motion, complete with sound-effects.

'You'd jump off Wunji Cliffs if she told ya,' said Voodoo.

'I wouldn't,' said Rippa. 'But, well, she is my girlfriend.'

'You and who else's?'

The other two's giggles grew harsher at this.

Rippa bristled. 'What was that?'

'Settle, Gretel.' Voodoo cracked another can. 'And put on the kettle.'

'Not my fault you're jealous.'

'Fark off I am. Wouldn't touch her with a bargepole.'

Rippa had seen the way his supposed friend looked at his girl — or more like leered at her — but he wasn't pursuing it. Voodoo was a near impossible person to reason with at the best of times, never mind when he was on the tail-end of a 24-hour bender. Rippa had never been able to party for that long and neither had the others until recently, and he wasn't sure how they managed it.

He picked up the Coke bottle bong next to the ashes and saw it packed with green. He wasn't planning to imbibe until later, he had a busy day ahead, but he could never say no. Weed was a part of the fabric of life down here, as much as the sun, sand and surf.

'You missed out last night,' Voodoo told him.

'How's that?' Rippa lit and inhaled, drawing deep. The dad saw and quickly gathered the ball and led his Socceroo singlet-wearing son down the beach far away from them. The boy gave a quizzical look to the murky bottle in Rippa's hand while his father shot him a frosty, disappointed one.

Rippa felt kinda bad. They had blow-in written all over them, and the father probably spent his days in the city choking in a shirt and tie and voting Liberal or worse. But he knew that the town needed more of these sorts up here, spending their weekends and splashing their dollars if Merri Bay was going to pick up and survive, and maybe one day even thrive. That's what his own dad always reminded him.

'We farkin egged old Bingley's pad,' Voodoo said. 'The roof, the walls, the windows, letterbox, the lot. Month-old ones as well. Bet you it smells like a dead dogs's arsehole now.'

'Yeah,' cackled Muggs. 'His missus was at the front door at two a.m. with her rollers in and dressing gown on. Her wrinkly jugs flapping about. Thought she was gonna scream or cry or shit herself.'

Rippa let out a little laugh but only because the smoke was taking hold. He liked Mr Bingley. Their old principal had been stern and often humourless, but he'd stuck his neck out and let Rippa graduate despite him turning up late and missing too many days because he was stood here with a bong or was out there on the waves. Mr Bingley told Rippa he had the brains to push on and get out and be the marine biologist he'd once claimed he wanted to be. This was back when he moved to Merri Bay halfway through Year 8 and sat quaffing jellybeans from the jar on the desk as his father signed the admission forms.

'You still playing cricket later?' Jacko asked him.

'Dunno. Got that gig.'

'Playing with that farkin mongo who plays the bongos,' smirked Voodoo.

'What did you say?' There was little in life that riled Rippa but making fun of his best friend and bandmate, Cal, who had mild cerebral palsy, was that one thing.

'Fuck that boyband shit,' Voodoo added quickly, massaging his right bicep. 'We need you. We're playing those Jilling Gully wank-stains, and my bowling arm feels shithouse.'

Rippa thought that everything about him and the other two looked *shithouse*. Newly shaved heads and blotchy DIY tatts, they'd all packed on the pounds from a bad diet of milk bar grub and Bush Chook beer and what else. Rippa was glad that he lived off barbecues and honeydew melon and didn't smoke tobacco or sink piss like it was water.

'I'll see.' Now Rippa only had eyes for the ocean. 'You heading in?'

'Fark no,' said Muggs. 'Too gnarly today. You'll never stay up.'

But Rippa had already lifted his board and was heading for the shore.

'Don't farkin do it,' growled Voodoo. 'We got the game.'

Rippa wasn't listening and waded into the cool blue, eyeballing the chunky five-footer gathering steam. It was choppy out, especially for this time of year, but this was what Rippa lived for. Without a second's thought he caught the tide just as it was about to let go and he was up and away, soaring like an eagle then shooting like a bullet over the foamy waves.

And in that moment he had no thoughts about the surf club's problems, or Old Man Bingley and how he could have been that marine biologist, or Sabrina and whether or not she was coming down to meet him. No thoughts of his mother who he hadn't seen in six years and whether she was in Perth or back in London or wherever. And in that split second before the wave broke and crashed hard upon the sand, he sensed many eyes watching him from the dunes and heard their cheers.

Joey Rippa thought it might have been the high from the stronger hydro they'd started to source from those bikies up in Geraldton. But now, almost out of his teens, he felt he knew for sure that on this board and with his girl by his side, that here in Merri Bay, he'd already made it. Life didn't get any better than this.

Chapter 4

Rippa arrived at the Merri Bay Surf Club, late as usual. He knew the band's gear would already be set up and he felt a twinge of guilt at not pulling his weight. And sure enough, there was Cal tightening his snare alongside Rippa's Gretsch guitar and Marshall amp, which the smaller guy had somehow lugged onstage and plugged in and no doubt tuned.

'Where've you been?' Cal asked. He was dressed in new ironed Levis his mother had bought for the occasion and his best purple check shirt that he'd made sure to button up all the way saying it made him look like a young Charlie Watts, which it kinda did. Rippa was in the same boardies, thongs, and an old white Bonds chesty with a hole in the collar he always wore. Rippa knew that Cal rightly suspected that rain, hail, weddings, parties, anything, it would be impossible to get his best friend in anything else, even in winter.

'Been at cricket. Sorry.'

'Gig's in ten.'

'I know, I know. I'm here.'

'Y-y-y-you could've given that a miss for one day.' Cal's condition made it challenging for him to talk at the best of times, and when he got angry or frustrated it got worse, causing his words to slur and his pale features to flush. He had a point, though. Rippa peeked behind the velvet curtain and saw there were already fifty payers stalking the bar and waiting for them to start.

Still, he couldn't help defending himself. 'Yeah, but they needed me. Hey, I batted a half-century and bowled a hat-trick.'

'And you went for a surf,' Cal frowned.

Rippa rearranged his long wet hair. 'And I went for a surf.'

'A-a-a-and you've had a smoke.' Cal didn't like weed, and he could always tell by his friend's red eyes and languid movements when he was stoned.

'I needed to take the edge off. You could do with the same the way you're harping on.'

'This is our biggest show. And you're high.'

'I'm always high.'

And to this Cal had no comeback. His was a petty gripe as Rippa was one of those high-functioning stoners and it would, as it always did, relax him and make him perform even better.

Cal sighed and changed tack. 'I've been getting phone calls for you as well.'

'From who?'

'Your Uncle Warren.'

Rippa raised an eyebrow. 'Haven't heard from that cat in yonks. What's he want?'

'Wouldn't s-s-say. But he asked if you still had your footy boots.'

'Weird.'

Cal did a drum roll then nervously fumbled one of the sticks. 'Would've been nice to run through the set again.'

'We rehearse four nights a week and have done since halfway through high school.'

Cal went through his box-breathing exercises that his occupational therapist taught him. 'I really hope you're right. I gave up West Ham for this.'

'What, you gonna fly over and go in goal for them?'

This got a smile out of Cal, no doubt sharing the vision of him wheeling around between the sticks at Upton Park.

'C'mon, you serious? I mentioned it, like, five times,' Cal said. 'You really don't know?'

'I'm very serious. I really do not know.'

'They're playing in Perth tonight.'

'Oh yeah? What do you care but? You're an Everton fan.'

'Y-y-y-yeah but it's an English team. We always followed it. Well … used to. Bet you don't even know who won the title anymore.'

'Um … was it Everton?'

Cal's smile faded.

'Okay, fine,' said Rippa. 'Next time a team comes we'll head down for it.'

Cal shrugged. 'We won't. Still, it's a nice idea.'

Rippa peeked behind the curtain again and scanned the room for Sabrina. His dad, Stevie, leapt up to the stage, his beer gut showing but his gold loop earring still shining loud and bright. He brandished a jug of Old Stoney Ginger Beer with ice.

'You guys are gonna tear this joint a new one.' Then Stevie's grin died as he looked out at the empty dance floor. 'Which is more than I can say for this crowd.'

'It's early yet, Dad.'

'It's a fundraiser. It was front of the paper. We need folks to dig deep.'

'I'm not sure they've got it to spare anymore.'

'The change in their pockets won't be much good when this place is gone. They'll bitch and moan how there's bugger all to do in town, then they'll leave and it'll get even worse. Maybe you boys can start and we'll flush a few in from the beer garden.'

'Sure, Dad.'

'Come on fellas,' Stevie punched his boy lightly on the arm. 'A bit of enthusiasm, please. This could be the night. I remember our first show. We were supporting Midnight Oil at this beer barn in the Cross. Arvo show it was, a bit like this one, and that's when EMI snapped us up.'

'Sure, Stevie,' Cal chimed in politely, having heard this story a million times or more.

'Dad, I think there's a bit of a difference between playing a big venue in Sydney, alongside one of the best bands this country's ever produced, versus playing a surf club fundraiser in the arse end of civilisation.'

'You'll never make it with that attitude.'

'I know, Dad. Sorry, Dad.' Rippa had no intention of making *it*, whatever *it* was. But he still felt bad. His father was always bubbling with enthusiasm and exaggerated hope about every little thing, despite the surf club being on life support since he could remember. And this was Stevie's night after all, and a vital one if he was to keep the debtors at bay and the power on until the winter at least.

'You ready then?'

'We're ready, Stevie.' Cal nodded, though his knees were jittering so much they were making his hi-hats rattle.

Rippa nodded too. That last smoke had drifted through him nicely and he couldn't wait for the curtain to pull back and for them to get into it and finally play their first show. They would have played it long before if Cal hadn't been sick, and when he wasn't sick, he'd been making excuses to cover his nerves. Rippa was never sure what his friend was so nervous about, because Cal was the best musician in town by a country mile, the one who wrote all the songs, and the only one who could play every instrument going. Rippa may have been the front man, but he was a pretender, and deep down he knew it.

Stevie wrenched back the curtain and a hush descended. He touched the mic to ensure it was on, jumping back when he heard a piercing shrill of feedback. 'Testes, testes, one-two. Alright you ugly mob, big thanks to yous inside who've paid your bucks and showed up. And to youse in the beer garden — get your gold coins off that pool table and away from the durry machine and give 'em to the door bitch instead. Or I'm gonna have Rick Astley blaring out those back speakers quicker than you can say "pop will eat itself". Because you ain't hearing this for free.'

A few boos came from outside.

'Mutton, is that a hip flask I see?' Stevie zeroed in on the young man with long sideboards and leather jacket despite the scorching afternoon. 'Your pockets are tighter than that pool table out there — a bit like your old man's. Bin it and get up to that bar, pronto.'

The kid's features turned as crimson as the pimples dotting his sideburns and he did exactly as he was told.

'Now,' Stevie bellowed. 'Let's hear it for Dune Landing.'

The punters cheered.

'You good, Cal?' Rippa whispered to his drummer who'd turned white as the sand outside and looked anything but.

'I-I-I-I'm good,' he muttered, closing his eyes. Then, when he'd counted them in, Rippa went for his first strum and the bottom string of the Gretsch snapped in two. Cal looked like he was about to cry, scream, spew, or all three, and Rippa knew that if he stopped they'd never get started again.

'Keep drumming,' he mouthed to his friend as he jumped back in using the remaining strings. And then they were up, up, up and away, their bass-less two-piece surf-sounds soaring into the eaves as Rippa sang:

'Tonight we're getting high,
Tonight it is no lie,
Tonight we'll reach where the moon kisses the sky.'

Rippa turned and saw Cal's shoulders relax. Their eyes met and they shone. They both knew that Rippa had found his groove and no matter how many bongs he'd choked down, and no matter how late he showed up, he would never, ever let Cal down.

A gaggle of surf girls were up tight to the stage, swaying and gyrating their bodies in the sweaty room which didn't have air-conditioning or even ceiling fans because Stevie could never budget for it. Rippa's dad gave a thumbs up as guys and girls from out back emptied their pockets for the door girl, ignoring the stamp in her hand, and barrelling on in.

Sabrina was among them. Rippa stepped away from the mic stand towards the edge of the stage for his solo and the gig-starved locals whooped like this was Wembley Stadium. He looked to Sabrina to make sure she was watching but she was by the pillar, head turned the other way talking to someone he couldn't see.

Chapter 5

As the final chord of encore number three rang out, the afternoon crowd almost lifted the roof off the surf club's main room. Rippa looked to his friend — both their shirts were dipped in sweat. He held out his hand and brought him in for a hug.

'Well done, Rip,' Cal beamed.

'Well done, *me*? Well done you. They're your songs. That's what they're cheering for.'

'Yeah, yeah, but you can s-s-s-sing. And play guitar. And look good while you're doing it. They wouldn't be cheering for me if I was up front in my wheelchair.'

'You're the brains. They'll all see that soon enough.'

Stevie bundled up with another jug of ginger beer.

'Sen-*farkin*-sational,' he howled over the mix of feedback and applause. 'I haven't seen a show like that since we were supported by Little River Band at The Espy back in '75.'

'Thanks, Dad,' said Rippa, taking a glass and letting his father enjoy the moment.

'If someone from one of the majors was here tonight, you'd get snapped up for sure. Three-album deal, I reckon. Maybe even five.'

'That's the d-d-d-dream, Stevie.' Cal subscribed to all the music trades and had sent every A&R man on the east coast their first shaky demo, never getting so much as a rejection in return. He was always telling Rippa that it was indeed a dream and that there was little hope. Not until they got themselves a proper recording, one that wasn't taped on his ancient Akai ghettoblaster. And then they could head over east or overseas.

Rippa placed his guitar on the stand and peered out to the pillar for

Sabrina. She was gone and, in her place, stood the unmistakable beefy outline of a man he knew well. A shape which had never changed since Rippa was a little kid.

'Uncle Warren's here?'

'Oh, um, yeah,' Stevie said unenthusiastically. 'Meant to mention.'

Rippa skipped down from the stage past a few younger admirers decked out in way too much makeup for a daytime show in a country town. He shook his uncle's hand. 'You like the show?'

'What show? I've been trying to call you.'

Rippa had known he wouldn't have liked the performance and that any music which wasn't Chas & Dave was not his thing. In fact, he knew that for his London-born uncle, any activity which didn't involve football of the global variety, he gave a wide berth to.

'Called all day yesterday,' Warren said. 'Didn't your old man tell you?'

'No, he didn't.'

Stevie was sheepishly avoiding their glare while pretending to roll up a guitar cable. His uncle and father had never got along which was hard for Rippa as he loved his father and at the same time thought the world of his uncle, even if he'd rarely spoken to him since he'd moved here from Perth.

Warren stepped back and examined his nephew like a farmer would with a prized Angus, poking his ribs and squeezing his muscles. 'Not the best condition. Though you are surf fit.'

'I do it forty hours a week.'

'Hmm. The state team's come down with gastro.'

'Poor them.'

'I'm talking clear the drains, plug the gaps under the doors and call a tiler-type gastro.'

Ripper curled his lip and put down his glass. 'Cheers for that.'

'They need players desperately.'

'I see.' Rippa didn't, though. He was busy scanning the room. He thought maybe his eyes had deceived him and Sabrina hadn't been at the gig after all.

'Joey. I've been doing some scouting for them, and they know I'm here.'

'Uh huh.' Rippa felt too hot and sweaty to see her right now anyway. He'd head to the water first to cool down.

'Joey.' Rippa realised his uncle had both his paws on his shoulders, rousing him. 'We're playing West bloody Ham at the WACA in three hours and you're in the squad.'

'Ah, right, yeah. Dunno bout that. Surf tomorrow morn's meant to be the best it's been in weeks and I wouldn't wanna miss it.'

'All they need is a half. Coach knows you're rusty. At least I think he said that. He was riding the porcelain saddle tight when he called.'

'I haven't played in forever.'

'You were in the district's squad two months back. You were player of the tournament.'

Rippa had almost forgotten. 'I've got no boots, no shin pads, no …'

'There'll be boots there. And I've got shin guards for you. As well as a car that's blocking the drive out front, so let's skedaddle.'

Just then Sabrina emerged from the bathroom looking even better than she did this morning, with her blonde locks tied up and no bra under her pink singlet. Rippa was sure he would melt.

'Dunno, Uncle Warren. I've got things going on here. I've got a missus now.'

'You're 19, not 90. Where is she?'

Rippa pointed. He'd never known his uncle to even look at a girl, never mind have a girlfriend. But in her cut-off jean shorts and sandals, even Warren was blanching and stuttering.

'Well … well … just … just … I dunno, go and tell her. Although the way she was barking at me this morning on the blower, just be careful she doesn't bite a leg or two off.'

Sabrina was sipping a Coke, which she'd no doubt sneakily mixed with a small bottle of Bundy from her bag like most of the kids in town did. It was one of the reasons why the surf club was going under.

'Hey,' Rippa sidled up, pecking her on the cheek.

She moved back, her eyes absently scanning the room for something or someone. 'Oh, hey.'

'See the show?'

'Nah. Vic needed us to serve at the milk bar.'

'Really? Thought I saw ya here.'

'Wasn't me.'

'It was good.'

'Yeah?'

'Real good.'

'Good, then.' Sabrina still wasn't meeting his eyes.

'We're getting better.'

'That's good too.'

Behind her Warren was frantically pointing at his watch.

'My uncle's in town.'

'Right.'

'He wants me to play in some soccer game in the smoke.'

'Right.'

'Like, right now.'

'Right.'

'Is that all you can say?'

'Is there any cashiola in it?'

'Hey, Warren,' Rippa called over. 'They paying?'

'Five hundred appearance fee.' He jingled his keys to move the matter along.

'Whatcha waiting for then?' asked Sabrina. 'Voodoo's got this new shit off the bikies which is way better than mull and we could buy a load with that.'

'What is it?'

'Speed, he reckons.'

'Yeah, I'm not sure about that.' Rippa liked his grass, almost as much as he loved surfing. It settled him, centred him. But he'd heard about his new drug on the scene that got your heart racing and kept you awake and drinking for days on end and knew it wasn't for him. Rippa lived for waking up fresh and early and ready to surf.

'I'm going to my aunty's anyway,' Sabrina said. 'She's making rissoles.' She edged away just as Rippa was making moves to get closer to her. 'Go score a touchdown or whatever it is they call it.'

And there she left him, confused and more than a little crestfallen. His uncle, though, had already grabbed his elbow and was hurrying to the car.

Chapter 6

Rippa and Uncle Warren hit the highway, heading south in his old Kingswood station wagon.

'So, um, yes, I guess I'll play.'

'Of course you'll bleedin' play,' his uncle told him. 'We're an hour-and-a-half along the road.'

'I know, I know. Just confirming is all.'

'However — small disclaimer. Given how I put your name forward and all the detective work to find you, and the chauffeuring and all-round despair of having to come up to Morbid Bay or whatever you call it — I'll be taking 20 percent of your appearance fee.'

'Umm, I guess that's okay.' Rippa was not looking forward to telling Sabrina this.

Warren pressed a button to double lock the vehicle. 'And my central locking system shares the same sentiment. There's no escaping now, boyo.'

Rippa hadn't been to the city in such a long time. He hadn't been anywhere in a long time, so long that he couldn't even remember the last time he'd been in a car. The sun had started to dip but remained bold and strong. Rippa wished he'd had time to have a final surf to cool off after the show. Or, at the very least, that his uncle wouldn't keep snapping off the AC every time he pushed the switch, moaning about Arab oil cartels and spiralling fuel prices. He thought about smoking but knew his uncle would hit the roof if it was tobacco, never mind the devil's lettuce.

Rippa grew increasingly anxious. This was also the first time he'd spent this long with his uncle since his mum fled. He and Warren had been so close before the move. With his dad already in Merri Bay running his bar, and his mother working all hours as a registered nurse, it had been his uncle who taught Rippa how to kick a ball, later driving him to training and matches. And in between he'd screen every Spurs VHS available and read every *Shoot* and *Match* annual to him cover-to-cover.

'Heard from Mum?' Rippa eventually asked to break the silence.

Warren's hazel eyes glistened. 'No, boyo. And you know I'd tell you right away if I did. I want to be able to make that call and tell you that more than anything in the world.'

The silence returned. There was rarely a moment in which Rippa didn't think of her. And he knew her kid brother was the same. His free-spirited, Swinging London mother who found out she was pregnant to that touring Aussie bass player the week John Lennon married Yoko in Gibraltar. And then under duress, because he kept going on about how life was so much better there, she followed Stevie Down Under to give birth.

But she never ever settled.

Even when her little brother and now deceased mother followed her out, she still never settled. Hating the heat and the flies and how nothing much ever happened way out west, she vowed one day to flee.

Although neither Rippa nor anyone thought it would end like it did. Stevie wanting to move back to his actual home in the even more remote small rural town of Merri Bay was the straw that broke the back of their already precarious relationship. When their only child was aged twelve and about to hit high school — and without packing so much as a change of knickers, never mind a bag, or telling anyone where she was heading — she was out of there.

Western Australia, for all its beauty and its laid-back way of life, had a violent undercurrent throughout the '80s and there'd been a few murderers on the loose, both of the serial and the more random variety. When it came to the whereabouts of Pamela Green, this was something her nearest and dearest never wanted to contemplate. It was better to think of her in a new place and with a new life, even though that was still a bitter pill to swallow.

Chas & Dave on the tape deck was doing nothing for Rippa or his creeping anxiety which had really kicked into gear now that the bush had cleared, and they could see the outline of Perth's suburban sprawl lying in wait. He hated being away from the ocean. Instead, he reclined his seat and tried to relax, only the seat wouldn't budge more than an inch. He turned and found it blocked by an old bar fridge. There was a suitcase next to it, and next to that was a wafer-thin foam mattress with a pillow on it. Rippa got a whiff or something rank and fusty like old bait which had been left in the sun, yet he knew Warren had never fished. He lifted his left thigh off the seat and found a pair of oversized and very faded y-fronts.

'Uncle Warren, do you, um, like, live in your car?'

The older man's head drooped so low that his chin was pointing at his navel. 'I do, boyo, I do. But only for the moment. Lost a shit ton on the ponies this past month, and let's just say the scouting aspirations which I've harboured are taking a little longer to materialise into something worthwhile than I first envisaged.'

It saddened Rippa to think of his beloved uncle living like this. He studied him, hypocritically chain smoking as he sweated at the wheel. Probably fifty kilos heavier than Rippa and yet shorter by a good inch or three. Sometimes he forgot that there was only eight years between them.

'Sorry, Uncle Warren.'

'Not your fault, boyo, not your fault at all. But I'm in a hole, I admit. Not an ordinary hole but a ten-foot deep one with a thick layer of shit at the bottom. And there's another twenty-foot hole waiting beneath it. And I'm about one wrong turn away from slipping head-first into that.' Rippa thought it best to change the subject. 'So, is this team actually any good?'

'You mean is footballing giant West Ham United any good?'

'I guess.'

'Of course they're bloody good. Not having the best of seasons but they ooze class. They'll take ten off our lot. At least with you they have a chance of pulling one back.'

'And what exactly happened to the state team?'

'They went to a training camp in Bunbury. Stopped off at some country baker's along the way. The sign on the window said it was the home of the best vanilla slice in the south-west, which may very well be true. Although being a bit of a roadhouse connoisseur myself, I always dispute these things because every bakery in every bumfuck town in Christendom seems to lay claim to some bullshit prize or another. Anyway, I heard from Con the assistant later that the vanilla slice was suitably top drawer. That was not the culprit. The culprit was the steak and onion pie which was on special and should be labelled the worst in the free world because it still has them all shitting for Australia, or so I'm told. Lee Tran in goal has apparently lost two stone, though given that he's nearly my size that might not be a bad thing.' Warren lifted his polo to pinch his flab and joshed, 'Maybe I should take a detour on the way back, hey?'

'The state team must be pretty desperate if they want someone like me to play.'

'Someone like *you*?' Warren almost laughed and he rarely ever laughed. 'Boyo, if your loopy old man hadn't dragged you off to Misery Bay or whatever you yokels call it, you'd be the first name on the team sheet. And that's me talking here — your biggest critic.'

'So you say.' Rippa was sorry he'd stirred this particular hornet's nest having heard this so many times he could repeat it verbatim.

'Why he wouldn't let you at least stay in school in the city with me during the week I do not know.'

Probably because you were barely out your teens and didn't have a job and now live in your car, is what Rippa didn't say.

'Tragic loss to the game, so it is. You stuck up there wasting your time in the sea, strumming your guitar, smoking and drinking and doing God knows what else.'

Rippa had to laugh as he thought of his girl, his band, the surf club, the cricket team and that heavenly ocean which he spent every waking minute in or around. Rippa felt like the richest guy alive. 'You don't live there. You don't know it.'

'I know it's a place you should retire to, not spend your best years.'

'It's paradise, Uncle Warren.'

'Bullshit. Paradise doesn't exist and if it does it certainly doesn't last forever. Just look at the state of your old man and that dive he runs.'

'Please don't go there.'

'Alright, alright, I'm sorry.' They both knew the subject of his father and the other side of his family were off limits and vice versa. 'I'm just saying you've got a heaven-sent talent that won't last forever, and it makes me weep when I think of the things you could be doing with it.'

'I'll take it on board.'

'You say that. You always say that, but you don't and you won't. I follow districts, state league, NSL, the lot, it's my job, and I know what you have in your toolbox. And you're of an age now where you can do as you please and you could be playing at that level, easy. Make that any level.' Warren skilfully lit another cigarette using the light from the last. 'The things I would sacrifice if I had a big toe's worth of your talent.'

Giving up smoking tobacco nearly every waking moment would be a start, is also what Rippa didn't say. It was around his 40th fag since they departed, and Rippa was thinking that if he could make it through the warm-up without coughing up a lung from all this passive smoking then that would be a real miracle.

'I dunno. I guess you have to live there to understand.'

'Me, live there? They don't have a proper football team, never mind a league. You have to travel three towns away to find anything resembling a ground and even that's got a cricket pitch slap-bang in the middle.'

Rippa knew he'd failed his uncle. The uncle who'd sacrificed so much and pushed him so far in the game for it all to amount to nothing. Even if it was all his own dream and never, ever Rippa's.

'There's more to life than football.'

Warren's head swung round in a flash. He looked at him deeply, his sad, beady eyes leaving the road. Rippa knew that if his uncle smoked weed of the more enlightening kind, if he dated someone like Sabrina and rode the waves of Merri Bay night and day, then he might think very differently. Yes, there may be more to life than Merri Bay, but looking at the unhealthy state of this wheezing, perspiring oaf, and the look of his car which was now his home, football was hardly the answer.

Warren's eyes had left the road for a moment too long. There was a deafening screech of brakes as he violently jerked the wheel to his left only to feel a crash and a thud as a seven-foot kangaroo took out his bumper and almost rolled the car. The stout grass trees by the side of the road were the only things saving them from smashing into the much thicker jarrah ones and sending them to an early grave.

Chapter 7

The battered Kingswood edged slowly into the city through the Friday night traffic, an hour later than they were supposed to. And around twenty minutes before kick-off, with Uncle Warren still moaning about the long-wait for the call-out, and the demolished bumper, and the charge, and the mechanic's West Coast Eagles cap, and the size of his insurance premium.

Rippa, meanwhile, was just thankful they were alive.

As they neared the stadium a sea of claret and blue-clad fans in party-mode spread out before them. It still made his uncle grumble. 'Fucking hell, boyo. You're so lucky. I'd love to be handed a pair of size sevens and a licence to unleash fury on these East London wannabe-gangster tossers.' He beeped the horn. 'Off the road Pommie Kray.'

'Eat my willy, Spurs wanker,' replied the short man with the maroon mohawk, having noticed the 'We Love You Tottenham' sticker on the back of the vehicle.

'Tell you what,' said Warren as he looked for a park, 'I'd be sharpening every stud before I went on that pitch. It's a struggle not to mount the pavement, let me tell you.'

Rippa was feeling none of his uncle's antipathy to the away support, though he was strangely struck by a case of butterflies. He'd been nestled in the warmth of his comfort zone for so long he barely remembered what the queasy feeling in his stomach was. It had been years since he'd played in front of any sort of crowd, with the annual districts matches he occasionally starred in pulling the proverbial two men and a dog. The sand and the surf and the cricket and the scenery and the infinite number of other attractive options in the Mid West part of the state, pulled the locals in every other direction.

Rippa was waved in by a woman in a 'WA Soccer' polo shirt and found himself shoved into the Home dressing room. A cacophony of bad pop music, sweat and Deep Heat attacked his senses. His entrance didn't register among the testosterone-fuelled young men who were laughing and joking among their usual club groups. The Italians, mostly communicating with hand gestures, were up top. The Greeks with their well-greased hair were at the back. The mainly shaven-headed Slavs to the left, and the loudmouth Brits to the right. All speaking their own tongues, all psyching themselves up, some ramming their chests together, while two of the Slavs headbutted the concrete wall.

This scene really took him back. There were hardly any non-Australian-borns in Merri Bay. Rippa thought he might have recognised one of two of the players from his junior days, but with puberty and facial hair and body development and everything that went along with growing up, he couldn't be sure. He got a few glances in return, although with his long, ragged sun-bleached hair and stubble, there was little hint of recognition in their eyes and more of a look that went '*Who's this joker who looks like he's been washed ashore?*' Which wasn't too far from the truth.

An older Indigenous man thrust an ironed bundle of kit into his hands. 'You the country kid?' he croaked.

'I guess.'

'You got five minutes to get that on. The lads have already been for a run. You wanna duck out for a quick stretch?'

'Nah.' Rippa had never been one for warm-ups. But then he remembered something he needed to do. 'Oh, wait, yeah.'

He had his own warm-up in mind. When he changed, he went down the tunnel. From his backpack he loaded the small brass pipe with a pinch of green bud. Near the punters who were smoking fags behind the fence, he ducked behind a wheelie bin and quickly inhaled. He immediately felt glad he'd done so as the smoke ironed out the tense creases in his muscles from the car ride and centred his mind, sending it back to its natural default setting which was thus: *Who really gives a fuck about any of this?*

He glided back to the dressing room where he found the players lining up. Some were jumping on the spot, some were roaring, all looked like they were about to drag themselves out of the trenches into no man's land and dive head-first at the enemy guns blazing, like their very souls depended on it.

'Coach?' Rippa asked a balding Mediterranean man with a faded grey suit covered in sweat patches. 'I'm on the bench, right?'

'Where were you for the team talk?'

'Warming up. Or maybe pushing a Kingswood up a hill.'

'Pardon?'

'Doesn't matter.'

He looked at his clipboard. 'Joseph Rippa, hey?'

'Um, yeah.'

'You're on the left flank. Watch out for their right-back. Whippet-quick and a nasty bastard as well. He's Wales-capped and doesn't know the meaning of the term *friendly*.'

Well, it takes two tango, thought Rippa, as he took his spot at the back of the lineup. And Rippa was not in the mood for any sort of dancing whatsoever. He was in the mood for doing his time, picking up his 500 bucks (or 400 as it now transpired) and getting the hell away from the Big Smoke and back to the surf.

The match was under the lights, and a crowd of around 10,000 had gathered inside the famous cricket oval on this balmy Saturday evening, a venue which had previously hosted greats such as Bradman, Richards and Botham. The atmosphere was a carnival one with fans singing the national anthems and fireworks alighting at both ends of the ground as the teams entered the reconfigured oval. Rippa looked over at their opponents expecting to see a well-oiled tight-knit group of elite athletes ready to teach their colonial underlings a painful lesson. What he saw was their two strikers being prised apart by their captain as they swore and swung at each other's noses. Meanwhile, their centre-back was falling to the floor in drunken hysterics at something his defensive partner had pointed out to him that was happening pitchside. Their goalkeeper clutched his stomach and puked up something bright blue.

They looked a spent force, and the game hadn't even kicked off.

WA got proceedings underway. The ball was switched right then back to the centre and then over to Rippa. This gave him an early chance to test this full-back. The Wales-cap who apparently didn't know the meaning of friendly jogged languidly in Rippa's direction. Rippa could see the tan-lines in the shape of Wayfarers around his eyes. A red-headed bloke, every inch of his skin was a painful shade of scarlet. He made a half-hearted lunge for the ball which Rippa easily evaded. And just like that, he was motoring away.

The West Ham skipper — probably the fittest-looking of the lot — was on him. Rippa shipped the ball inside to one of the Greek-Australians who returned it straight away. Rippa then glided between the centre-half and sweeper who'd only just stopped giggling. The keeper gingerly moved off his line hoping to intercept. With the goal behind him gaping, Rippa thought he'd do what he used to do back in the juniors. He dug his left toes into the turf and scooped the ball high over the stranded goalie. Then he ran by, easily tapping it into the empty net.

There was barely a minute on the clock and the minnows from West Australia were ahead against footballing royalty and the crowd — even the Hammers' fans, some of whom had travelled all the way from England — were in awe as they applauded the exquisite skill they'd just witnessed. In truth, given the dimensions of the cricket ground, all were too far away to see the actual state of their heroes, never mind smell the stench of beer and shooters on their breath which helped facilitate this one-way show.

Rippa was having the time of his life. He was feeling relaxed and sharp. And his natural pace, which had always been one of his greatest assets, was making him un-markable in the eyes of his drunk/hungover/out-of-shape opponents. He was first to every ball and skinning his marker at will, while his left foot was showing no signs of rustiness as he pinged in quality ball after quality ball which had the West Ham defence scrambling. And when that avenue was blocked, he was equally at ease using his pace and artistry to drill into the centre, putting the backline on the backfoot as they were forced into making desperate blocks and barges and not-so-subtle blows to his body to halt this one-man onslaught. Given the richness of the supply, if the WA striker from the Slavic end of the dressing room hadn't looked so nervous on this, his first State outing, he could've scored a barrowload.

There were no such qualms for Rippa who had never been so high before a game and never felt so much at ease. As the first half progressed, he continued to terrorise the Hammers' defence time and time again — to such a degree that the Wales-capped full-back was dragged on the half-hour. However, the youth they brought on in his place made little difference as his thighs began cramping from jet lag almost immediately. West Ham boss Bobby Noll tried the centre-back at right-back, then the sweeper, then the captain, but all lacked the pace and know-how to stop the young Australian by any legal means.

And it wasn't too long before Rippa made it two. Collecting the ball from a half-clearance, the opposition this time stood off him, wary of the havoc he'd wreaked, half-expecting him to run at them again. Instead, Rippa took his time, lined the ball up and rifled a left-footed drive from thirty yards into the top right-hand corner getting every fan of every persuasion off their bums.

And Rippa could swear he heard his uncle above the crowd whooping like he'd scored the winner in the World Cup final.

It was only the woodwork which was providing any resistance. From kick-off, the state side won the ball, knocking it long, and Rippa's half-volley crashed against the bar denying him a first half hat-trick. Then West Ham hooked the clearance upfield and Scottish striker Frank McAvennie, not long on as a sub, was onto it. He ran clear, rounding the WA keeper right on the half-time whistle to give the visitors some respite.

But it was a half the Hammers would want to forget and that thousands would remember forever due to the display of one man.

Chapter 8

Rippa followed his teammates back into the Home dressing room, grinning as his name was chanted by the crowd, with even the West Ham fans getting in on the action.

Uncle Warren was kinda right — he *had* missed playing.

Once inside his presence again barely registered as his teammates returned to their state league cliques and gabbled away to each other in their native tongues. The coach was about to close the door and commence his team talk when it swung back open, knocking him so hard that his toupée flipped up.

'Oh my word, oh my God, oh my sweet mother of Holy Jesus. Where — is — he?' It was Bobby Noll, and he was frothing at the mouth.

'Where's who?' asked the state coach, hurriedly patting down his hairpiece as a Mexican wave of sniggers circled the dressing room.

'Kim Wilde on the wing, that's who. Well, Kim Wilde if she hadn't shaved in a week, eaten in two, and never left the sun. And of course, if she was a young man and not a pop star and could actually play football.'

The West Ham boss spotted Rippa in the corner. He had an orange slice in his mouth and was removing his borrowed shin pads and Puma Kings.

'There he is, there he is. The man of the moment, all 45 of them because there was a memorable one in every minute you spent out there, my son.' He clamped a hand on each red cheek and brought him in close. 'Oh my days, where have you been hiding, sunshine? You've been hiding away here *in* the sunshine, presumably, because I have not seen a showing like that since Stan Bowles at Roker Park back in '73.'

'Thanks, I guess,' mumbled Rippa through the orange peel, having no idea who this crazed man actually was.

'You're faster than Flash Gordon. Braver than Popeye. You've got a left peg on you that could crochet a sweater, gift wrap it and place it carefully under the tree.'

'Thanks again.' By this time Rippa had his thongs, board shorts and Bonds chesty back on.

'Where the heck are you scarpering?'

'I'm only down to play the first half.'

'You're on a hat-trick, son. They're all out there chanting your name. Heck, even I was.'

'That's really kind of you but I need to head ASAP if I want to be back for my morning surf. I've heard there's gonna be a six-metre swell.'

'A six-metre what? Bloody hell, are you winding my clock? Sonny, I'm Bobby Noll, manager of the famous Cockney Boys. I'm coming back from this place with a couple of boomerangs for the grandkids, a tin of Anzac biscuits for the missus, a suntan like Louis Armstrong, and you. Yes, you! Preferably stuffed into my hand luggage so you can't ever get away.'

This woke Rippa up. 'You want to sign me?'

'Do dingos love the taste of babies?'

'Huh?'

'Course I want to sign you. Right here and right now.' He put out his hand to shake.

Rippa politely waved it away. 'That's really nice of you Mr ... Ball.'

'Noll.'

'*Noll*. It really is. But, y'see, football isn't really my thing. Surfing is.'

'We have surfing in England. Newquay's the spot. Beautiful town. Can't say I've sampled the pursuit myself, but the grandkids do like a bash with the old snorkel set when we take them there in the caravan every second summer. Tell you what, I'll send you there a day a week as part of the deal.'

'You would?'

'Sure as Ned Kelly was a thieving convict bastard, so I would.'

'Hmm.' Rippa scratched the back of his head, suddenly nervous.

'We'll develop you. Nurture you. We'll give you a handsome signing-on fee too. Anything you want, you just say the word.'

'Cool, cool. That's nice and all, but I really gotta head.' Rippa swiped his shaggy fringe from his face which indeed did make him look a little like the English pop star Noll mentioned. He slipped his old canvas backpack over his shoulder, graffitied with bands like Jane's Addiction, Metallica and Hoodoo Gurus, then he made for the exit.

'I'll sign,' piped up one of the Italian-West Australians, this one with a bumfluff goatee.

'Who are you?' asked Noll.

'I played right-wing.'

'And what did you do out there?'

'Um … had one shot which got blocked. Oh, and, um, put in two crosses too.'

'That's right. One took out the ball boy and the other took out a floodlight. Pipe down, Plastic Pacino. You though,' Noll turned back round and thumbed Rippa hard in the centre of his chest, pressing a business card into the young man's palm. 'For the good of the nation, you should think long and hard about this.'

'I already have, Mr Noll. Have a great trip in our fair country and do visit Merri Bay should you get the chance.'

All eyes were on Rippa now as he sauntered out the dressing room and away from what each and every player would have decapitated their own nonna/yiayia/grandmother for.

A professional football contract.

In the car park, Uncle Warren was even more incredulous. In fact, without his customary cigarette dangling from his fingers, his nephew had never, ever seen him so angry.

'So let me get a grip on this,' he fumed. 'The not yet late and still super great Bobby Noll practically chops down the sheds to get in and beg you to sign a pro deal for a Division One English club — one of the bigger clubs at that —and basically lets you name your price. And you give him the old brush off?'

'Yeah, it's not for me.'

'It's West Ham United. It's for everyone.'

'What do you care? You're a Spurs man. You hate anything with United or Ars or *enal* in it.'

'I don't care if it's ruddy Middleby United.'

'Who are they?'

'Jesus, help me.' He finally lit a cigarette and composed himself. 'It's a big offer. You could put Australia on the map.'

'I think it's already on the map.'

'I meant the football map, thicko. What the hell have you been smoking up there? This is your ticket to ride.'

'I don't want a ticket to ride anywhere, Uncle Warren. Wait a minute, you're right. I actually do need one right now in fact. Straight back home. When you're ready, of course.'

The big man exhaled a thick plume of smoke out his nostrils like a fearsome yet vanquished dragon. Rippa could've sworn that in his eyes he saw another dream which had crashed and burned and died.

'See this?' Uncle Warren held his thumb aloft and made Rippa do the same. 'Walk out that door and down that street and keep doing it. Because that, boyo, is your only ticket to ride now. All the way back to Maudlin Bay or whatever you muppets call it.'

'Hmm, I see.'

'And you can forget all about that appearance fee as well. You can thank that bastard roo for writing off my new home.'

Chapter 9

It was over an hour before a driver paid heed to that thumb and finally pulled over on the highway. And then another hour before Rippa actually found someone going in the direction of Merri Bay. He was amazed that every car that stopped had no idea where it actually was. But finally, a Supa Valu truck climbed onto the curb and the driver said he was going by there. He had to make a half-dozen drop-offs along the way, yet Rippa figured that as it was now night-time it would give him a chance to doze to the dulcet tones of AM radio leaving him fresh for his dawn surf. However, he understood the Hitchhiker's Code and knew that he'd first have to exchange a series of pleasantries with the man at the wheel. As the stocky Indian grinded his teeth, slapped his cheeks and chugged iced coffee by the glugful from the carton, Rippa could sense he hadn't slept in days.

'Are you tired, mate?' he asked as Rippa got comfortable.

'Been a big day even before I hit Perth. I surfed, played pub cricket, then our band played its first show.'

'You pulling my third leg? No way could anyone fit all of that in.'

'Um, yeah, guess you're right.' Rippa really didn't want to tell him about the football as well, as he snuggled into the makeshift pillow that was his backpack against the cool glass.

It was when he was drifting off and the driver was droning on and on about how he had driven up from Albany and how he spent 80 hours a week on the road and how his wife had left him for her yoga instructor that a sports report came on the ABC mentioning the match.

Rippa's match.

Turns out West Ham had brought on all their stars at half-time — the more professional ones who hadn't been solely drinking and sunbathing since they touched down — and they turned it round winning the game comfortably 5-2. *Comfortably*, the news report claimed, because WA had mysteriously been reduced to ten-men when their stand-out star Joey Rippa didn't reemerge after the break.

So, Uncle Warren's 10-1 prediction had only been half as bad as he'd imagined.

'That was me,' Rippa muttered.

'Who was?' the driver asked, rolling down the window to get more fresh air to keep him awake.

'I scored those two goals.'

'What two goals?'

'The two goals against West Ham.'

The driver almost swerved off the road in shock. A Harley coming the other way tooted its horn and gave the truck the finger. 'You bullshit me, my friend. You bullshit artist. Why aren't you back there?'

'Because I live up here.'

Then the driver started laughing. Really laughing. Laughing so hard that Rippa feared he might have to reach over and take the wheel, and he hadn't driven anything since passing his test on his 17th birthday as you could walk everywhere in Merri Bay.

'I've picked up some freaks along the road but that takes the biscuit. That takes the whole packet.'

'I'm serious.'

The driver's laughter halted, and he peered over at him suddenly looking very serious. 'If that is the case you can add a few notes to that. Big juicy red and yellow ones.' He pointed at his ashtray featuring a smattering of silver coins layered in sand and sweat which Rippa had dropped in as a courtesy during their fuel stop.

'Nah, you're right mate,' Rippa concurred. 'Just pulling your third leg.'

It was first light by the time the truck made its deliveries of mostly canned goods and two-minute noodles, and they finally passed through Merri Bay on the way to the driver's final destination. Rippa was home. He thanked him and secretly praised the heavens above for arriving back in one piece, resisting the urge to kiss the tarmac as he disembarked.

'West bloody Ham,' the driver giggled as he sped away. 'Had my third leg pulled many times by hitchhikers but that's the funniest one yet.'

Rippa smelled smoke billowing up from the sand below and heard the melody from Cold Chisel's 'Cheap Wine' playing on the radio.

'It's the farkin soccer hero himself.' Voodoo was sitting next to Sabrina by the fire among the few stragglers who were too wired to sleep or had nowhere else to go. Rippa found it strange seeing his girlfriend sit so near to Voodoo as they always went on about how much they hated each other. 'Where the fark have you been?'

'Playing soccer. At the WACA.'

'Haha. Yeah, right. And I've been here getting loaded with Bon Scott.'

Rippa realised he was still wearing his black and gold WA shorts. He'd have to get his Billabong boardies on sharpish so he could really feel at home.

He flopped out on the sand next to Sabrina. She had a towel hunched around her shoulders and was shivering. She looked pale, her usually luminous blue eyes were dull and tired. He stole a kiss on her cheek. She didn't smile, but then again, she rarely did anymore.

'Thought you were at your aunty's?'

'I was. But she goes to bed at, like, eight o'clock.'

They sat in silence as Chisel played on the stereo and Jacko and Muggs played a violent game of Slaps which degenerated into a more brutal game of Knuckles as the pair beat down on each other's hands hard.

'Hey. Can I talk to you about something?' Rippa asked Sabrina.

'Can't it wait?' She lit a cigarette, one of the few things that turned him off about her as he hated the smell.

'I guess.' But Rippa didn't know why it did. Why nearly anything he wanted to say to her *always* had to wait.

'You want some whip?' she asked.

'Some what?'

'Speed.'

She showed him a small plastic wrap which contained grains of something that looked like dirty washing powder.

Rippa grimaced. 'Shit looks nasty.'

'Don't be such a cube. Best I've felt in a long time.'

'I'll stick to grass, thanks.' He packed his pipe.

She organised a line of the white stuff on the back of a cassette case and snorted. Her pupils ignited and her jaw began to grind.

Rippa lit and inhaled. The smoke took him back to his cosy place where tiredness or girl troubles no longer mattered. He looked out longingly at the waves and saw the sun was nearly up. 'Can you come with me to grab my board?'

'Why?' Sabrina asked, like it was the oddest request for a boyfriend to ask.

'I told you. I wanna ask you something.'

'You're not gonna ask me to get hitched, are ya?'

'Woooo,' the others goaded, suddenly overhearing.

'Our Rippa's getting to be one clucky ducky,' joshed Muggs.

It was getting to Rippa that the only time he got to spend with his girlfriend these days was always with the fellas around. 'Nah, nah, don't be silly.' Though if she hadn't laughed, and if he knew he had half a chance of her saying yes, then he would pop the question in a second. 'Just … please. Come with me to get my board.'

He took her hand and this time she let him. It may have been the difference in drugs, but he'd never felt more distant from her. They walked up the dunes with more woos and worse from his so-called friends. He wrapped his fingers around hers so tight like he would never let go. But despite the warm January morning, he found her hand limp and icy.

'I played a blinder by the way,' said Rippa.

'What?'

'The game. The one I played in.'

'Right.' The speed was making her agitated and jittery, but it certainly wasn't making her more talkative. 'You get the money?'

'The what?'

'The five hundred.'

'Oh, um, it's coming soon.' he lied. 'Funny story. They want me to play soccer. In London.'

'Congrats, I guess.'

'But don't sweat. I told them I couldn't.'

'Why'd ya tell 'em that?'

'Well, a lot of reasons. But mainly coz of you and me.'

'They'll pay you but?'

'Course.'

'How much?'

'Dunno. I guess pretty well.'

'You're a dickhead. I'd leave this dump in a second.'

Rippa stopped dead in the sand. 'What d'ya mean? This is home.'

'Nothing ever happens here.'

'Yeah, and that's what's so good about it.'

'Maybe for you.'

'What about us?'

'What *about* us?' Sabrina stopped too and her eyes finally met his.

'Well, would you wait for me if I did go for a bit?'

'How much would you be making?'

'Dunno. Some players there get six figures.'

She did the math on her fingers. 'That's more than a thousand bucks a week.'

'Yeah.'

'Yeah, then.'

'Yeah then, what?'

'Yeah then, I'd probably wait.'

They continued walking as Rippa asked,' *Probably?*'

'That's what I said. You deaf?'

'Cool, cool. It's not really an issue though as I already said no.'

'You *are* a dickhead.'

Rippa now had his surfboard under his arm, and they were back at the beach. The sun was up and a few of the partiers had nodded off, while others were preparing to leave.

'Heard the gig wasn't too shit,' said Voodoo, cracking another tinny.

'You shoulda come.' Rippa was glad that he hadn't.

'Fark that. Had a hundred better things to do.'

'Fair nuff.'

'You must've been happy.'

'I was.'

'You must've been doing cartwheels that little Cal didn't have a full spazz-out in front of the whole Bay.' Jacko and Muggs rolled around laughing as Voodoo collapsed onto his back and writhed and kicked, pretending to have the mother of all fits.

'Get fucked, Voodoo.' Rippa tried to remain as cool as he could in front of the bigger guy as all remaining eyes fell on him.

'Oh sorry, rockstar. Or is it faggoty-arsed soccer star now? Did I hit a little nerve?'

This used to be his best friend along with Cal. All they did together was surf. But it had been the start of last summer since he'd seen him or the others out on the water. They didn't even smoke weed anymore, preferring beers and the speed which were taking over their lives. And with no jobs he didn't know where they were getting the cash for it. Though his dad had mentioned a rumour that Mr Bingley's lawn mower was missing from the other night so he was getting a pretty good idea. And they looked like shit — gaunt and unshaven, not even bathing in the ocean. And getting a new pair of shorts never happened for them — they always stank. He hoped Sabrina would never fall this far.

'You don't sit up onstage,' Rippa told him. 'You don't sit anywhere but here on your dole bludging arse.'

'Listen, you little prick. Only farkin try-hards and wannabees play that big girls' game or get up in their dad's shit bar and sing and dance in a boyband with some cripple.'

Cal had put up with enough abuse over the years said to his face and didn't need it said behind his back too. But Rippa let it go, like he always did, like he did with everything. He packed the pipe again, had another toke, and felt much better about life, same as he always did.

Rinse and repeat.

Then he grabbed the board and got away from Voodoo and the others. He hit the water, the cool blue bringing clarity to his dreamy haze. Maybe he should go to London after all. He was young enough for a new adventure. There were worse places to move to, half his family were from there after all, and though he didn't know it well, at least he'd been. In the back of his mind was the thought, or rather hope or dream, that it might be where his mother had gone. And there were much worse things to be doing than kicking a ball. Plus, no one ever said it had to be forever.

He swam out further so that he could no longer hear Cold Chisel or the laughter of his so-called friends. Where he could only hear the hypnotic crashing of waves and cawing of sea birds and nothing else. And then he saw that big swell rise up like a mountain and felt that familiar tingle of inspiration. He caught the wave just before it reached its peak and swivelled around to face Merri Bay. He took in the seaside town in all its glory, with the sun bursting out from the horizon and reflecting on the cliffs either side, dotted with lush, resplendent jarrah trees, turning their large leaves an iridescent orange. And he knew then that he'd made the right decision when he told West Ham thanks but no thanks.

But as the wave swept him furiously to shore sending his board flying from his grasp and flipping him onto his back with a heavy thud, he looked up to the beach and noticed Sabrina passed out next to the dying embers of the flames and snuggling into Voodoo who was smirking down at Rippa.

Despite all this serenity, there was something still nagging him big time.

Chapter 10

'They wanted you to do what?' Stevie was sweeping up the ring pulls, fag ends and broken glass from last night's festivities.

'Sign for them,' his son replied.

'Why would anyone go over there?'

'Exactly.'

'I hated Pommy Land.'

'I know, Dad.'

'France, Spain and Italy were alright. Shit, so was West Germany and Holland. But England? They reckon Churchill was a hero. I think he was a silly bastard. He shoulda done a deal with the Jerries and got them all out to safety.'

Rippa had also heard this a billion times before.

'Your East Pork United or whatever they're called should've toured The Bay. Then they'd have understood why you gave them a body swerve. They'd never have went home themselves.'

'You're right, Dad.'

'You got a job here for life. You know that.'

'Cheers, Dad.'

Among the debris lay a broken stiletto heel, a pair of Oakleys, and two broken teeth but this was standard fare for a Sunday morning. It was no way near as bad as the wooden leg and glass eye his dad claimed they found following a show he played back in Bondi in the '70s.

'How'd it all go in the end anyway?' Rippa asked.

'Good, good, real good,' Stevie scooped up the remaining items into a pan, a set of keys with a rubber dildo keyring now amongst it. 'Although not great if I'm honest.'

'How come? I thought it was busy.'

'It's just not busy enough, that's the thing. Kids now, they've got the cinema which has opened over in Winnenara. And there's their video games and their home video setups. And outside of that they don't have the spare moolah that I had when I was a young bloke to come and have a few beers or bourbons and a catch-up at the club. Not with the logging and fishing dying off. And tourism isn't what it used to be. Families are getting to Bali for less now. And there's drugs on the scene here too, and not nice mellow drugs. But cheap, nasty ones that can wreck communities.'

Rippa nodded only too aware.

'And that new coastal road heading for Broome means we're off the beaten track. Out of sight, out of mind.'

Rippa felt bad about yesterday at the beach when that father saw him light up in front of his kid. 'How short are we?'

Stevie sighed and leaned on the broom. 'I'd say ten K for this financial year.'

'Shit, Dad.'

'I know, son. I'm not gonna be able to pay you your full whack this week either.'

'That's okay.' It really wasn't. Rippa was already overdrawn from buying Sabrina that silver ankle bracelet at Christmas which he was yet to see her wear. Plus, Valentine's Day was coming up and her birthday was the same week.

Stevie got back to sweeping. 'But things'll come good, they always do. A few more of these fundraisers and some solid traffic at Easter and we're back in the game. And we'll get there together, hey.' He lovingly squeezed his son's arm and Rippa tried to ignore the quiver in Stevie's voice.

'Sure we will, Dad.'

Cal was onstage packing up his cymbals and placing them carefully away in their cases. Rippa always found this to be a strange ritual of his because Stevie had said they could practise here whenever they wanted and no one else ever used the stage.

'How'd it all go when I left?' Rippa asked him, helping.

'Well,' Cal began, 'Jenna Turby told me i-i-i-it was the best gig she'd ever been to.'

'How good's that?' Jenna was possibly the second-best looking girl in the Bay and Cal had been going on about her since Year 8.

'But then she told me the only bands she'd ever seen were on *Telethon* or *Rage*. And then this guy who looked a bit like Hendrix shouted me a beer and his girlfriend said that I had …' Cal suddenly shook his head. 'Actually screw all this, what happened to you?! You played against West Ham!'

'Oh, yeah, I did,' Rippa said, almost forgetting. 'I wanted you to come. I couldn't find you.'

'Sorry, dude. I was feeling a bit under the weather after the show.'

'You okay?'

'Post-gig comedown and all that.'

'I wanted to wait longer but Warren was in a mad rush. Which is probably justified considering it was nearly kick-off when we got there.'

'So, c'mon, how'd it go?'

'Scored two.'

'Fuck off.' Despite his mother's hippy roots, Cal MacCallum's father's side had been strict churchgoers and Cal never swore unless something got him going.

'Yeah, the coach or whoever came in at half-time and asked me to sign.'

'Fuck right off.'

'I told him no.'

'What the actual fuck?!' His friend was squealing and latching onto his neck now.

'C'mon, Cal. We've got the band. We need to save for a new recording.'

'Do you know how many recordings you could pay for if you were a

First Division star? Can you imagine what Jenna Turby would say to me then? How well did you play?'

'I didn't think I did all that good. I mean, I haven't trained or anything in months.'

'You should shelve the whole music thing. At least for a little while and focus on football. You should be back in Perth at the very least.'

'Nah.'

'I mean you're good with a guitar, but…'

'Nah, nah, this is what it's all about. This and surfing. All this here,' he extended his arms wide. 'This is home.'

'Yeah, a home that isn't g-g-g-gonna be here soon. Your dad was in tears this morn when he was counting the takings.'

'Fark.' Rippa had never ever seen his father cry.

'I can't believe Bobby Noll wanted to sign you.'

'Is he a big cheese?'

'If you have to ask that question then maybe you did make the right decision after all.'

'Thanks for the heads up.'

'How much did they offer you?'

'Dunno. I got the impression that I could kinda name my price.'

Rippa took out Bobby Noll's official West Ham business card from his waistband. It had the club insignia featuring the famous Boleyn Castle, with Noll's name and details embossed beneath in that even more famous claret and blue.

Cal snatched it from his fingers. 'We gotta call him.'

'You really want rid of me that bad?'

'N-n-n-no, Joey. It's because you're me mate. Me only mate in a town of bums, bullies and bogans. And I want you to go and get out, at least for a little while, and experience something special. Do something remarkable. You threw uni away as well. You could've been a marine biologist, hands down.'

'Every kid within thirty clicks of the coast wants to be a marine biologist.'

'And every kid outside of this dead-end village wants to be a pro-sportsman of some description too, so don't throw this chance away as well.'

Cal wheeled in the direction of the back office. He began dialling the other number which was scribbled on the back of the card in biro which Rippa hadn't even noticed.

'Dad'll go spare if you're ringing overseas.'

'It's a local number. The team's still here. It'll be his hotel.'

'He'll still have a moan.'

'Hi, B-B-B-Bobby Noll please…Yes, it's urgent. Tell him it's on behalf of Joey Rippa.' Cal put his hand over the receiver. 'When your dad sees the offer, he'll be screaming for joy.' Cal returned to the call. 'M-M-Mister N-N-N-N-Noll. It is an absolute honour to speak with you. I-I-I-I've been a huge admirer from afar since you won the FA Cup in 1980. And then when you made McAvennie and Cottee gel together, I mean, that was really something. And then as a player, all those appearances and goals and awards and that tackle you did on Billy Bremner in that friendly, a-a-a-and…Oh, who am I? S-s-s-s-sorry. Cal MacCallum . Best mate, or rather advisor in all things business and leisure to Joey Rippa. Y-Y-Y-Yes, he's here and keen to sign but we have a few requests, or rather demands…There's a few things he wants. Scratch that — there's a few things he needs. For starters his dad requires ten thousand to save his bar.' Cal waited a beat. Then his eyes lit up and he covered the phone again. 'He said yes.'

Rippa grabbed the receiver. 'And I need another ten grand for my uncle to get a new car. And then another ten grand for flights and studio time for my pal here, Cal. Sorry *business and leisure advisor*…Oh, and I need to go to Newquay one day a week as well like we talked about.'

Rippa waited. And he waited.

'Yes,' Rippa finally answered. 'That's all dollars…Yes, that's all.' He listened and he waited, and then he waited some more. He wasn't excited like Cal. He was shitting himself.

Did he really want to do this?

Finally, he lowered the phone telling Cal plainly, 'He says he's faxing the papers through right away.'

Cal was almost leaping out his wheelchair.

'Thank you, Mr Noll. I look forward to working with you.' Rippa finished the call and hung up.

'And I'm going to London to record?' Cal was beaming like his Lotto numbers had come up. 'You didn't have to do that.'

'Course I did. The band's still a priority. You said we needed a better recording and what better place to do it than London?'

'I'll have to wait to get the nod from the docs. Which could take a couple of months, but, like … wow.'

Rippa leaned on his Marshall trying to process what had just happened. 'I don't know if I can do all this, Cal. I'm not a footballer. I mean, sure, I can play a bit, but that life's not for me.'

'Trust me. If the great Bobby Noll says it's for you, then it's for you. Look what you've just done. You saved the bar.'

'True. And I got Uncle Warren a car. Might even get a thank you from the miserable git.' Then his brief smile faded as he thought of his friend and those bullies like Voodoo on the scene. He knew what went on when he wasn't around to protect him. 'What about you here?'

'Worry about yours-s-s-self and making this work. Just call me every week. And write, too, once in a while.'

'I promise I will.'

Rippa would miss his friend. He'd miss Sabrina too. And as he peered out the window and watched the waves glisten from silver to gold to diamond tinted, as they kissed the shoreline of Merri Bay, he knew he'd miss them most of all.

Chapter 11

**WEST HAM PICK UP A DUTY-FREE BARGAIN
ON THEIR AUSTRALIAN TRAVELS**
By George Kostas
Soccer Week
January 13, 1989

West Ham United have rounded off their mid-season tour of Australia by announcing the surprise signing of free agent Joey Rippa on a two-and-a-half-year deal.

The little known teenage winger notched a brace and put in a standout performance in the exhibition match at Perth's WACA Ground, despite the English side running out 5-2 victors.

West Ham manager Bobby Noll said prior to the trip that he was not seeking new players whilst abroad but couldn't resist this deal, claiming he was blown away by the unknown Rippa, who holds a British passport through his English-born mother.

'Explosive pace, energy and a left foot that could open a can of Heinz Baked Beans and serve it on a platter to Her Royal Highness. The kid's exactly what we need. He'll bring a bit of fizz to the flanks and, once he's settled, he'll have Upton Park off its knees and on its feet.'

Residing in the small town of Merri Bay, 300 kilometres from the state's capital city of Perth, Rippa has flown under-the-radar, never previously featuring at national or state level. He is currently unattached to any club and has been picked up for a modest signing-on fee.

'He's a different breed,' enthused Noll. 'Most kids want a flash car or a new wardrobe when they sign. All he wanted was his dad's lecky bill paid, a second-hand campervan for some uncle, and a recording session for his

skiffle duo. Hey, I'll take that from a young player any day over bubbly and page three models, thank you very much.'

Following the announcement of the deal, Rippa sounded slightly more downbeat about the prospect of leaving his hometown.

'I'm gonna miss the beach and my girlfriend and my band and the perfect weather which runs all year round. But I've been told that East London is a beautiful part of the world with…with…with its…hmm. Actually no one has told me anything good about the place. In fact, what I've read is nothing short of terrifying. Muggings, beatings, traffic and grime. I'm shit-scared. I've barely slept a wink.'

Rippa also hasn't endeared himself to his new supporters with the revelation that he is a boyhood fan of West Ham's London rivals, Tottenham Hotspur. Despite this, Noll says the club will do all it can to make this move work and help him settle.

'Have you been to West Australia?' Noll asked reporters. 'It's paradise, absolute paradise. I see the kid's point and then some. But we're giving him a day off a week to build sandcastles or sunbathe or do whatever it is these Aussies do out Cornwall way and he seems okay with that. Tidy spot down there, so it is. I might even go with him. I had the best 99 Flake I've ever had in my life there one May Bank Holiday, so I did. And don't get me started on the battered sausage I had before it. I'd be here all day. Actually, I'd be there all day, every day, if I could.'

Bobby Noll also apologised to supporters over the The Sun *exclusive regarding his players and allegations of casino splurges and hotel romps during their trip to Australia.*

'Is it good what I read? No. Was it how I planned it? No. Would I do the trip again? Definitely. I've got a cousin in Queensland and I'm dying to see her bit of the world so let's hope young Joey works out and we can shoehorn another trip there next year. Maybe even two of them.'

Chapter 12

The BA 747 jerked and rattled in the angry sky as the wind and rain battered down on it. Rippa huddled under the complimentary blanket, hating every moment. The journey conjured up nightmares of his last jaunt to London with his mother when they had to turn back following a stop-over in Singapore after one of the engines failed. Then they endured multiple aborted landings due to an incoming typhoon.

It didn't help this time that Rippa was positioned right behind the rancid smelling toilet which had been used, or rather abused, numerous times by a pub darts team on tour. Or how he was sandwiched next to a sweating, overweight businessman with a greasy quiff, drinking tumbler after tumbler of rum and hacking away on a laptop, elbows jutting every which way. Rippa cursed himself for not requesting a first-class ticket off Bobby Noll. Instead, he swirled the melting ice in his glass of Coke, wishing for once that he liked drinking and wishing way more that he was allowed to smoke something of the green variety. It had been about half a day since his last and it had long worn off.

The British Airways air hostess was up ahead. She was short and nimble with pixie-esque blond hair and large blue eyes, and Rippa thought she looked a little like the Griswold mum in *National Lampoon's* who he'd always had a secret thing for. She glanced over at him as she poured a cup of coffee for another passenger and gave a little smile. Then she replaced the jug on the cart and sashayed over to him. Rippa quickly rubbed his eyes and patted down his hair. Her arm reached down and assertively pushed his elbow out the way, turning off the switch on his armrest.

'You've hit the assistance button,' she said.

'Sorry.'

'Yet again.'

'I'm really sorry.'

'And you've got your feet up on the seat in front.' She looked down with disdain. His thongs were kicked off, showing grubby soles and black toenails, cracked and broken. He found it funny that these were the tools sending him halfway around the world. He never washed them, he never bathed, period. Having a proper shower with soap was the rarest of things for him. The ocean was his bath.

Rippa lowered his feet apologetically and noticed the nun in front relax her fingers which had been holding her nose to block out the smell. Then she blessed herself. Maybe it was time to reappraise his hygiene habits now that he was no longer living a stone's throw from the water.

He thought this act would be enough to appease the hostess. Instead, she leaned in and whispered short and sharply, 'And if you could stop staring at my bum for the entire duration of the flight that would be a big help also.'

'Yeah. I'm really, really sorry about that too.'

God, he was bored. The film above starring that guy around his age, Keanu something, in a time travel thing was probably alright, but it was doing nothing for him. In truth, he'd never had much time for pictures. Though he had fond memories of *The Goonies* and that one with the green alien with the oversized head. He also didn't mind that *Dirty Dancing* movie with Patrick Swayze in it that Sabrina loved so much and rented every week from Vic's Milk Bar (though he could never admit this to any of the boys). He wished they made more surf movies. Imagine Keanu Reeves and someone like that Swayze dude in a surf-heist flick where there were shoot-outs and explosions? Now that's something he would watch.

Rippa cracked. He pressed the button, this time on purpose.

She was back like a flash. 'Next time you accidentally press that, you'll be getting a visit from the captain, so help me God.'

'I thought the English were supposed to be polite.'

'You're thinking of the Irish. Or the Dutch.'

'I meant to press it.'

'What for?'

'A Bundy and Coke please. A double.'

'Will it keep you still for more than five minutes?'

'I think so.'

'Here. Have a triple then.'

She gave him two. He threw them down double-quick and immediately settled. The man next to him was becoming a real drag with his girth and his flailing arms as he typed and propped up his ridiculously high fringe. And with his pea-sized bladder which meant that the moment Rippa got comfortable he had to get up to let him queue for the amenities behind the darts guys. What was worse was that while he was thump-thumping away on the keyboard, he'd now taken to mumbling to himself, things like, 'How good is that?', 'Bonanza,' and 'Tickety boo'. Eventually he started talking to Rippa, and being a nice guy, Rippa had no choice but to engage.

'How's this economy?' He was pointing at a black and white bar graph on his computer screen which Rippa couldn't make sense of having never seen a laptop computer up close before. 'It's a lot better than *this* economy,' he gestured to the section in which they were confined. He handed Rippa his business card, with silver letters on a white backdrop. 'Martin Vasey, Agent to the Stars.'

'Um … Rippa.' They shook hands.

'Just Rippa?'

'You got it.' He looked at the card closer. With its Comic Sans font, it was nowhere near as posh as Bobby Noll's. 'Who do you represent?'

'Well…no one you'd have heard of yet. I'm all about nurturing talent. Stage, screen, you name it.' The man moved in closer which was really saying something as they were already wedged so tight that Rippa's ribs were bruising. Then he whispered, 'I'm actually off to Paris then New York but gotta do London first. Shouldn't be saying this but I have a meeting with a certain Jason and Kylie when we land.'

'Who are they?'

'Have you been living under a rock?'

'You could say that.'

'What about yourself, squirt? You doing the whole backpacker thing?'

'I wish.'

'You wish?'

Rippa really did. 'Signed a professional contract.'

'For what?'

'For football.'

'Football?'

'Soccer.'

Martin Vasey was all ears and eyes and everything now and somehow managed to lean in even closer, the rum pulsating from his breath making Rippa feel the weight of those triples of his own he'd just thrown down the hatch. 'Tell me more.'

So Rippa did.

'I could represent you,' the businessman gushed. 'I was just saying to the partners in the firm that we needed to expand into sports. I'm envisaging endorsements for you. Coaching clinics, brand engagement, ambassadorships. I'm talking about putting your capital to work. I'm thinking about stocks and shares and establishing your own property portfolio. Diversifying your wealth. The sports landscape is changing. The days of athletes like yourself sacrificing their time and their health for a halftank of petrol and a stubby of beer are gone. This is the dawning of the age of Aquarius and you, my friend, are heading to the right place.'

'I am?'

'I mean, anything north of Finchley is basically third world, a complete waste of time. But not London, that's a metropolis, a sporting Mecca in the truest sense.'

It sounded almost plausible. Believable. Yet all a bit strange as even Rippa could recognise that the man's accent was distinctively northern English.

'But first,' Martin Vasey continued, 'Have you heard of Amway?'

'I think so.' Rippa remembered his mum going on about the sales fad before she disappeared and how she lost a chunk of Stevie's funds which he'd put aside to set up the surf club.

'We can get you on top of the pyramid. Imagine those 30,000 fans in the stands not just cheering *for* you but buying *from* you, and essentially working for you.'

'Buying what exactly?'

'Everything from brake fluid to toothpaste and even birth control. Just imagine it.'

This, Rippa could not.

Martin Vasey held out his chubby, slimy right hand once again. 'So, have we got a deal?'

'Wait? What for?'

'For me. To represent you.'

'Oh, no. Oh, no, no, no. I mean, best of luck with it all. I'm sure you know what you're doing. But no thanks.' Rippa was being kind. He was certainly no style icon himself, but the man's shirt was about three sizes too big for him and he smelled of something rank which didn't come from rum or feet or the toilet in front. And he was sweating like a burst banana which had been left out in the summer sun.

'Thank you, Mr ...' Rippa looked at the card, 'Vasey. But I didn't even want to sign my football contract, never mind one for a pyramid scheme.'

'Young man, this goes beyond pyramid selling, taking it into a whole new paradigm. I'm talking leverage. I'm talking asset allocation. I'm talking ROI.'

'With all due respect, sir, if you're meeting with Johnny or Karen or whoever they are, then why are you here in cattle class?'

'Only a poser would cough up good money for business seats. That's an extra couple of grand in my skyrocket right there. That, my young friend, is good financial management personified.'

'All I'm really into is surfing. Speaking of which,' he pointed at Keanu on the small screen, now playing air guitar. 'Here's an idea. How about using your contacts and making a surf movie starring — get this — Keanu Reeves and Patrick Swayze and maybe even that baddie from *Lethal Weapon*?'

Martin Vasey looked at Rippa like he'd just grown another head. 'That would never in a million years work. Maybe you should just drop out and stick to the beach lifestyle after all.'

The man gruffly returned to hammering away on his keyboard, pressing the button on his armrest for yet another rum. Rippa did the same, really hoping for a quadruple this time that would knock him out for good.

Chapter 13

Rippa waited by the luggage belt. While his fellow passengers were seeking their suitcases, Rippa was looking out for his dayglo surfboard cover and guitar case. He wasn't completely unprepared — his smalls and a spare t-shirt were stuffed into his old backpack. He'd also brought along his stonewash Levi jacket which was draped over his shoulder. He knew the club would provide him with new boots and shin pads now that he was in the big leagues.

Bare essentials of board and guitar in hand, he trekked towards the taxi rank. When the automatic doors of the airport opened, the January English air with its wicked cocktail of wind, rain, sleet and a hint of snow bowled him over like a 22-wheeler. So much so that he had to grab onto the door frame to catch his breath. The last time he'd been in the UK was in March, and while certainly not tropical, it had been nothing like this.

As he shivered waiting in line for a cab at the congested rank, he spotted the *Evening Standard* headline at the paper stall:

DIVISION ONE MANAGER SACKED AFTER HORROR RUN

Geez, thought Rippa. Imagine struggling a bit at your job and then having your dismissal plastered over the front pages for millions to see. Britain was a colder place than he remembered in more ways than one.

He had to wait nearly an hour in the raw elements before finding a black cab big enough to take his oversized items. Even then, the cabbie moaned all the way to Upton Park about what the corners of Rippa's possessions were doing to his upholstery, and the traffic on the M-whatever, and the price of fuel, and the unending strikes gridlocking the nation, and Kerry Dixon's miss for his beloved Chelsea against Blackburn which had burst his coupon and ruined his month. Rippa just nodded. He'd bought new batteries and was listening to INXS's *Kick* on his headphones hidden under his long hair to shut out the reality of where he was and what he was doing.

When they pulled up at the ground, Rippa told him he was looking at a flatshare nearby, not wanting to get into how he was about to turn out for the surly cabbie's most-hated rivals and really spoiling his day.

He struggled out of the car with the board and guitar, getting no assistance.

'Can't help you, mate,' the driver told him. 'If I step out on manky Green Street, I'd need to zip home for a bath and a change of threads — and I'd have to burn the old ones. You'll understand soon enough.'

Rippa gave him a five-pound tip anyway and hopped over the puddles and up the stadium steps. He gratefully threw open the ornate double doors, immediately struck by a cascade of claret and blue. The carpet, walls, the drapes, the front desk awning. Even the frames of the photographs of past players, a few of them showing some big guy with a mop of blonde hair who he remembered seeing holding the World Cup trophy once, and another fella in black and white scoring in the 1966 final. His uncle would know who they all were, but Rippa wasn't sure.

What he didn't know about football could fill the stands twice over.

Despite this, Rippa couldn't help but feel the nostalgia, the prestige and the history baked into these foundations. He couldn't wait to see the pitch. And it was now that finally the magnitude of this opportunity — what he'd done and what he was about to do — kicked in causing, those butterflies to flutter again. Cal was right — he'd have been a maniac to have turned this down. Through his lack of sleep, and the craving for a real smoke, Joey Rippa from little Merri Bay had signed for one of the big cheeses in the world game and now had his chance to become one of its greats and make himself immortal.

'Can I help you?' the older woman at the desk with the chewing gum sneered.

'I hope so. I'd like to see the manager, please.'

'Oh Christ, not another one here to complain. Listen, the chairman has clearly outlined his reasons and there's to be no further comment.'

'No, y'see, I'm the new guy.'

'The new steward?'

'No.'

'The new kitchen hand?'

'No.'

'You can't be the masseuse. I was told to expect a Chinese chap.'

'Nope. The new player.'

She looked at his attire. Then she cackled. And then she pointed back to the street. 'Cheeky little time waster. Off you pop.'

'I'm serious.' Rippa rummaged through his old backpack for the contract.

'I'm sick of you Jeremy Beadle-types hobbling in here to have a laugh at my expense.'

'I swear it's here somewhere.' He was sweating now, despite the cold.

Suddenly she was round the desk and on him, twisting his arm and directing him out. 'I haven't got time for this. I've a transfer list as tall as a witch's hat to type up, quotes for the program, and Christening invites for my great-nephew to take to the printers, so if you wouldn't mind …'

A barrel-chested middle-aged man in a baseball cap and a Scoreline anorak marched out. 'Here's the updated transfer list, Rhonda.' He paused, noticing what was going on, then grabbed Rippa by the scruff of his denim jacket. 'Another Millwall thug in here to stir us up, hey?'

'Ouch,' winced Rippa as the much larger man squeezed and bent his arm in ways it wasn't supposed to go.

'Lad says he's here to see you, Mr Burke,' said Rhonda.

'Who?' he asked, gold-fillings gleaming.

'The lad you've got in a headlock.'

'Not you,' Rippa managed to gasp as the door was opened and he was about to be flung down the frosty steps. 'I'm here to see Mr Bobby Noll.'

The man paused. 'Do you not watch the news?'

'There it is.' Rippa had managed to reach into his shorts' pocket and produced the scrunched-up contract, complete with a claret and blue letterhead.

The man dropped him to the mat and skim-read the document, mumbling and shaking its head at its main points. 'Two-and-a-half-year deal...room and board...to report to Mr Noll on Tuesday the 31st at 10 a.m.'

'And I'm half-an-hour early.' Rippa got up, adjusting his jacket.

'Jesus, Mary and Joseph,' the man muttered. 'Rhonda, you might want to tell the directors that Noll's reign of bumbling incompetency was worse than we thought.'

'I will do, Mr Burke.' She headed straight for the boardroom.

'And tell them I'll resolve it.'

With a beady eye kept on the ragamuffin before him, Burke picked up the phone and dialled. 'Chapman Cole...Yes, Ron Burke...Yes, yes indeed...I'll send one to you today ... Oh, it's something straight out of the box alright.'

Rippa put down the surfboard and guitar he was still holding and gave his sore neck a stretch.

Burke hung up. 'Sure you're a footballer?'

'Not really.'

'Beg your pardon?'

'I mean, um, of course.'

Burke began jotting something on a blue Post-it Note. 'Heard of Middleby?'

'Nope.' Then Rippa thought. 'Actually, yeah I have. Not sure from where though.'

'You'll know all about it now. Because it's going to be your home for the next four months.'

'What?'

'Your biggest fan Bobby Noll has left the building. Was booted out to put it bluntly, following a string of gross misdemeanours such as this. And there's a new sheriff in town.' Burke thumbed his own chest. Then he handed Rippa the address scribbled on the note along with a National Express voucher. 'And this sheriff is sending you to the little leagues.'

'Little what?'

'You'll see.'

'Hmm, right,' sighed Rippa. 'You'll be keeping tabs on me, though? I'll be coming back, right?'

'You're a Hammer now, or so that scrap of paper says. You're one of us, a prized asset. Of course, in two decades of management I've never brought in a player from a division below. And never mind an Australian. And definitely not in a million years from the GM Vauxhall Conference.'

'The what?'

'Non-league football, Croc Dundee. I can tell by looking at you that there's 101 things you need to learn before I let you polish a pair of boots here, never mind wear them.'

'Middleby? Right? Do I get a bus there?'

'No, you get there by Kangaroo Airways.'

'Kangaroo what?'

'Of course by bus. Gee, you Aussies really are a dim lot. The ticket's there, the address is all you need.' Burke had a strong arm back on his shoulder and, though he was gentler than before, this time he was making sure the boy got all the way outside.

'What exactly is Middleby like?'

'Gorgeous spot. Family area, salt of the earth people. Birthplace of the common nettle, Myra Hindley and the clap, or so I'm told.'

'Right, but, but …'

'So catch ya later, alligator. Do keep in touch.'

And with that the door was slammed and bolted and Rippa was back on the street. He looked down and saw the cab from before pulling out onto the road and accelerating far away from him.

Chapter 14

If getting his surfboard and guitar case into a London cab proved tricky, getting them onto the Underground and then onto a coach bound for Carlisle (via Middleby) proved near impossible. The National Express driver flat-out refused his luggage, reasoning that there was no room in the undercarriage.

'Got a classful of Luxembourger exchange students up top. The amount of shite they've brought with them, you'd have thought they'd invaded.'

'Could I take it on-board and rest it on my seat?' Rippa asked.

'Against union regulations. You'll have to dump it here.'

'Please. It's a thousand-dollar board. And the guitar was once owned by the frontman of Mental As Anything.'

'Mental as what?'

'Doesn't matter.'

Cal and his dad had both told him it was daft bringing them. Rippa searched his pockets. He had £6.24 in change, half a packet of spearmint LifeSavers and a travel pack of Kleenex. He handed it over to the driver. 'It's all I've got.'

The driver's permanent scowl broke into a smile. 'This will cover the week's union dues and my breath after that cheese and onion pasty I just wolfed down. And help clean up the mess after. You have yourself a deal.'

Rippa struggled on with the eight-foot lump of fibreglass and thick vinyl case, clipping at least three Luxembourg students in the face.

'Arschgeige!'

'Scheizer!'

'Achtung, baby!'

While the students were indeed all positioned up front, the back was a motley crew. There was a young and clearly heartbroken goth crying her eyes out as The Smiths spilled out of her headphones. There was also a kindly old man with a grey labrador onboard which Rippa didn't even know was allowed.

'Heya, girl.' Rippa lowered his hand to pat it. The dog went feral, barking and trying to chomp Rippa's hand off and had to be restrained by its owner.

'Harmless thing,' the old man told him. 'But absolutely detests the hairies such as yourself. Don't take it personal. Apparently, her paternal great-grandfather worked in drug reinforcement in the sixties. Brian Jones tried to pat her on Carnaby Street once and very nearly never played guitar again.'

Rippa sat in the back row behind a couple old before their years, their grey skin, sunken eyes and teeth like condemned buildings showed the ill-effects of every kind of vice going.

'You moving house too?' the woman turned, rolling a cigarette.

'You could say that.'

'Good old National Express,' her partner wheezed. 'Cheapest house movers in the land.' Rippa saw he wasn't the only one the driver and the Luxembourg students had been complaining about as the couple had somehow sneaked on a washing machine, microwave, single bug-eaten mattress and 24-inch TV complete with stand, which were all jammed into the seat across.

Rippa settled next to three men in red-and-white hooped rugby shirts and flat caps sharing a bottle of Diamond White. The bus shuddered forth as they chatted away to him. Rippa didn't understand a single word, the tip of his board pinning him to his seat and making it impossible to move, never mind breathe. The window was steamed up meaning he couldn't see out either. Whereas moments before he was shivering from the cold, now he felt sick from the heating and was wishing he'd removed his jacket before he'd boarded. He didn't have any space to move his hands and put them over his ears when the drunks started singing 'Rule Britannia' over and over as he fell into a cursed sleep, driven by jet lag and panic about where he was and what horrors lay ahead.

In his dreams he was out on his surfboard, except it wasn't Merri Bay. The water was black and icy and he was getting whisked around like a top loader so hard that the board escaped his grip and there was no sign of the shore. Wall-to-wall with waves, he was sucked down deeper and deeper until there was no way at all to breathe and he felt all life squeezed from him like a tube of toothpaste.

He awoke with a piercing scream, varnished in cold sweat, which had the Luxembourgers, the goth, the junkies, the drunks, and even the driver spinning around to check that someone wasn't being hung, drawn and quartered in the backseat. Rippa gave a little wave to let them all know that he was semi-okay, and they were on their way.

After three storms, a near head-on collision with a bin lorry, and an emergency stop so that the men next to him could get off for a pee and a chuck, Rippa heard the call from the driver, 'Next stop, Middleby.'

As he struggled with his belongings, he accidentally swiped someone else four rows ahead with his guitar case, someone he hadn't noticed yet. It was the guy, the businessman or agent or Amway seller or whoever from the flight. Martin something. He was huddled in a seat near the middle, his quiff now flat and lifeless, his features hungover and teary.

'Vasey. Vasey!' Rippa gasped, remembering.

The man eventually turned and looked around in mock amusement. 'Um, who?'

'Thought you were heading to Paris after London?'

'My name is Leroy Cummings.' The slight northern twang was gone, replaced by a strong Harlem one.

'How did you go with Jimmy and Cheryl? Are you gonna get them on the telly here? Are you gonna get them a hit single?'

'What are you smokin, you crazy mofo? I'm a tourist, man. Here to soak up all this fine nation has to offer.'

'You know who you should sign? Tom Carroll. He's a surfer, the most underrated in the sport. Now there's a cat with star potential.'

'Sir, I don't know you, but you need to back-da-fuck away.'

'What? I know you. I just spent 24 hours jammed up against your moobs. Your computer thingy is in there.' Rippa pointed to the bag at his feet. 'I've still got your business card.'

'You need to control yo ass, muthafucker.'

'But, but … you said The North was a third-world shithole.'

'He said The North was what?' the entire bus turned on him. Even the teary goth and the Luxembourg students.

The bus pulled into the station and just as they were about to devour the man who Rippa was sure was Martin Vasey, he had no time to pursue the matter. The door clicked open, and Vasey quickly gathered his laptop bag and forced himself outside and fled into the nearby bushes.

Rippa departed the vehicle at a more leisurely pace, this time only striking two of the students instead of three.

'Dickkopf!'

'Schwanzlutscher!'

He thanked the driver and the doors squeaked shut behind him leaving him alone at the stand. He looked at his watch. It was still the afternoon and yet the sky was already as dark as coal. Rippa was thinking that he might be struggling from cosmic withdrawals due to a lack of THC in his system. Then he remembered his dad telling him that this was how things were here.

As miserable as sin itself.

He clutched his board. He wanted a smoke. He missed the waves already. He missed the band. At this hour they'd be finishing up rehearsal. He missed Cal — the smartest guy in the Bay by a country mile. He missed it all. He trundled into the cold dead of night, or quarter–past-four in the afternoon as it transpired. He thought about 'Rule Britannia' and 'God Save the Queen' and 'Land of Hope and Glory' and all those other odes of pride and conquest he'd endured over the past four hours, and he couldn't help thinking that his poor dad was right and the English really were full of shit.

Chapter 15

Rippa moved the congealed grey-brown sticky mass of whatever the hell it was that filled his cracked and grubby bowl. He thought that some sort of potato of the mashed variety may have been involved, though with the thick rubbery and very salty sludge covering it (he thought this might have been gravy) it was hard to tell. And then there was something else at the bottom of the bowl, something deep-fried. Animal, vegetable or mineral he couldn't say and thought Sir David Attenborough himself would struggle to label it.

But Rippa didn't mind. He was indoors. With no one there to collect him at the station, and no taxi large enough to carry his two prized, though cumbersome, possessions, he'd staggered for an hour through the rain, sleet and cold on the icy pavement, toward the council estate address scribbled on the Post-it Note, trying not to injure himself before he'd even made his debut. Then after he'd navigated his way past the congregation of latch key kids asking him for change, or fags, or booze or all three, and a pack of rabid Yorkshire terriers who looked like they hadn't been fed in weeks, he was safe and sound.

He wasn't warm though, the heating appeared broken or switched off. And he didn't know if he was actually safe. The graffiti and the numerous booted in doors and smashed windows on the trip here attested to that. He was now sitting at a dinner table with some English soap blaring in the background. The couple — his new landlords — sat across. They were of indeterminate age. The woman had coarse patches of hair across her cheeks and chin and was so overweight she had to prop herself up with a walking frame when she attempted to shuffle from one side of the room to the other. The man, in contrast, was a tall and wiry fellow with a pencil moustache and Rippa thought a draft from the windowsill might be enough to knock him off balance.

'How long you here for then?' the woman quizzed, somewhat aggressively as she scraped away on her plate, the colourless concoction collecting around the bristles on her top lip.

'Till the end of the season.'

'You like it over here then?'

'Just got in. Hard to say.'

'What's Australia like?'

'It's heaven?'

'Heaven?'

'Especially in terms of the weather. And it's so bright and clean and there's so much to do.'

'Too many sharks and crocodiles for me.'

'I have to say I've never seen them.'

'I wouldn't leave the house there, what with all the skin cancers and creepy crawlies and such.'

'You would.'

'I wouldn't,' she hissed.

Rippa backed off. 'You're right. You probably wouldn't.'

'Surprised they even play football there.'

'Ruddy great big game for shiiiiirtlifters,' the man added threateningly, before repeating the insult. 'Shiiiiirtlifters. Want to be playing a real game. Like rugger. They'd make a man out of you. Sort you right out so they would.'

'Hmm, perhaps.'

'Getting paid good money to hoof a bloody bag of wind around a field? You should be down pit with me twelve hours a day. That'd put a rug on your chest.'

'He's eating very slowly, isn't he, Albert?' Morag said to her husband.

Albert nodded. 'That he is. '

'Do you not like food?' she asked.

'Not everyday's a ruddy regent's banquet around here, you know,' Albert tutted.

'I like food,' said Rippa. 'It's just … well …'

'Well, what?' asked Morag.

'This oughta be good,' Albert leaned in.

'I only really eat fresh food.'

'Fresh food?' asked Morag.

'What the bloody hell does that mean?' said Albert.

'Barbecues. Grilled vegetables, rice, sometimes pasta. Lots of fruit. That sorta thing.'

Albert slammed the table with both fists making Rippa jump. 'Did we lose a war?'

'No, we did not, Albert, dear,' clucked his wife.

'Are there Japanese tanks on our street starving us into submission?'

'No there are not, Albert.' She reached over and put her hand over his to calm him.

'My old man didn't storm the beaches of Normandy so we could cook bastard barbecues.'

'It's … it's fine,' Rippa reasoned.

'Don't think that he thinks our food is good enough for him,' Morag simpered.

'If it was good enough to build an empire, then it's good enough for the likes of him.'

'It … it's not that. I'm happy to cook for myself.'

Morag shrieked and clutched her ample breast. 'That kitchen is my sanctuary.'

Albert put an arm around her and eyeballed Rippa. 'You … you … thankless bastard.'

'I didn't … I really didn't mean to …'

'Room and board is what it said on the ad and room and board is what you'll get,' Albert stated.

'I didn't mean to offend. Forget I mentioned it.' Rippa took a small mouthful and willed himself not to gag.

'That's more like it,' Albert nodded. 'Although whilst here you'll still be expected to pull your weight. We're not slaves.'

'That we are not, Albert.' Morag wiped away her tears then removed a sheet of A5 lined paper from her pinny, smeared in grease. 'We're a family. And here's what we ask of you. Monday is window washing day. Tuesday you scrub and iron your clothes, as well as ours. Wednesday is gardening day. Thursday is sweeping and mopping. Friday you do all the bedding. And weekends are for new projects.'

'I'm building a basement,' Albert proudly stated. 'So we can help more poor and needy like yourself.'

'Poor and needy?'

'There's barely a stitch on you, lad.'

Rippa looked down at his bare legs covered in goose pimples and couldn't really argue. 'You see … I'll be playing a lot of football so I'm not sure how much time I'll have.'

'We know what time you'll have, won't we, Morag? You're not the first footballer we've taken under our wing.'

'I'm not?'

Morag's head gyrated on her shoulders. 'Oh, no. We have another right this minute, don't we, Albert?'

'Goal-stopper or whatever you call them. Kiwi chap, I do believe. I imagine the two of you Antipodean cousins will get on like a couple of kookaburras in a gum tree.' Down the hallway, the front door slammed. 'And here he is, the man himself. Better late than never.'

'Hello, Dwayne,' Morag cooed coquettishly.

Dwayne was as tall as Albert but younger and better built. He was already balding.

'Sorry I'm late. Had to give the gaffer a lift to the library after his racer got a puncture.' He spoke with a harsh New Zealand edge to his vowels.

The couple rose like they were part of a choreographed dance routine, waltzing over to Dwayne and hugging him. Rippa thought it was like he'd returned from the front line after years of active service.

'He's one of your lot,' Albert pointed at Rippa, a thin smile across his lips.

Morag collected her and her husband's plates. 'We'll leave you two alone for a moment and let you get better acquainted.'

Albert helped his wife to her walking frame and away they went with the dishes, hocking and limping as they did so.

A silence fell which Rippa, despite being the new arrival, felt duty-bound to break.

'Joey, Joey Rippa.' He extended a hand. 'Friend and foes alike call me Rippa.'

Dwayne ignored the gesture, instead sitting and buttering the end of the loaf. Rippa had already surmised it was not actually bread at all, possessing the same density as something you'd pave the driveway with.

'I've heard all about you,' Dwayne said, not making eye contact.

'That's good then, I guess.' Rippa looked around at the spartan decor and the beige and brown colour scheme, which did indeed look like it was last updated during the war. He tried to lighten the mood. 'What about this joint, hey?'

'Pardon?

'At least there's nice high beams to hang yourself. How long you been living with the Addams Family?'

'Addams Family? They're called the Gristles. And I've been fortunate to call this haven home for the past four-and-a-quarter years.'

'Geez. Yeah. Only kidding. Nice spot. Where exactly are we anyway?'

'Middleby. Jewel of the north.'

'Is it near the coast? I brought my board.'

Dwayne allowed himself a smile, though it was not a kind one. 'I hope you mean an ironing board. It's the most landlocked town in the whole of the north of England.'

'Crumbs. What do you do for fun then?'

'There's all you'd ever want in Middleby and more. There's bingo and pubs. There's bridge Mondays and Wednesdays. Darts Tuesdays and Thursdays. Dominoes Friday. And there's an impersonator who plays in town every Saturday. It's like seeing the real thing. Elton Jack and Bloody Holly are my personal faves.'

Rippa tried not to laugh. 'Sounds rad.'

'*Rad*? What's that supposed to mean?'

'Never mind. So what's on Sundays?'

'Church. And if you don't like that then there's sleep.'

Rippa was wondering what he'd got himself into. The pair sat there, Dwayne gnawing and greedily slurping away at whatever it was that lurked in his bowl. Rippa couldn't think straight, especially with the evening soaps humming away on the screen in the corner, this one particularly dreary and set around some farm.

Rippa cracked and sprang up. 'Let's see what else is on.'

'Don't do that,' Dwayne ordered.

But Rippa had already flicked it to the news. The US was getting a new president and Rippa thought that 'Bush' sounded a particularly peaceful moniker, and no wars would surely ever be instigated by someone with such a green and leafy surname.

Dwayne snatched the control and changed it back. 'TV's for *Emmerdale* and *Emmerdale* only. And maybe *Songs of Praise*.'

Rippa sat back down as Dwayne recommenced quaffing the bread and

Morag and Albert began the mother of all arguments in the room next as furniture and crockery was flung around.

'Well,' Rippa muttered to himself again. 'At least the place has nice high beams.

Chapter 16

Rippa lay in bed after an uneasy sleep, shuddering to the sounds of World War III droning and whirring above him. He leapt to his surprisingly clean windowpane and looked up and saw that it was RAF planes doing routine exercises, looping uncomfortably close to the rooftops. He'd overheard at the bus station that his new home was just three miles from their base.

Breakfast at the Gristle's was slightly more appealing than the previous night's fare — but only just. It was two pieces of what he presumed to be Weet-Bix. Despite there being no sugar, honey, bananas or even milk to go with it, he wolfed it down in the lukewarm water it arrived in like it was a death row meal.

As it was Tuesday, he scrubbed his clothes, along with the couple's. The skid marks on Albert's y-fronts proved particularly stubborn and the parachute-sized bloomers of Morag's took longer than expected. After he hung them up he waited outside for Dwayne in time for training. He'd noted the run-down black Cortina in the parking spot out front that wasn't there when he first arrived and presumed it was the goalkeeper's.

'Alright, D. Dawg,' Rippa chirped as the bigger man emerged from the building. 'You wouldn't mind, would you?'

'Mind what?' Dwayne replied dolefully, getting in the driver's seat.

'I'll sort you out with some petrol money. It's just till I get some wheels of my own.' Rippa tried the door. It was locked.

Dwayne rolled down the window. 'Firstly, my parents Christened me Dwayne, not D. Dawg. Secondly, I don't like you and never ever will. And thirdly … well, I don't have a thirdly yet, but I'll soon think of one.'

Maybe it was the country bumpkin in him, but Rippa had never met anyone quite like this.

'Haha, funny joke.' But when Rippa tried the handle again and still found it locked, the penny dropped. 'C'mon, bro. We have to stick together us lot. Being so far away from home and all. We're practically the same you and me.'

Rippa watched as the keeper's face angrily burst open like a peach that had smashed onto the floor. He feared the keeper would implode, explode, or eject himself through the roof. 'We — are — not — the — same! You lot, you effing lot, you think you're so much better than us.'

'Which lot?'

'Your lot.'

'My lot?'

'You ever even been to New Zealand?'

'As in actually go there? Um, nah. Too far, mate.'

'Exactly.'

'You been to Oz?'

'Wouldn't piss in the place. The sooner we separate from you and gain our freedom, the better.'

'Just so that we're on the same page, we are talking about Australia, right?'

'That place,' Dwayne turned his head and gobbed out the window as he said it. '*That* place … I can't even bring myself to utter the word. I pray every night for the day to come that you savages are pinned to the walls, and we get to wipe you off the face off this fine earth.'

Like maths, history was not Rippa's strong point. However, he thought he knew a thing or two about the past and was fairly confident that in terms of goalkeepers, Dwayne was as bat-shit crazy as they come.

'"Advance Australia Fair"?' The Kiwi continued, revving the Ford's engine. 'Advance Australia this, fuckface.'

He gave him a V-sign, tall and proud. Then after a long, drawn-out and over-cautious three-point turn, which saw him navigate around a kid's rusty scooter missing its front wheel by a hair's width, and then knocking over a dustbin filled with fleeing rats, the Cortina was skidding off out of there.

With no bus stops, never mind taxis, within sight, Rippa huddled into his denim jacket and dragged his feet. At least this time he didn't have his surfboard or guitar to lug with him. His teeth were chattering in his shorts and thongs, but his toes were toasty ensconced in four pairs of grey flight socks he'd pilfered from the backs of passengers' chairs when he disembarked the craft.

The rain tilted horizontal, and the scenery appeared bleak to say the least. Factories were crumbling and bordered up, cars were rusted through, sitting up on bricks with their engines and re-sellable parts long ripped out. And the people he came across appeared weak and emaciated from a lack of sun, with concave eyes and popped pink capillaries, as they wandered aimlessly around the cracked pavements.

Eventually he made it to the ground which appeared everything that Upton Park and the WACA weren't. A busted-up sign with CLAPPERS LANE hung from it. There was only a single stand running along one side of the pitch that looked more like a draughty cattle shed than something fit to enclose humans for an afternoon's entertainment. This stood, jagged and unsteady before the pot-holed and near-grassless pitch with a slope running right to left which made it seem more like a hill from some ancient and brutal battle.

When Rippa entered the front office there were no claret or blue drapes. There were no drapes at all. Just a worn and discoloured carpet and mismatched fittings that made it look about as inviting as an air raid shelter. At least there was a kindly old face to greet him along with an enthusiastic handshake.

'Chapman Cole,' the man said, tall glass of gin and tonic in hand even at this early hour. He was wearing an outrageous black velvet top hat and matching morning suit over a waistcoat and looked the double of The Fat Controller from *Thomas the Tank Engine*. 'I'm the chairman, the custodian, the emperor himself only with clothes on. And you, my good man, must be Joseph the Rippa himself.'

'Rippa, yes,' he said, recovering his arm, surprised to find it still attached.

'Rippa indeed. And how was your trip to our fair town?'

'Not so good, Mr Cole.'

'Good to hear,' Cole replied, not hearing at all. 'And your lodgings?'

'Can't imagine how they could be any worse.'

'Splendid, just splendid. And I've also heard some equally splendid things about you. An Australian footballer? As rare as the Tasmanian Tiger. Young man, I've a mind to put you in the museum or the Middleby Zoo. If we had either of those kinds of things here, that is, which of course we don't.'

'Right. Thanks.'

'Nope, I didn't think there was a specimen in existence such as yourself. Then again, I haven't been out of the country since VE Day, so what would I know? Anyway, don't let these modest surroundings fool you. Please come up to my office.'

He led Rippa up a rickety staircase covered in dust and cobwebs and creaking like a haunted house. But the old man wasn't lying. It was far more impressive. There was a small, simple antique desk to the far corner in front of a bay window which looked out onto the ground. Except this wasn't what caught Rippa's attention. It was the model train set covering the entire room.

'Do sit down.'

Rippa would have but there was nowhere to sit. There was no space for chairs, what with all the miniature villages, bridges, forests and trains, and of course, reams and reams of train track spread out.

'Actually, it has gotten a little out of hand,' Cole admitted as he pushed a button on the control and made the trains move. 'Perhaps just perch there on the desk.'

Rippa did so.

'This is the largest track in the North,' the chairman said. 'And the seventh largest in Western Europe.'

'It's a life's work.'

'It is, my boy, it is. You a model train enthusiast yourself?'

'Can't say I am.'

'Hmm, I'm sure you have other competing pursuits down there in the land of milk and honey. What girders your loins?'

'Surfing, Mr Cole.'

'What in damnation is that?'

'You don't know what surfing is?'

'I told you, I haven't left these isles since the spring of '45. No need to rub it in.'

'Sorry, Mr Cole. It's where you take a fibreglass board out on the water and ride the waves.'

Cole grimaced. 'Sounds decadent.'

'It can be, I s'pose. I find it peaceful, something that centres me. Which reminds me, it was in my contract that I get one day a week off to hit the beach.'

'My dear boy, we're the most landlocked town in the North.'

'I know. I'm to head to Newquay.'

'Well, you'd have nothing to fear there.'

'Good.'

'Especially as there is now way on this green earth that it is going to happen.'

'Huh?'

'It might be in your West Ham United contract but it's not in your

Middleby United one. I need you here at the coalface 24/7 if we're going to break free from the shackles of this farmer's league.'

'24/7?'

'It's an expression, a slight exaggeration, but you know what I mean.' Cole pressed a button and the big red train let out a whistle, followed by a puff of steam, and was on its way. 'You'll thank me later. When you don't have hyperthermia and jelly fish stings.'

'I'm not sure about that.'

'Why you young folk would want to go anywhere else I can never work it out. Middleby simply has it all. The pub has even started getting those little Babycham things in that all the yuppies in the South like. And the chipper now has curry sauce as an option. Forget your Grimsbys and your Scunthorpes, it is becoming positively cosmopolitan here. We'll be donning cigarette holders and berets next.'

Rippa noted a pillow and a single mattress beneath the desk. 'Do you, um, sleep here as well, Mr Cole?'

That dragged the chairman's attention away from the controls. 'Are you trying to insinuate that Mrs Cole has told me to sling my hook?'

'No, sir.'

'That she asked me where I have misplaced my marbles?'

'Not at all.'

'That I'm spending so much time here at the station and writing to my pen pals at the International Model Railway Association that she ordered me to pack a bag and move in permanently and is in the drawn-out process of taking me to the proverbial cleaners?'

'Not in those exact words.'

'Well she has, in a way. And being left with a mere half of this sporting club will mean being left with nothing much at all. It is therefore imperative that we bounce back up to League Football at the very first attempt if we're all to cushion that particular blow.'

'Sorry to hear that.'

'Don't be sorry, boy. Just promise we'll cut that six-point gap and get back there. I'm not giving up my model train universe. Sorry … I meant football club. No way, José Rippa.'

'I'll do what I can, Mr Cole.'

'Make sure you do.' He put down the controls. 'Time to go and meet your general and your fellow troops in the trenches. Life in Middleby isn't all lollipops and signal stops, you know.' The train got caught on a loose bit or track and ground to a noisy halt before keeling over. 'Though sometimes I really wish it were.'

Chapter 17

Sitting in the boot room in the bowels of the stand and having his head cradled by the Middleby United manager, was not how Rippa imagined his first day as a first professional footballer would pan out.

'Phrenology,' the boss Rory Brady hummed, eyes closed.

'Pardon?'

'What we've been doing here would take us a thousand lifetimes to experience. I have walked inside your head. I have dirty danced with your hopes and wrestled with your deepest fears. We have spanned a universe sitting here and achieved something that mere mortals only dream about.'

He lifted Rippa's head up to its usual position and stared deep into his eyes. Rippa's hair was now even shaggier than usual, in contrast to his manager's long, greying barnet which was swept up into a neat ponytail.

'You ever read Seneca?' He reached back and glided his fingertips across the bookcase behind his desk, picking out a title. 'How about Confucious? Sun Tzu? Sid James?' He held up an unauthorised biography of the *Carry On* star.

'Can't say we covered any of these in Senior English,' said Rippa.

'Football isn't about what team scores the most goals.'

'It isn't?'

'Matches aren't won on the pitch.' Rory laid down a stack of titles, Anthony Robbins's *Unlimited Power* perched on top. Then he touched his own temple lightly. 'They're won in here.'

'I see.'

'And now that I've cradled your cranium, now that I feel that I truly know you, we're ready for anything. Questions?'

'Can you show me the dressing room?'

'No, you're not ready for that yet.' Rory shook his head. 'I'm so glad that they've put you up with Dwayne. What a good stoic he is. A leader, a humanist, and a bloody good laugh as well. Must make you feel so much more at home lodging with a fellow Anzac on our fair shores.'

'You have no idea.'

'I love you Australasians. I had an aunt who emigrated to Australia. Or was it New Zealand? Or Norfolk Island? Hmm, or was it an uncle? No, no, I know. It was an aunt who became an uncle. Anyway, doesn't matter. Your people are full of substance.'

'We're full of something.'

'And that's all that matters.'

'Good-oh.'

Rippa forced a smile as Rory laid his hands back on his head. The manager studied him intently, his eyes now boring into his very soul. After what felt like an hour, though was probably little more than a minute, he gave one final squeeze and then let go.

'And now I think you're ready.'

The coach put an arm around him, and they headed out.

'I'm not like Old Man Cole. I have no Pollyanna complex when it comes to Middleby. I know the place has its problems. I've plied my trade from Aberystwyth to Aberdeen — or rather worked with those who have — and let me tell you, you'll never meet a nicer bunch anywhere. Or a coach as meticulous as me. So,' he pondered, scrambling with his notebook. 'Which position did you say you play again?'

'I didn't say anything. I thought with that phenology thing you found out everything.'

'It's *phrenology*. And I'll level with you. There are a few cosmic glitches that I'm trying to iron out.'

'Left-winger is my favourite spot.'

'Marvellous. Our current one's about to have a spell on the sidelines.'

'Why's that?'

'Emergency vasectomy.'

'Couldn't that wait until the end of the season?'

'Not for our Giddsy. Nine children by seven different mothers. Or is it the other way around? Doesn't matter. He spends that much time in the maternity ward that giving him the snip now will save us time in the run-in.'

'Hmm, I see.' Rippa didn't at all.

'Any other questions?'

Down the tunnel they watched as the rain came down in thick buckets, turning the surface into a turgid soup bowl.

'You know that phemology thing?' Rippa began.

'*Phrenology.*'

'I don't think it's up to much.'

'Why'd you say that?'

'Why didn't it pick up how desperately unhappy I am here?'

'Desperately unhappy? You've been here five minutes.'

'I know, but I can just tell it's not going to work out. Let's call it a sixth sense, y'know?'

'I do know. And I'll tell you what you don't know.'

'Which is?'

Out his back pocket Rory brought a series of palm cards cut from the back of a Sugar Puffs packet. He flicked through them before selecting one and reading words he'd carefully printed on it.

'No man whose testicles have been crushed or whose organ has been cut off may become a member of the Assembly of God.'

'Beg yours?'

'Wait, sorry.' He shuffled again. 'This is the one: A person often meets his destiny on the road he took to avoid it.'

'I don't really get it.'

'Listen, this destination was selected for you for a reason. By a higher power. To build resilience, fortitude … balls.' Rory made a squeezing motion with both hands. 'So give it all you've got.'

'Sure thing. But I'm still a bit down about the whole Newquay thing.'

'You leave that with me.'

'Okay, Rory.'

'And now I think you're really ready.'

They walked towards the dressing room.

'You'll just love these blokes,' Rory told him along the way. 'Millsy, Boonsy, Dawson. Clarksy. Comics the lot of them. You might have trouble running as your sides will be in stitches.'

'As long as that's the only thing in stitches.'

'Nearly nabbed another winger from Scandinavia before you showed up.'

'Yeah?'

The manager paused and looked at him closely. 'Yeah, he was a pretty Swede guy. Haha. You geddit?'

'I geddit.'

Rory was laughing so hard, Rippa thought he might have to hold him up. 'And another from Helsinki. He was quite the Finnish article.'

'That's humour right there.'

'Get used to that kind of banter because that's how the lads round here roll. Mad as meat axes, every last one of them.'

Rory opened the door. 'Knock, knock. Here he is, you mental-men. All the way from Australia, Mr Joey Rippa.'

Fifteen hairy and misshapen males were in a state of undress, some showering, some shaving, some brushing (hair or teeth), some whipping each other's bare buttocks with damp, rolled-up towels. The room fell silent as they took in this exotic creature in the middle of winter, wearing flip-flops, shorts and a t-shirt with cut-off sleeves. No one knew what to say.

Then they burst into laughter.

'No way is that a footballer,' a voice shot out.

'No way did Chapman sign that.'

'No wonder Bobby Noll got the bullet.'

'Hilarious, Gaff,' said a shaven-headed, cube-shaped short man, his arms, chest, legs and even his face covered in tattoos. This was Millsy, the captain. 'Now where's the real new signing?'

'This is he,' Rory implored. 'This is him. Don't judge every potato by its jacket.'

'He's built like a woodbine.'

'He's got hair like my missus first thing in the morning,' said another.

'He's that piss-weak he looks like my toddler could knock him over.'

'Listen, you lot,' Rory told them. 'He's the fastest thing on two legs and has a left boot that could carve marble. Or so I'm told. So let's show him some respect and turn on that famous Middleby charm. He's one of us now.'

He pointed Rippa over to where there was an empty peg. A straight-faced beast built like a wardrobe and known to all as Boonsy was standing next to it shaving his back.

'I'm not laughing,' he told Rippa in a monotonous voice. 'I'm not laughing at all.'

Rippa edged back. 'Hmm, yeah, doesn't look like you ever have.'

'I think it's awful what you people have been doing to that poor man Mandela.'

'My people?'

'Your people. And this apartheid will not wash. I learnt all about you people after Live Aid.'

'I agree, mate. I really do. But I'm Australian, I'm not —'

'Exactly!' Boonsy seethed, spit flying. 'Bloody Australians.'

An equally stocky man with dreadlocks powered over. He had a bath towel draped around his neck and his wedding tackle jiggling every which way as he thundered, 'That's my fucking peg!'

'Sorry Curtly, simple mistake,' Rory said, quickly helping to move Joey's backpack along.

'I travel all this way, give up my home, my job, my kids, my whippet, my wife, and a functioning affair, only to have some chancer rock up from their volleyball game and shit on my peg.'

'Our mistake,' Rory said again before turning to Rippa. 'Oh, my, we all do seem a little tetchy today. That's what happens when you're four games without a win. Anyway, the lads are done for the day. Wasn't planning on playing you this week anyway so don't worry too much about missing the session. There doesn't seem to be any training gear for you yet but you're already donning a rather sporty combo.' Rory felt the weight, or rather the lack of it, in Joey's backpack. 'Where are your boots?'

'The thing is, I don't actually own any.'

'No boots? They're like a hammer to a carpenter, a brush to a painter, gloves to a heavyweight champ.'

'I get all that. But I thought your phelology —'

'*Phrenology!*'

'... Phrenology might have picked this up. I haven't owned a pair since I was 12.'

'That shall have to be amended posthaste. Great footballers come in all varieties, I do suppose — is what Nietzsche might have said if he'd been a football fan. Wonder who he'd have supported? Probably Borussia Monchengladbach, though I'd like to think he'd have harboured a soft spot for Middleby.'

Rory put an arm around his young charge and led him out of the room and back up the tunnel. 'Tell you what, as it's just you, how about we get you limbering up with a few laps of our hallowed ground and make you feel right at home?'

'Could I have a ball?'

'A what, sorry?'

'A football.' Rory was looking at him like he was asking for invisibility powers. 'Like, a football … to kick. Like, what I've been brought here to do.'

'Why would you want one of those things?'

'To dribble. To pass. To shoot. Also, as I can no longer surf first thing in the morning anymore, I could get up early and practise with it.'

'Well in all my years in football working with players from Boscastle to Boddam, I've never heard of such madness.'

'You haven't?'

'You won't want the ball on weekends if we hand you one to boot around willy-nilly. We need to keep you hungry. Diogenes himself would be turning in his tomb at the thought of such decadence.'

'I thought I was here to develop.'

'This is developing.' He gestured out at the mud patch. 'And where better place to do so. Football's a thinking man's game nowadays. Weights, drills, sprints, even ball work will only get you so far. Same as your everyday coaches who worship at the temples of Cloughie, Robson, and Venables. But these fellows right here …' he pushed a selection of Stoic, Gandhi and Churchill books — as well as the Sid James biography — into Rippa's chest. 'These will push you upwards and onwards towards the mantle of greatness. Not practising with a ruddy football.'

The wind howled right through the tunnel. The rain had stepped up and the pitch was now looking like the aftermath of the Battle of Towton.

Rippa peered dolefully down at his flip-flops. 'You really want me to run in these?'

'I'm sure the Spartans themselves wouldn't have flinched. Made in Taiwan? That would have been a luxury for them.'

Joey lifted his denim collar above the nape of his neck and set off at an unsteady canter, which is all he could manage, weighed down by all those books, as mud gathered around his shins and his footwear sank into the thick mud.

Chapter 18

'Rippa! Your time has come.'

Rory had assured his new recruit that in no uncertain terms he would not be featuring in the league game at home to Kidderminster Harriers. Because of this, on the day previous, Rippa ran a half-marathon on the boggy pitch-side track, then stayed up till three a.m. through a mix of jet lag and trying and failing to make sense of Andrew Carnegie's *How to Make Friends and Influence People* which he'd been given. Then he'd spent his whole morning lugging lumber from the local timber yard to Albert and Morag's for the proposed basement conversion. And all he'd eaten were two Weetabix and water, leaving him neither energised or inspired.

But, sitting there on the bench on the hour mark of the drab and 1-1 match, he was willing to answer the call.

He pulled up his socks, then he tightened his boots. Well, as much as he could. They were old ones that had fallen down the back of the lockers. Despite half the *Middleby Evening Times* having been stuffed into his toes, and wearing the four pairs of flight socks and three pairs of Middleby United ones, the size 13s still flapped around at the ends like a kite caught in a storm.

'I thought Giddsy was playing quite well, boss,' said Rippa. He had, indeed, already scored to cancel out an early goal by the visitors.

'He has. He is. But we just got the call that his new squeeze has gone into labour and he has it in his contract that we have to take him off. Don't worry, his op is booked for Tuesday, so never again.'

It was also the Middleby fans who thought he was performing well as they mercilessly booed when the board showing number seven was held aloft. The boos became even louder when they saw Joey stripped and ready to take his place.

'Hear that passion, feel that love,' Rory whispered to him.

'That doesn't sound like passion where I'm from.'

'The best fans in a twenty-mile radius. The only, mind. There's only rugby clubs round these parts. But they're still the best.'

'You really think?'

'Drink it in. And get ready to write your name in the Middleby book of greatness — if such a thing existed, mind.'

Rippa wasn't quite ready. He was still trying to swipe his hair from his eyes, having misplaced both his brush and elastic band in the cramped home dressing room. However, he was glad to get his bum off that freezing bench and to have an excuse to move around. His team tracksuit hadn't arrived, and his denim jacket was offering no protection.

Rippa had never played in rain and mud like it. It would be an achievement keeping on his feet, never mind trapping a ball and attempting to do something constructive with it. He thought back to his first summer when he arrived in Merri Bay. The bigger boys, Voodoo among them, laughed at his mullet and said that no way could a city slicker like him make it out in the ocean. Six months later he was the best youth in the area and eighteen months later he won the all-ages surf comp covering the entire Mid West.

If only West Ham was a surf club instead of a footballing one, then Bob would indeed be his uncle.

With these memories circling his mind and the boos in his ears, he clapped hands with Giddsy, stepped over the white line, and immediately went arse-over-tit and face-first into the mud. Now the fans' boos switched to laughter, which then spread to the players and even the match officials. Boonsy gave him an arm up.

'Another disgrace to your nation,' he said. 'Even the Afrikaners would be pissing themselves at the state of you. And they don't laugh at anything.'

Rippa dug the thick mud from his eyes and took up his position, confident of showing them all.

'It's The Great White Shark,' said a fan in the stand.

'It's Young Einstein,' said another.

'It's Kim bloody Wilde,' joked a fat man eating chips at the back.

On the wing nearest them, Rippa was finding it hard to shut them out.

'Is this was what the whip round at the family picnic day was for? To raise funds to sign this freak?' said another.

'Who's Kim Wilde?'

'That bloody West Ham reject right there.'

A ball was sprayed out wide for him to run on to and Rippa set off like a hare. But the surface met his footwear and sucked him down making it feel like he was running on treacle. The heels of his boots were piercing the surface deep, and the toes, with no bones actually filling them, had nothing of substance to pull him out. In the family section, children cursed and shook their heads, while one made a cutthroat gesture. Over in the disabled area, punters waved their walking sticks in anger, as an elderly lady waggled her prosthetic leg.

'Kim Wilde in high heels would be bloody quicker,' she moaned.

The full-back easily collected the ball and nudged it back to his keeper.

'You still jet lagged, Oz?' asked Millsy.

Rippa shook his head. He was a little, but he was more so struggling to adapt to the surface and the hundred-mile-an-hour style of play. Because of the heat down in Australia the game there had a slower, more measured build-up, while this was more like kick and rush meet British Bulldog as bones clattered and blood splattered.

It was another few minutes before Rippa got a chance to make amends as he followed Rory's strict instructions to stay wide and not venture inside. The ball was played out to him by Dawsy. This time he got there before his marker. He took a touch and played it ten yards inside to Clarksy and then ran on for the return. Level with the eighteen-yard box he looked up and saw a sea of grey shirts darting towards the goalmouth. He managed to strike the ball well with the side of his boot, but he'd misjudged the gale-force wind and the ball swivelled and sailed away from the keeper, landing on the roof of the net for a goal kick. This time it was the turn of his own players to lay into him.

'Waster.'

'Keep it lower, would ya?'

'Kim Wilde? More like ...' Millsy paused. He clearly had little to offer. 'Kim ... Riled. Which is exactly what you've made me.'

Having never played in front of a large crowd aside from his man-of-the-match showing at the WACA, and never having played since he could remember without smoking grass to calm his nerves, Rippa felt his knees knock and his cheeks fill with colour. He was a fish out of water, suffocating on the banks of the river, no question. But he was also raised to be a fighter and no way would he choke and hide. He took a deep breath and fronted up, and when a long clearance from Dwayne hit the sky, he was onto it. This time, though, he thought he'd do something different and run at his marker. He dribbled the ball along the touchline and got his legs pumping and sailed past his opponent who attempted a trip. Their midfielder then raced over and slid in, studs up. He got a chunk of the ball but it fortunately broke in Rippa's favour. He was now racing through into the final third, gliding along the turf instead of sinking into it, and had the Middleby strikers in support making it three against two. He took another touch and was about to play in the big number nine when he felt a painful crunch from behind.

Both his legs were taken clean from him as he was booted through the air like a crash test dummy, landing with a dull thud in a puddle the size of the Thames as the ball trickled to safety. Rippa lay there, unable to move, as the players and fans raged, not at the referee but at Rippa for not playing the ball sooner. Their fury only abated when the physio was eventually waved on and the howls turned to whistles and catcalls as the players also got involved.

'I've got something you can rub,' said Boonsy.

'Fancy massaging my bollocks after?' said Dawsy.

'There's a giant bone in my pants that needs resetting,' added Millsy.

Then Rippa, face in the mud, heard a woman's voice bite back. 'Judging by the lack of penetration out here on the pitch, you useless arseholes wouldn't know what to do in the bedroom.'

Rippa struggled round and wiped his eyes and saw that the gruff voice did not match the angelic view. Hair and eyes the colour of milk chocolate, framing a delicate moon-shaped face, the physio was more classic '50s film star than beach babe, which was the look Sabrina and all the Merri Bay girls rocked.

'Where's it hurt?' she asked, gently wiping his forehead with the ice-cold sponge.

'Everywhere,' Rippa groaned.

He felt her lift down his shorts a little and examine the lower part of his back, right near his bum. 'You're fine. It's just a bit of bruising.'

She was stockier than Rippa and helped him onto his feet with ease.

'Look at that,' smirked Millsy. 'He didn't even have to buy you dinner and you're already on him like a rash.'

She hit right back. 'Keep it up and the next dinner you'll be eating will be through a straw, ya tubby fuck.'

'I don't think I can play on,' Rippa told her.

'You can. You have to. You're in Middleby now and if you don't play with heart then this lot will rip yours out and feed it to their young.'

Lost in those chocolate eyes, Rippa suddenly didn't feel so sore. He did a little stretch and found he was moving even better than before. And with both subs used there really was no chance of coming off.

The game entered the final ten with Middleby pinned back in their own half and Rippa finding himself trying to screen the runs from the overlapping right-back as The Harriers smelled blood and pressed for a winner. The crowd was tetchy, bordering on furious, as the chance to go back into the top three was slipping against their mid-table opponents.

In injury time, Middleby finally made a foray forward. With the Kidderminster right-back still upfield and toiling from his offensive exploits, Rippa found himself in space.

'To me! I'm open! Switch it left!' Rippa begged.

But his teammates were intent on keeping the ball as far away from the debutant as possible, already viewing him as a liability. With all other options marked, the captain finally lobbed the ball over to the free man out wide. Rippa collected it but his marker had tracked back and was now on his tail. Rippa steadied himself on the tricky terrain and quickly stabbed his boot at it. But he did little to dispute his teammates' opinion of him as he again skied the ball high and seemingly wide. The groans were deafening this time.

But the ball had nicked the right ear of their centre-back on the line and Middleby were awarded a last-gasp corner. The boos for Rippa were now replaced with a hearty 'C'mon, Middleby! C'mon, Middleby!'

'Up, up, all you up!' Rory ordered as even Dwayne streamed forward into the opposition half for the final attack. Rippa jostled at the back stick sensing his chance. Millsy swung it in. The ball hung in the wind. The Kidderminster keeper came off his line for a punch and missed it completely. Boonsy stuck out a knee and it was blocked on the line again by the jug ear of their centre-half. It pinballed out into the powder keg of players striking shins, chests and more ears before spinning out to Rippa who remained free at the back, three yards out with only the keeper to beat.

Their number one dived down to block at his feet. Instead of side-footing it either side of him, Rippa elected to treat the fans to one of his trademark scoops. The type that had Bobby Noll frothing and drawing up that contract. However, this time Rippa didn't have his size eights on. This time he got under the ball alright, but the extra-long toe of his left boot burrowed deep into the soft turf, and he got under it way more than he planned. And because of this he sent it spiralling up, up and up, and it kept going over the keeper and didn't stop, looping over the goal and even over the two stray travelling fans behind the hoardings and out for a goal kick.

Rippa slumped to his knees as he felt his body sink deep into the filthy mire. This he didn't mind as it was covering his ears from the full-time whistle and the abuse from the crowd. No one had ever called him a wanker before, but 2,000 of his own fans were now doing so over and over.

Along with every last one of his teammates.

Chapter 19

Australian winger Joey Rippa's fairytale move to English powerhouse West Ham United has turned into a nightmare. With Hammers' manager Bobby Noll getting sacked when the ink on the deal was still drying, Rippa was immediately farmed out to non-league outfit Middleby United. And things have gone from bad to worse.

Since signing on loan for The Clappers back in January, Middleby haven't won in their last six matches, drawing three and losing three, which has seen them drop to fifth on the GM Vauxhall Conference ladder. Rippa is also yet to play a full 90 minutes. In last night's loss at bottom-side Aylesbury United he was handed his first start but was subbed at the break having registered just five touches. A report suggested that his removal had more to do with a death threat which was phoned into the ground saying that if he wasn't pulled, then he would be missing a knee-cap via a sniper's bullet.

Middleby manager Rory Brady remains philosophical about the impact the new loanee has made.

'Let me tell you about someone, with unruly hair not unlike young Joey, who also made a slow start on the stage of life. That man was a certain Jesus Christ. For 30 years — bugger all. Less than bugger all. Just a load of carpentry, mystical ramblings, and petty crimes down the markets. Then all of a sudden — boom. Miracle after miracle, bringing folk back to life, walking on waves, turning water into wine. Let's face it, the ending was a bit car-crash, let's hope our Rippa doesn't go there. But, long story short, it's not over yet. It's just beginning. And for the record I'm not actually comparing Rippa to Jesus. He probably can't walk on water but if you do see him paddling around out there in the middle of Clapper Lake next time you're walking your dog, then you heard it here first.'

With no goals and no assists to his name, Rippa himself admitted that the move had been a struggle.

'The pitches, the food, the housing, the weather, the scenery, the people. I could go on. I mean, it's not just another country, it's another galaxy. And, sorry, but it's a third-world one at that.'

Rippa then went on to downplay reports that he'd lost a stone-and-a-half. And that he'd fled to Manchester Airport in the dark of night attempting to board a flight back home.

'Nah, mate,' he said sheepishly. 'I've got a cousin in town visiting who looks exactly like me and it was most certainly him.'

Geoff Harrow, secretary of the Middleby United Supporters Association and editor of the fanzine, *You Fat Bastard*, believes the club could have bought in three players for a similar sum to the loan fee they outlaid for Rippa as he questioned the club's recruitment policy.

'We've got a right-back playing left-mid. A sweeper playing up-front who hasn't scored since October, and a stopper whose voice hasn't broken. Put simply, there were other priorities above signing some unknown winger who's never played in England, never mind this league, or for any team in Australia for that matter. Bobby Noll was clearly tanning way too much Foster's on that trip and didn't deserve the axe. He deserved hanging.'

Asked if he thought Rippa had what it takes to make the grade, the fan who hasn't missed a match since the outbreak of WWII was less than optimistic.

'He runs like a girl with two legs down the one knicker and spends more time swiping his girly mop out from his eyes than looking at the ball. I wouldn't say he's been our worst signing ever, mind. We had a fellow, Bert Tilderman, who we got from Walsall in the late '40s. He had a wooden leg, an eye patch and a hook for a hand. And he was the reserve keeper. And don't get me started on the players we bought in the mid-'40s when some of the townsfolk wanted to stay in Europe and keep fighting rather than come home. They were horrendous. So if you want to be kind then this Rippa chancer is nowhere near as bad.'

With a crucial six games remaining, Middleby United must win them all to have any hope of a return to the Division Four at the first time of asking.

At the time of going to print there has been no interest from any NSL clubs keen on bringing Joey Rippa back to Australia and ending his nightmare.

Chapter 20

Rippa sat alone in the booth of the busy pub, The Orient Express, and forced down his dinner — a packet of greasy pork scratchings, which was the only delicacy the pub had on offer. Still, they were far tastier than anything Morag dished up.

Rippa took in the decor of the hostelry. It featured train-themed everything — booths in carriages, tiny tables you struggled to fit your knees underneath, and framed pictures of every locomotive imaginable. Even the staff wore caps, blazers and money belts just like conductors. He was sure this was the place the players met every Tuesday night before their day off, to bond as they called it. The first two Tuesdays no one had bothered to tell him about this, the third he had a dodgy stomach from the poached eel Morag had prepared, and the next few he'd come home from training feeling so lethargic from depression more than anything, so he took a tablet and slept right through his alarm until the next afternoon.

This week, though, Rory had insisted that the players invite him so he could get to know the real them away from football and Rippa reluctantly agreed. Despite his efforts, he'd had no interactions with his teammates except trying to solve who had sliced denim jacket into strips, who'd put his flip-flops in the sandwich press, and who it was that kept blaring Men at Work from the street outside his bedroom window at midnight every Friday which, if he was honest, was annoying Albert way more than it was him.

'Long-haired, pug-ugly Kim Wilde wanker,' said a passing drinker in Coke-bottle glasses.

'Happy to be here,' replied Rippa, growing more accustomed to these insults, as he drained his cola through a straw.

He looked at the vintage railway clock above. Rippa elected to go. Not that he had anywhere else to go to, but he'd been waiting half-an-hour and had been insulted by so-called fans four times now. Morag would have *Emmerdale* blaring and the only thing to do in the house was watch it, though even that had to be better than this. He slung his newly re-stitched denim jacket on. He was walking to the exit when he heard a crowd of drinkers crammed into the far booths suddenly hush. He looked and there was the entire squad silently hiding behind an old railway crossing barrier.

'Ah, bollocks,' moaned Millsy, slapping Dawsy on the back of his head. 'I knew you were lighting your fags too loud.'

'Guess you'd better join us, Rippa.' said Curtly reluctantly lifting the barrier. The others moodily budged over to make room on the end of the bench. Rippa relented and got one cheek sat down. He'd never seen so many ashtrays and drinks spread out across the table, everything from wine to shots, to cocktails, to beer steins.

'What are you drinking?' the barman called to him. He was dressed in coal-stained overalls like a fireman on a steam train.

'Just a Coke, thanks.'

'A Coke?' they all bellowed.

'I … I don't really drink.'

The table went silent as if he'd just told them he was dying.

'Not even a whisky toddy when you're ill?' asked Dawsy.

'A Blue Hawaiian in summer?' asked Curtly.

'A sherry by the log fire at Christmas?' asked Boonsy.

'What is it you do then?' Millsy enquired.

Looking at their sensible hair and shoes, one thing Rippa wasn't about to do was tell them that he smoked pot. 'Guess I'm pretty square.'

'Guessing fucking right there, Oz,' mumbled Dwayne cradling one of the frothy steins.

'Fuck that, get him a snakebite, Robbo,' ordered Milly to the barkeep.

'Coming right up.'

'What's a snakebite?' Rippa asked.

'All the kids drink it.'

'So it has no alcohol?'

'It's the ticket.'

As the barman plopped a fizzy purple pint in front of him,

Chas & Dave's 'Snooker Loopy' came on the jukebox and it reminded Rippa of his Uncle Warren and why he was here.

'The rule round these parts is,' Millsy told him, 'You gotta drink it in one.'

Rippa relented. Despite his dislike for the club, the town, and everything in it, a part of him still wanted to fit in.

'Skol, skol, skol!' the players chanted, hammering down on the table as shot glasses and hot ash sailed to the ceiling.

'Skol you fucking koala shagging bastard,' yelled a young Girl Guide selling boxes of cookies at the next table.

Rippa did so with surprising ease, feeling his teeth ache but enjoying the immediate sugar hit. It was the most flavoursome thing he'd consumed since disembarking the plane.

'You like that?' asked Millsy.

'Love it. Another please, barkeep!' He turned to Millsy. 'And you say there's no alcohol?'

'You big girl's blouse. Anything that isn't behind the optics doesn't count.'

'Hmm, right. Why don't you drink it then?'

'Because I'm not a big girl's blouse. I stick to vodka, me. Fat-free it is. I'm a model pro after all.' He threw down another of the clear shots as his tummy jiggled with all the excess weight.

'Model pro, my arse,' said Curtly. 'You've a belly like a waterbed.'

'Bollocks.' Millsy sucked in hard and patted his stomach. 'Doctor said I've the physique of a twenty-year-old.'

'Yeah. A twenty-year-old hippopotamus,' Curtly quipped.

Another pint was placed before him and Rippa demolished that too, finding them refreshingly moreish. 'I Should Be So Lucky' was put on the jukebox, apparently to take the piss out of him, but Rippa didn't mind as he still had zero idea who the singer was. He was in a great mood. Then for the benefit of the players he got up on the table and started waltzing about to Rolf Harris's 'Tie Me Kangaroo Down Sport', a song he really knew. But even though he was a light ten stones, the small table couldn't support him and it flipped and he fell, sending glass and ash hurtling all over the room.

'Will I get barred?' he asked, bouncing right back up.

'No chance,' Dawsy replied. 'Chapman Cole owns this joint.'

So Rippa got up again and kept dancing when 'Great Southern Land' came on next.

The night was certainly helping them all bond. Tilesy, the left-midfielder who Rippa thought might have been from Liverpool as he rocked a giant Zapata moustache and always knocked about in an Everton tracksuit, sat next to him when Rippa had climbed down for a rest and refuel.

'How you settling in, fella?'

'You know, it's not so bad.' The snakebite was certainly making Rippa feel perkier.

'Middleby's okay but I bet it doesn't compare to the lovely part of the world you're from.'

'You mean you've been?' Rippa asked, surprised.

'We used to go there every summer.'

'You did?'

'Yeah, la. Me mam and dad and nine brothers and six sisters. We used to take the caravan and drive across.'

'Really?'

'Those big snow-capped mountains were something else. And we used to hammer that *Sound of Music* cassette so much that we had to buy a new one at the Esso every year.'

'Hmm. You're talking about Austria aren't you?'

Tilesy darkened. 'But you fuckers have a lot to answer with that Adolf fella. Flattened Merseyside, he did. Killed my old man's childhood bunny with a shrapnel wound and he never got over it.' He pointed sadly to his heart. 'And I've still got the emotional scars to prove it.'

'I'm sorry about that but I can assure you that Hitler was no close relation.'

Dwayne was on his other side and Rippa made another stab at friendship with the big Kiwi. 'You planning on heading home this summer?' Rippa asked.

'This is my home now. I can't go back since you Australians,' he almost vomited the word, 'have ravaged it economically, politically and spiritually.'

'I'm really not sure it's as bad as that, hey?'

'The oppressor would believe that. Now if you'll excuse me,' he turned the other way. 'I'm here for a relaxing beer. A relaxing non-Australian beer. So hooroo or whatever it is you savages say.'

A gaggle of not-so-young ladies had joined the table. Their faces were heavily made-up, and with their beehive hairdos, faux silk scarves and ¾ length granny coats, they were dressed like Rippa's own grandmother might've done down in London if she was still alive.

'You alright, duck?' One of the red-headed ones screeched into his ear above the music. She put her hand on his knee, and he jumped so high he nearly flipped the table again. 'Ooh, you're a Nervous Nellie. I only asked if you were alright.'

Rippa burped and then mumbled, 'Yeah, I guess. I mean, definitely. Perhaps. Actually, not really. I think that drink went down the wrong way.'

'No wonder,' she pointed at the row of empty pint glasses. 'You've shifted about ten.'

'Aren't they good for you?'

'Let's see if you're saying that in the morning. Who knows? Maybe I'll be there to find out.' She put her hand on his thigh, and he jumped again, knocking the table and causing the glasses to tumble and smash. Kim Wilde's 'Kids in America' was so loud, and the players so preoccupied with the other ladies that no one even noticed.

'Sorry, sorry,' Rippa slurred to her. 'I actually have a girlfriend.'

'So what? I have a husband and four littlies.'

'Shouldn't you, um, be home with them?'

'Tuesday's my night on the razz. Along with Thursday, Friday, Saturday and Sunday afternoon.' She looked at her watch. 'So are we gonna stop jawing and start necking or what? I didn't come here for a blue rinse, y'know.'

She removed her bubblegum, attaching it under the table.

Then she lunged towards him, mouth gaping, her teeth a crooked mass of nicotine, tea stains and shiny fillings, her breath unspeakable.

'I … I think I've gotta go.'

Rippa jumped up again and his knee smashed the table yet again. Only this time it stuck on the gum and he had to give it a big heave-ho to separate it from the red sticky mass.

'Where you going, Oz?' asked Millsy.

'Things to do.' He gripped the pillar suddenly feeling woozy.

'We're off upstairs once we've knocked off these slappers. Old Man Cole's laid on Marmite sandwiches and a load of strippers. Way better than this lot.'

Rippa raced out the door as Chas & Dave returned to the jukebox with 'Rabbit'. He immediately spewed a geyser of blackcurrant into the gutter, so much of it that he thought the surge would never end.

Chapter 21

Out in the fresh air, Rippa immediately felt better. He moved unsteadily down the street, his pockets jingling pleasantly with the sound of copper. He passed a phone box and knew he needed to speak to Cal. He'd promised to call and write but had been so caught with the move that he hadn't managed to once. Then he remembered that he really had to call Sabrina too. He'd tried ringing her every day at all different hours but she was always out. He wished there was some magical device people could keep in their pockets or handbags and he could speak to her no matter where she was, or somehow type a sentence or two to say that he missed her.

He went in and dropped the coins into the slot and dialled her home phone number. It rang and rang. He was about to hang up again when she answered.

'Hello,' she rasped.

'It's me.'

'Who?'

'Joey. Joey Rippa. Um … your boyfriend.'

'Oh, right. How's London? You meet the Queen?'

'I'm not exactly in London anymore.'

'How's that big pro team you're playing for? I ain't seen ya on GWN news.'

'I'm not exactly playing for them anymore, either.'

'So what exactly is it you're doing over there again?'

'That is a really good question. How's The Bay?'

'Sun, sand, surf, repeat. You know how it is.'

'Oh, I know.' He was buckling at the knees he missed it so much. He heard voices in the background.

'I gotta go,' Sabrina said.

'Why?'

'All that sun, sand and surf, I guess.'

'Have you been, like, um, faithful?'

'Have you been, what?' The line was turning fuzzy.

'I mean, I've been faithful. Just in case you were wondering. We're still going to wait for each other, yeah?'

'I can't hear you, Johnny. You're breaking up.'

Did she just call him Johnny? Did she just say they were breaking up?

The phone went dead. Rippa's good vibes from the sugar high had well and truly worn off and now he felt drunk and weepy. He had to talk to Cal. But the phone offered no change and that jingle-jangle in his pockets had ceased. He lifted his collar high and headed out into the wind and cold, the brown moccasins he'd bought for fifty pence from the Cancer Shop at least offering some resistance. Out on the high street a couple in matching grey and white Middleby tracksuits greedily snogged. To his left was a queue snaking around the chip shop where a gang of teens younger than him punched on — fists and boots flying — but all were too inebriated to do much harm. Despite the bleakness of it all and the homesickness lying heavy in his soul, Rippa still had no desire to go back to his lodgings and face those people. And Tuesdays was the only night Albert and Morag relaxed their curfew at Dwayne's behest.

Down an alleyway off the main drag, Rippa heard a girl singing soft and delicately, her voice dripping in sweet honey. She was performing a song his mother used to sing to him on rare nights back in suburban Perth when the weather was wild, and he couldn't sleep. It was 'Shelter from the Storm' by Bob Dylan. He walked away from all the shouting and breaking of glass, and car alarms and police sirens, and down towards its source. It was a small establishment named The Middleby Working Men's Club.

He opened the doors. The glow from the open fire warmed his insides. In the corner of the quiet old man's pub was a small stage and up there was the club physio picking an acoustic guitar. It sounded ethereal, angelic, not of this world. Well, that was until her bandmate — a tubby bearded thirty-something with long matted hair, wearing a green velvet cloak that made him look like a wandering wizard from the nearby woods — began thrashing around on a djembe, completely out of time and way too close to the mic. But the physio seemed used to it, and the smattering of folk heads with beards and braids were too polite to let it phase them as she finished to polite applause. Rippa slipped in quietly and sat down at an empty table enjoying the end of the set and savouring the contrast in surroundings to the hell which raged outside.

'That was incredible,' he told her when she was packing her guitar into its soft case.

'Oh, thanks. Joey Rippa, right? I'm Jane from the club. Did not expect any Middleby players within a mile of here. Isn't it your big night out at The Orient?'

'It is. Or it was, rather.'

She wrinkled her button nose. 'You smell like you've had a skinful.'

'Nah, must've been something I ate. I was drinking these things called snakebites. Full of nutrients and goodness.'

'I hate to tell you this, love, but that's one of the strongest tipples going.'

'Serious?'

'How many did you have?'

'Maybe ten pints? I lost count.'

'And you're not a drinker?'

'Not really.'

'Well, I wouldn't expect you to be able to read anything that Rory Brady has put on your list until at least the weekend.'

Rippa felt faint and really needed to sit down. He parked his bum on a drum stool until he was grunted at by the bearded giant who was her bandmate.

'Magnus doesn't really like people going near his drums,' she said. The wild man snarled. 'He doesn't like speaking much either.'

Rippa was getting used to being disliked in these parts and apologised, grabbing a chair instead. 'Between you and me,' he said, sitting, 'I'm really more of a smoker than a drinker. Pot smoker that is. But that doesn't seem to be a thing here.'

'It's a thing, alright. Especially this scene here.'

Rippa looked at the happy bunch nursing half-pints of real ale and sat in a circle jamming with guitars, fiddles and harmonicas.

'We meet here every Tuesday,' Jane said. 'Heard you like your music.'

'Don't tell anyone this either but I like it way more than football.'

'And I like music way more than I do rubbing down a bunch of sexist, misogynist, man-babies and you can tell that to whoever you like.'

'Sorry.'

'Not your fault. You're one of the good ones. Probably the only one.'

'Why'd you do it then?'

'I'm a sports physio. It's either that lot or the rugby team. And trust me, the rugby lot are far worse.'

'Can I buy you a drink?'

'I don't think you can.'

'Course I can. The bar's right there and we just got paid.'

'I mean, you can hardly stand up straight.'

Rippa tried to rise and found the carpet spinning and suddenly felt like vomiting all over again. He swayed towards the floor, clamping onto the djembe for support. As Magnus rushed towards him, Rippa moved back and bounced off the side of the stage, just managing to launch himself out the exit. Into the clogged gutter he puked up more of the ten pints and the packet of pork scratchings. The couple in Middleby tracksuits broke from each other and peered down the alleyway at the commotion.

'Fucking disgusting the way some people lead their lives, hey, Gaz,' the woman told her boyfriend. Then she recommenced mauling him all over again, tongue down his throat, her chipped and oversized hot pink fingernails everywhere.

Chapter 22

Before he opened his eyes Rippa could already feel the throb in his head, spreading down to the rawness in his guts, and leading to the weak, withering feeling in his core. And then there were the numerous bumps and bruises from stumbling for half the previous night.

And he knew, he just knew that someone was watching him.

Aided by the hard heel of both his hands, he unpeeled both his eyelids. Then he let out a scream as there, hovering mere inches from his face, was Morag's toothless, hairy face and its many chins.

She stood back. 'It's alive. And more's the pity.'

'W-w-w-what are you doing?' Rippa scrambled half up, covering his bollock-naked body with the threadbare duvet and feeling the cold. It was always so chilly in this house, like death itself. The thumping pain in his brain was like a pneumatic drill making him even more disorientated. He was sure he'd double-locked the bedroom door.

'I am trying to teach a harpsichord lesson. Except, it's a little difficult with all the snoring coming out of this room. It's like we've chained up a wild animal in here.'

Rippa wasn't even aware that he did snore.

'The state you came in here last night,' she cooed suddenly, lightly massaging at her breasts and looking anything but annoyed. 'You kept me up all night.' Then her fingers crept into her bloomers as she whispered, 'All — night — long.'

'What the bloody hell's going on in here,' Albert boomed, appearing in the doorway.

Morag threw herself away from the bed. 'Oh, Albert. He dragged me in here, so he did. I said I had a lesson, and he wouldn't hear of it. He was more beast than man, lying here in his birthday suit our saviour made.'

'What?!' Rippa shrieked. 'In no way whatsoever, at any time, in any state, in any dimension, in any alternate universe even, would any of that ever happen.'

'You calling my missus ugly?' Albert demanded as he cradled his sobbing wife, helping to cover her exposed bosom with her red silk gown. 'Are you calling my partner for all eternity a fat, sweaty sow? There, there my sweet, sweet petal, picked fresh from God's garden. Daddy's here.'

'No, but …'

'You're on your last legs, young man. The state you waltzed in here last night. Partying like it was bloody 1999. Bringing a lady of the night home as well.'

'That was Jane. The physio. From the football team.' Rippa just about remembered the lift home she gave him and how she helped him in before leaving straight away. Then he remembered getting a glass of water and going to bed as quietly as he could. Dwayne had still been at the pub when he left there. He wondered if he was getting the same treatment.

'And look at this, Albert.' Morag wept as she pointed to a Polaroid of Sabrina next to his bed in her bathers outside the surf club. Alongside this was the 1989 *Sports Illustrated* calendar which his dad had got him every year for Christmas. This one featuring Stephanie Seymour in a tasteful cream lacy number. 'Bringing the devil into our home. The devil! Oh, Albert, what did we do to deserve all this evil?' She nestled deeper into his stick-like arms.

'There, there, love.' Albert then turned on Rippa. 'I've seen the perverse way you look at my queen. And I tell you, this is your last warning. Your very last.'

'I wasn't aware there'd been a first.'

'You go back to your lesson, my flower. I'm heading to the market to buy a fat hog. And as for you — while I'm away I want those profane pictures burned to cinders. And get that lawn mowed and that fresh blood and bone down right away.'

'Yes, Mr Gristle. It won't happen again, Mr Gristle.' He'd have agreed to anything just to have them gone.

'It better not. Oh, and this came for you.' Albert tossed him a postcard.

With the pair gone, Rippa eagerly read it. It was from Cal.

Dear Joey,

How you going, mate? Been buying Soccer Week (when I can find it) and watching the English highlights but heard nothing about how you're going there?? Are you injured? Pls give us a number so I can phone (I'd say write but I know you won't!)

The Bay misses you. I've realised I have no other real friends here. Voodoo and his mob are more annoying than ever!! I get my leg brace off next month and will be able to walk. Soon as the doc gives the all-clear I'll be over, and we can start recording and I can maybe even get a flat with you. If that's still alright??? But then I guess you probably have all that sorted and already have a cool pad of your own. Never mind.

Please let me (and your father) know you're okay.

Your pal, Cal.

Rippa lay in bed reading the tiny scrawled words over and over, missing his friend and his home so much. And then he flipped it over and looked at the image of the coast of Merri Bay and those waves baked in sunshine, his heart breaking like it never had before.

He'd call his friend right away and make those plans and get the wheels in motion. He got up, threw some shorts and his grey club polo on, and went out to the hallway. He'd have to ask Albert where Sabrina's postcards were. Maybe they'd gone missing? There's no way she wouldn't write. She had time on her hands. He'd written almost every day, and he was busy and was certainly no writer.

He heard a stuttering, spooky tune coming from behind the living room walls and thought it might have been the theme from *Psycho*. Then it stopped and through the walls came the crack of a cane or worse.

'It's a C-minor, Henrietta,' Morag hissed. Then he heard a young child sob. 'It's an effing C-minor.'

With Albert gone, the coast was clear. He tiptoed down the hallway. He picked up the phone from its cradle ready to dial. He put his ear to the receiver and waited for the dial tone.

But there was only dead air.

His fingers followed the line of cable. The end didn't reach the wall. It had been hacked off. Strange, as he always paid his board on time and phone use was part of the agreement. He'd have to brave the cold and go to the phone box instead. But first he'd make his life a little easier by getting his jobs done.

Jacket and shoes on, he crept out back hearing the snip-snipping of shears from the neighbour's hedge. In the tiny brick structure which was the shed, he found the lawnmower under a sign above which read CLEANLINESS IS NEXT TO GODLINESS in bold lettering. There was a bag of pungent blood and bone next to this. Rippa caught a whiff and made it outside just in time to vomit up another purple stream from last night right over the orchids. He'd give the fertilising a miss for now and wheeled the lawnmower out onto the grass.

The snip-snipping from over the fence paused.

'How's old Adolf and Eva treating you?'

'Who?' Rippa looked over. An old bearded man in a grey and white Middleby bobble hat grinned at him from between a tall hedge.

'Your landlords,' the man said.

'Could be worse.' Then Rippa paused and thought for a moment. 'Actually, I have zero idea how it could be any worse.'

'Oh, it will get much, much worse,' the man chuckled. 'You're that United lad from Australia, yeah?'

'You gonna tell me to hang myself as well?'

'I wish the entire team bloody well would. Lifetime fan here for my sins.'

'Sorry for being so, well … shit.'

'Hardly your fault. We've always been shit. And as long as the earth revolves around the sun, we always will be.'

'No silver-lining there then.'

'You're young. There's a bit of spark about you despite what they all say. You can rise above it.'

'Thanks for your optimism, but I'm really not so sure.'

'First you've got to get away from Mr and Mrs Twit in there.'

'I'm getting that vibe.'

'Let's just say,' the man lowered his voice to a dull whisper, eyes darting everywhere, and suddenly very nervous, 'Apart from that big streak of nothing that plays in goals, I always see lodgers arrive, a new one every month. But I never, ever, see them leave.'

'What are you getting at?'

'Look around you.'

Rippa looked. The lawn beneath his feet was green and lush. He didn't know of anyone else's round here that needed mowing each and every week. The roses, likewise, growing like nothing else did in Middleby.

'It's not natural,' said the man. 'It's not natural is all I'm saying.'

Rippa thought of the basement Albert was renovating and felt a cold shiver creep up his spine.

'Why don't you sell up then?' Rippa asked.

'I've tried. We've all tried. But word's got around far and wide. No one will touch anywhere near Jack Sprat and his wife.'

'Joey!' Albert suddenly called from inside. 'Where's my hacksaw, Joey?'

The man panicked and dropped his shears. 'We never had this conversation. We never spoke. You can't prove anything. I'll deny it all.'

And with that the old man was sucked back through the hedges.

Chapter 23

Rippa was hard at work in the boot room, polishing Curtly's Diadoras. He had the rest of the squads' all lined up in a row, neatly scrubbed and shining bright. Rory entered and looked immediately startled.

'What you doing, Rippa?'

'My job. It's my turn.'

'Who said?'

'Millsy and Boonsy. And Greggsy and Barnsey. In fact, all of them did.'

'We have YTS kids to do this. Not first-teamers.'

'Oh.' Rippa's shoulders drooped and he put down the pair. 'I've been had again, haven't I?'

'It's the only reason we have the YTS kids. By the time the big teams in the North have scooped up the talent pool, the ones we get couldn't tie the laces on those things.'

'Oh, dear.'

'C'mon, Rippa. Chin up.'

'Sure, Rory.' But with his long face, he didn't look like he was about to anytime soon.

'I know what'll cheer you right up.' From his kit bag he pulled out a bright red and green knitted sweater with a reindeer pattern. 'It's a present. To keep you warm.'

'Thanks.' Rippa held it up to him. It looked about several sizes too tight even for him. 'But it's not Christmas.'

'Sorry bout that. It did take me a wee bit longer than expected. The wife doesn't want it anymore. But hey, the collars and sleeves are triple stitched.'

'Thanks, Rory,'

'Don't worry, you're gonna make it, Rippa. The great Captain's Cook career was littered with things that didn't quite work out.'

'Wasn't his body boiled and eaten?'

'I thought you Aussie's were an upbeat lot?'

'Sure, Rory. It's just … it's been a tough time with Newquay being KO'ed, and my living situ, and now I've been underpaid. I really need to see the chairman.'

'Well here's some good news. We're about to play the YTS mob in a bounce game. No running today. And Chapman Cole will be there.'

Rippa loathed running. He always had. Back home, surfing, cricket, and occasionally riding his BMX — and very occasionally playing football — kept him fit. But all this team did was run. Uphill, downhill, sprints and cross country. From Monday to Friday, they still never saw a ball. Rippa kept raising this with Rory, but the boss insisted there was no other way over here and reading the great philosophers such as Bill Odie would stand him in better stead than mere ball work. And the players, even seasoned veterans like Millsy with more clubs than Jack Nicklaus, told him to get back on his kangaroo and go back to Australia if he wanted that. Because this was the home of football, and this was how they did things.

Rippa put the lid back on the tin of Cherry Blossom and trailed behind Rory towards the training ground.

'I understand it's tough being away from home,' said the boss. 'I'll add Dostoyevsky's *Crime and Punishment* to your list. Four years he was in Siberia and look how he thrived. And, c'mon, Middleby's hardly Siberia.'

A plastic Co-op bag was whisked up by the sharp wind and landed right in Rippa's face. 'That's one opinion,' he muttered, struggling to tear it off.

'And it's not easy moving to a new place. I'm basically a foreigner myself, y'know.'

'Where you from?'

'Chifly. Seven miles west. I tell you, the looks I got when I set up sticks here were nobody's business.'

On the pitch the players of both sides were already stretching and preparing for the whistle. And all laughed when they saw Rippa turning up late. And then they really laughed when they noticed the flecks of dark polish around his ears, eyes and nose giving him the look of a giant panda, and they all tried to outdo each other in the shit-joke stakes.

'You moving to Warsaw to play with the *Polish* national team?' said Boonsy.

'You did a *ripper* job on those boots,' said Curtly.

'Rise and *shiiiiine*, it's Joey Rippa time,' added Millsy.

Rory put an arm around his shoulder. 'Don't listen to them. Get out there, get to that byline and show me the real left boot I've heard so much about.'

'Where exactly do you want the ball?'

'In the mixer. See The Schnozz?'

'Who's The Schnozz?'

Rory pointed at the gangly striker sporting the biggest and reddest hooter Rippa had ever seen. 'Just back from nose reduction surgery. You could see that thing from where you're from.'

Rippa nodded and jogged into his position, glad to finally be allowed to kick a ball during the week. This was, after all, what his new life was meant to be all about.

Well, he was glad until Rory blew his whistle, and their opponents came at them.

The kids were around sixteen, but most had thick facial growth. And all were shaved-headed and wide-chested with crazy eyes. They didn't speak, they looked incapable of it, communicating instead with each other via a series of verbal tics and growls. Rory had been right about their negligible footballing ability as they struggled to hit the ball with any panache, preferring the direct big toe method. And without the ball they were even more savage, using every method — pushing, punching, kicking, and the occasional elbow — to throw their older opponents off their game.

There were few causes in which Rippa might put his health and well-being on the line for — Merri Bay, Sabrina, Cal and his dad among them. But a meaningless training game on the other side of the globe was not one of them. Every time the ball came near, the hulking full-back with no neck, scabby tic marks covering his bald head, and a left shoulder looking decidedly higher than his right one, would stomp towards him thundering 'ARSE MUNCHER!'

It was enough to give Rippa skid marks without having to go near the mud.

So instead of trying to round him or go anywhere near his vicinity, Rippa elected to play the ball safely back to his own full-back. After twenty minutes of this, though, his own teammates were getting restless with his negative, self-preserving play.

'Boring Bugger,' said Boonsy.

'Negative Nigel,' said Curtly.

'Backwards passing bastard!' screamed Millsy.

Rory wasn't much happier. 'Look alive, Rippa. You're meant to be the creative fulcrum. Skin him. Whip it in. Aim for The Schnozz!'

The Schnozz himself trotted over to the touchline. 'C'mon, Rory. I've already reported the club to the PFA twice about the jibes regarding the dimensions of my natural and not in any way abnormal nasal cavity.'

'Sorry, Simon.'

Rippa watched Chapman Cole take a seat on the sideline and light a cigar the size of a baby's arm. He was looking less than impressed by the fare on offer which he was paying for out of his own pocket, as he wriggled and sighed and occasionally looked away, probably wishing he was near his beloved model train track.

Jane, the physio, was packing up her medical bag next to him. She gave

Rippa a hearty thumbs-up as she departed. Suddenly Rippa knew what to do. The next time the ball came to him he swung his body goalwards instead. His marker screamed and steamrolled forward, studs primed to inflict the maximum amount of pain. Rippa gulped down his fear and leapt over the flying boot heading straight for his standing leg.

Then he was off, pedalling down the byline. He glanced towards the box. There was a melee of bodies all wearing the same grey and white stripes (it was too cold to play in skins and the club had never gotten round to buying bibs). And there, sure enough, shining out among it all was that schnozz, looking even redder and more bulbous than the one on the jumper Rory had knitted him, shining bright in the cloudy surroundings. Rippa's left foot was wound back ready to land the ball neatly onto it, when he heard a runaway train come hurtling from behind. It was then that he realised all too late that his marker possessed pace as well as brutality. And the last thing he saw was an oversized shoulder and then a flash and a searing pain as it smashed right into his nose.

When Rippa came to, he was clutching a pack of thawing peas and seated next to the chairman watching the rest of the supposed friendly match. Cole by this point had given up on the spectacle and was perusing this month's edition of *Railway Modeller* magazine instead.

'What happened?' asked Rippa.

'You got clattered by a juvenile delinquent with a sailor's tongue on him,' said Cole. 'Don't worry, lad. The physio does a half-day on Thursdays, but we've sent for her to come back.'

Rippa's bloodied nose felt like it was twisting upwards at the full moon which had begun to appear. 'I think I need a hospital.'

'You've obviously never been to Middleby General. If you're not seeing the Pearly Gates, then you don't want near the place. Because after a trip there — no matter what's wrong with you, even if it's an ingrown toenail

— to Saint Peter you shall soon be heading.'

Rippa tried breathing out his nose but couldn't. 'Can I ask you something?'

'You may, young man.'

'I'm meant to be on seven hundred quid a week.'

'You are? That's more than my rail bonds yield.'

'And in my pay-packet, I'm getting one-twenty-five.'

'That's more like. That's some nice hamburger money right there.'

'Only my board is a hundred. So that's not leaving much to clothe myself, or to pay to use the phone.'

'You can use my telephone.'

'To call Australia?'

'No, you cheeky bugger. 0-8-0 numbers only.'

'To spell it out, Mr Cole, I'm meant to be a professional footballer and that wage doesn't really cut it.'

The old man placed the magazine down. 'The way you played out there? The way you've been playing? I wouldn't give you £12.50.'

'That's not fair. I know I've had a few teething problems but …'

'Do you have any idea how much track I could buy with £125 per week?'

'Not really.'

'The answer is a bloody lot. Seven hundred quid was your West Ham contract. That's in Division one where gates can exceed 40,000. And you'd have to start every week to get that. You'd have to win. And you'd have to score a bloody hat-trick.'

'I see.' Rippa knew he should have got Cal or his uncle to read the small print on his deal.

'Now I took you on a basic wage. We don't pay bonuses at Middleby. Pulling on that shirt, being part of the fabric of a world-famous town, should be reward enough.'

'I hadn't even heard of the joint till I arrived.'

'You hadn't heard of what?'

'Never mind. It's just, I can't live off that.'

'When I was your age that sum would've kept me in penny whistles, Woodbines and waistcoats for weeks.'

'With all due respect, Mr Cole, that was about a century ago.'

'Half a century ago. Forty-five years to be precise. Cheeky bugger.'

Jane appeared with her medical bag. 'Sorry, Joey. I was at the shop.'

'That's okay.'

'They do you one, did they?'

Despite the throbbing pain running across his face, the sight of her couldn't help but make him smile.

She assessed the injury with her big kind eyes and her long, soft fingers. 'I'm gonna have to reset it.'

'Oh, Jesus, God, fark, no.'

She gripped the septum and the bridge. As she did so, another scream came from the pitch as Rippa's marker scissor tackled Greggsy. 'And it looks like I'll have to be quick. You ready?'

'Jesus, God above, no!' he scrambled for something to hold onto and settled for Chapman Cole's bejewelled fingers. The chairman tried and failed to pry him off.

'Sorry, love,' she told him. 'But we have to.'

'Okay. But only if you agree to hang out with me tonight.' Rippa wasn't sure where this came from having never given it any thought. But out it came.

'Can't,' she told him.

'Oh.'

'There's something I always do on Thursdays.'

'I see.'

'You could come along, I s'pose.'

'You're on!'

'You don't know what it is.'

'Doesn't matter.'

'You won't like it.'

'I can guarantee you it's a billion times better than anything else on offer.'

'I'm really not sure you'll want to.'

'Why'd you say that?'

'Not after I do this.' And with a twist and a crack so loud that even his marker twenty feet away flinched, Rippa unleashed a yelp so extreme that Chapman Cole was compelled to give him a reassuring cuddle.

But in no way whatsoever was he giving him any extra cash.

Chapter 24

'Up to tricks — 46,' announced the deadpan bingo caller from the stage.

'Thanks for coming,' said Jane.

'I told you, there's nothing I'd rather be doing in Middleby,' Rippa replied, a strip of tape across his nose and his voice returning to something nearing normal.

'It's just the only thing that brings her any lucidity at all. Bingo and Middleby United.'

'Man alive — five.'

Jane's nan nestled between the pair, ink blotter in hand, cheerfully blacking out the numbers on her multiple cards as she sucked noisily on a paper bag-full of white toffee bon bons. It was true. The older woman hadn't uttered a word on the drive here, but as soon as they entered the old draughty town hall she was asking him all about Australia, and giving him the story of her school friend who migrated back in the '20s, and telling him how her week had been and how she was trying out a new pair of dentures tonight.

'Downing Street…' said the caller.

'Bingo!' yelled out a tattooed man in a beer-stained singlet near the front.

'You didn't hear the number,' continued the caller.

'But you're gonna say 10 and I have 10.'

'How do you know I'm going to say 10?'

'10 Downing Street is where the PM lives.'

'Maybe, but there are more houses than that on it. Downing Street…' the caller went on, '11.'

The man leapt up, his fist shaking. '11? 11? It's 10. It's effing 10! I never even went to secondary school and even I know it's 10.'

'10's the number of times you've been thrown out of here and that will change to 11 too if you don't pipe down.'

Merri Bay had its share of characters but even Rippa's eyes were widening at this other scene. 'Is it always this rowdy?'

'This is actually quite civil,' Jane replied. 'I've seen chairs thrown, and tables set alight. The police usually appear. The night is young.'

Rippa sipped his 20 pence cup of tea and munched his 30 pence Golden Wonder salt and vinegar crisps, delighted to be somewhere where his meagre pennies had a little mileage and where he felt warm and dry. Then, sitting under the harsh strip lights, he was suddenly saddened thinking of Sabrina back there in the sun, and how it was coming into the cooler autumn months where you could now surf all day, even in the height of the afternoon. And he thought of Cal, and how they would've had another couple of gigs by now and got a lot better, and how he really should get the wheels in motion for that recording.

'Get up and run, 31.'

'This is probably the most exciting thing in Middleby,' Jane told him over Nan's shoulder.

'I've been here two months and I know it is.'

He scanned the room taking in the other bingo players and noticed there wasn't anyone in the building who could be described as healthy. They were all wheelchair or Zimmer-frame bound, or grossly overweight, and all were eating or drinking or smoking something that should come with a government health warning.

'How long you been coming here?' Rippa asked Jane.

'Since I was a little girl. My parents … I never really knew them. My nan and pop brought me up.'

'I'm sorry.'

'Don't say that. People always say that when I tell them, but I had the happiest childhood. And it all revolved around here and United. But Pop passed two years ago, and Nan's never been the same since the Alzheimer's got its claws in.'

'Have you ever thought of leaving?'

'Dirty Gertie — 30.'

'Bit rude,' she scoffed.

'No, no, it's just … y'know, it's a big world out there and life is short.'

'I'm joshing you.' She smiled and Rippa melted. Then she whispered behind her nan so she wouldn't hear. 'There isn't a day, an hour, a minute that I don't dream of it. Believe it or not this isn't what I planned. This wasn't what I stuck in at school for or passed up all those parties and holidays in the Med to do. No way. But I could never leave Nan. This place is a boulder around my neck. Still, it's home.'

A man with rows of army medals pinned to his chest and who looked so old Rippa thought they might have been from the War of the Roses, limped up with his walking stick. 'You alright there, Violet?' he asked Nan.

'I am thanks, Alf, love. Are you coping?'

'Me tinnitus is back with a bang. It's like a bloody orchestra of crickets have made their home in my ear canal and they're doing Last Night of the Proms each and every night. My frozen shoulder's returned. I've got raging sciatica, and this new heart medication has me pissing like a racehorse.'

'Oh, deary me.'

'And our bloody Jim's only went and written off his white van again. The third in three years. Barry's been thrown out by the girlfriend, so I don't know when we'll see the grandkids. And our Ruth's remand has been put off indefinitely.'

'Oh dear, oh dear.'

'But apart from that, I'm bloody marvellous.'

'That's good to hear.'

'Listen, you don't think you could give us a run home, could you? Jim's down south looking at van number four. I give it a month until that one's at the wreckers n'all.'

The old lady turned to her granddaughter.

'Course we can,' Jane nodded.

'Edna, Agnes and Jerry were relying on me too. I know it's a lot to ask …'

'Don't you mention it,' Jane told him. 'I'll make two trips.'

'God bless you. See here lad,' the old man winked at Rippa, 'Making an honest woman of her would be the wisest thing even the greatest of men could ever do.'

'Oh, come on now, Frank,' Jane blushed.

'You might be right there,' Rippa agreed.

'I am right,' the old man said. 'And getting the occasional cowp might even help your game. Something bloody has to. You've been on fucking holiday since you pitched your tent here. And as much as I love the place, Middleby is a shitehole of a town to holiday in, so get your bloody finger out of your arsehole and start playing.'

And with that he was wobbling away on his stick back down the hall to finish his card.

'So sorry about that,' Jane tutted.

'Don't be,' said Rippa. 'Happens everywhere I go. That was one of the more amicable encounters.'

'This town's known for a few things but good manners it ain't.'

'Young and keen — 15.'

Nan grabbed her granddaughter's sleeve, a grin as wide as the Pennines spreading across her face.

Jane looked at her card. 'You've gone and done it, Nan. You've got a full house.'

'Full house!' Nan shouted.

'We have a winner,' said the caller.

A smattering of polite applause was drowned out by sounds of chairs pushed back and groans of 'bugger' and 'bastard' as Jane helped Nan up to the stage to collect her prize.

The old lady glowed when she proudly returned cradling a brown paper bag.

'What did she get?' Rippa asked.

Jane examined the contents. 'A bag of beer nuts and a box of PG Tips.'

'Oh, no.'

'No, thats a good one. Someone last week got a doorstop and a half-dozen bog rolls.'

Nan returned to her sweets and her blotters and her happy place.

'What are you up to tomorrow?' Jane asked him.

'Apart from scrubbing sheets and dreaming up new and inventive ways in which I can end it all?'

'Well, it's a bit of a drive, but I've heard you love your surfing. How about we check out Newquay?'

'Fark yes!' Rippa was ready to hit the floor and kiss her feet.

'I know it's in your loan deal that you're not meant to leave the county, but I won't tell if you don't.'

'I certainly won't.'

'Nan's at the community centre all day doing her crochet class so we could spend a few hours.'

'I'd crawl there just for a few minutes.'

'Won't it be too cold to swim?'

'I don't care if the waves are frozen solid. I'm getting on that board and riding them.'

'Are you two talking about the old in and out?' asked Nan, doing a finger and circle motion.

'Eugh, Nan! We are certainly not.'

'I used to like sex, me.'

'I'm glad to hear it, Nan,' laughed Rippa.

'1939 being a particularly rampant year.'

'And I think that's our cue to get you home.' Jane gathered the geriatric mob for the ride back.

Chapter 25

They hit the M18 on what was another dreary day in the North, but Rippa wasn't caring as the ocean beckoned. Although he did feel a little bad that they had to drive in the bitter cold with the front and back windows open so that Jane's small Escort could accommodate his surfboard.

'I got you a little something,' she told him, from behind the wheel. 'It's in the glove box.'

'The glove box? Didn't you lot know that the glove box is a place specifically designated for the use of gloves and gloves only?'

'Very funny.'

'You didn't have to get me anything. This trip is more than enough.'

'You do know that you're paying for petrol.'

'Bummer.'

'So open it.'

He did. Inside was a long roil of foil. He unwrapped it to reveal one of the thickest joints he'd ever seen.

'No way. How'd you get this thing?'

'I am part of a folk club, y'know.'

'Thanks so much. You mind if I light this bad boy? It's pretty well-circulated after all.'

'Fill your boots.'

'You wanna imbibe?'

'I used to back in uni, but honestly it's not my curd tart.'

Rippa rolled the window down as far as it would go and lit up using the car lighter. He inhaled and immediately smiled as the pleasant aroma of spliff filled his lungs, spreading to the tips of fingers and his toes.

After three puffs he carefully stubbed it out feeling that his tolerance had been lowered from the hiatus. He was getting happier with every mile they were away from Middleby and, despite still being a hundred miles from their destination, he swore he could smell a hint of salt in the brisk breeze. Looking out, the smoke was bringing colour to the mundane motorway, with its beat-up cars and dishwater sky, smoothing out the edges and making everything seem softer and warmer. The melodic sounds of New Order's *Technique* on the tape deck was helping each step of the way.

'You've missed it, haven't you?' she said looking down at the spliff which Rippa had carefully rewrapped.

'How can you tell?'

'Because you haven't said a word in twenty minutes. Just stared out the window, grinning.'

'Sorry.'

'Don't be. Nice to see you happy for once. I can get more if you want?'

Rippa paused. 'I've missed it. I don't know if it's the lack of munchy cravings, old Morag's cooking, or Rory's training, but I've lost five kilos and feel stronger and more mobile than I ever have.'

'That's great. You don't have to smoke that.'

'Nah, I will for sure. It's been such an integral part of my life for so long. Since I was 13. To the point where I can't imagine life without it.'

'How about a life without surfing?'

He laughed. 'Weed I can go without. But I know I will never, ever, feel that way about surfing.'

Jane held the wheel steady with her right hand while she ejected New Order on the player. 'Can I play you something?'

'Please.'

'It's a bit shit.'

'I bet it's not.'

'I mean really shit.'

She put a new tape in and pressed play. He was immediately startled by that voice, *her* voice, which he'd fallen in love with at the Working Men's Club. It was a demo of her covering Bob Dylan's 'Shelter from the Storm.' Jane's finger picking, too, was perfection to Rippa ears and the ideal accompaniment to his day. Except when her friend Magnus spoiled the outro with an extended djembe solo.

'You're really good,' Rippa told her. 'Like, really, really good.'

'Behave. I'm an aspiring musician. Actually, that's being a tad big headed. I'm more like a perspiring musician up there. I get way too nervous.'

'Nah, it's endearing. It's part of your act.'

'Not sure about that.'

'Where did you learn?'

'Pop taught me. He was one of the original folkies in town. Moved up here from London in a caravan after the war. Then in my teens I took lessons before they got too expensive. The guy wanted a tenner for each one.'

'Ten quid? Who was he, Eric Clapton?'

'More like Eric *Crapton*.'

Rippa giggled hard at this. It had been a while since he'd felt this relaxed around anyone.

Jane continued. 'And he always wanted me to take off my jumper during the lesson. He'd turn the heating right up before I got there so I'd have to.'

'Sounds like he needed that tenner to pay his bills.'

'I was only young, and he was a right dirty old bugger. The first time I only had a singlet on. The next times I made sure I had another three on underneath and he soon stopped.'

'That's awful.'

'That's life as a young lady in Middleby. Anyway, you really think it's good?'

'I do. But some advice?'

'Please.'

'Lose the big guy.'

'Magnus? He's a sweetie.'

'Maybe to you.'

'He's the reason I started getting up there.'

'That's nice. Though I think you'd sound better alone.'

'Sometimes I do think he sees my singing and playing as an accompaniment to his drumming.'

'Do you have any of your own songs?'

She reddened. 'Not telling.'

'I know you do.'

'There is no way you are ever, ever, hearing those. Not even Magnus is.'

'I'll work on it. I'll get you to crack.'

'They're going with me to the grave.'

The drive was five hours but after the smoke and the good tunes and fine company, the time flew by. When the ocean came into view, Rippa was like a puppy almost panting and clawing at the windows to get out.

Newquay was quiet for this time of year. It was nothing like Merri Bay, lacking the colour and vibrancy, not to mention the warmth of the Southern Hemisphere. It was drizzling, and the wind made it feel like those six a.m middle of July surfs back home.

Still, it was Malibu compared to Middleby.

Rippa was prepared and had brought two wetsuits to wear to ensure he remained well-thawed. After Jane had parked up, he grabbed his board and raced towards the sound and fury of the deserted beach. He skipped down the steps to the sand. It wasn't soft and fluffy. It was more like gravel which got wedged in his nails and between his toes. And the water was like ice, so cold it left him gasping. He swam out. Despite the climate, he felt the glow in his bones and in his soul. The waves held up well, choppy and flat in parts. Not necessarily better or worse, just different.

A wave came towards him. It looked slow and manageable but when he got close, he realised he'd completely misjudged it. He got his left knee up too late and soon he was tumbling and rolling as it wiped him out in a way he hadn't been since he was a beginner. It sent him flying to the shoreline in a crumpled heap, limbs pointing every which way.

'Are you okay?' Jane called over, clearly worrying she'd need to reset his nose again.

Rippa was too winded to answer, giving her a little wave as he coughed up a handful of the gravel and a string of brown seaweed. It had been so long and the surf here was so different that it was like starting again. The waves were shorter and quicker and more volatile making their patterns harder to predict. But after a few more turns he began to enjoy the novelty of the challenge and time lost all meaning as he glided across wave after wave, time after time, feeling whole again.

Eventually Jane beckoned him to where she waited on the seawall, cradling fish and chips and cans of something red called Tizer.

The food tasted so much fresher than the greasy mess which the chippy served in Middleby and even fresher than back in Merri Bay.

'So this is what all the fuss is about?' she said looking out.

'It's hard to explain.'

'I think I get it. I feel like that about music, about hiking the moors. Maybe not as intensely as you do but it's in the ballpark.'

Rippa laid down the piece of battered cod in his fingers. 'When I was twelve my parents split.'

'I'm sorry.'

'Actually, that's not true. It was my mum who just upped and split.'

'Gosh. I'm really sorry.'

'No one knows what happened to her. But I have a feeling she's alive and well and living over here.'

'Why's that.'

'Because she's a Londoner. Because she never wanted to live in

Australia. But Dad got her to, saying life would be easier. Some people don't want life to be easier. She was miserable out there and always talked of home. Missed the music scene, even missed the food. Then he wanted to move further out to Merri Bay and it was just too much. One day she went to the supermarket, and we never saw her again.'

'And you moved away with your dad?'

'I didn't want to. I was well into my football. Had my mates there. But I was still a kid, so I had to. At first, I was depressed like Mum. Thought of running away more than once. And then one day I found a board and it changed everything. I got good quick, and I got respect. It became an obsession. Out there on the surf, Mum leaving didn't matter so much, and football got pushed to the back of my mind. All that mattered was the waves.'

'Could you be a pro surfer?'

'Nah, I'm not that good. You'd have to be in the top point-zero-zero-one-percent or some shit. And I wouldn't want to. It's not about that. It would ruin it.'

'But you are in the top percentile for football.'

'Some might say. Actually, one might say — Bobby Noll.'

Jane tutted. 'Of course you are. You wouldn't be here if you weren't. You're head and shoulders above that lot.'

'It's just so much pressure. Out on the board there's none. And I don't feel like I have to *make it*,' Rippa used air quotes. 'Because out there I know I already have.'

'You can nail this too.'

'Nail what?'

'Football.'

'The town hates me.'

'Deep down they know the game and they can see how good you are. And they can also see that you've never really tried a leg.'

Rippa leaned back on the sand breathing in the fresh air. 'If I could do this every day, then I'd happily kick a ball around on weekends.'

'Go to Middleby and stick in. You can get back to West Ham. Anything can happen.'

'I guess.'

'At least there's hope for you. There's no hope for anyone else there.'

Rippa knew what she was saying was right, and yet his heart still yearned for home.

'Shit, what's the time?' He looked at his wrist for the watch he never wore.

'It's gone two.'

'I was meant to call Cal.'

'Who's Cal?'

'My mate. My bandmate.'

She jagged him lightly on the arm with her wooden fork. 'You never told me you played.'

'I'm in no way as good as you. But Cal is. He's the drummer and he writes all the songs. Damn good ones. He's gonna come over and we're gonna record and gig.'

'You dark horse, you.'

'I'm supposed to call but it's too late. It's always too late or I'm too busy. Or I just can't get my head together to do it because I know it'll make me sad and homesick. I'll do it tomorrow after the game.'

'Which reminds me,' she said huddling into her jacket. 'We should go. I have to be up early.'

'Why? Match isn't until three.'

'I also work for the club tuckshop. I need to bake three hundred sausage rolls for the game.'

'You're the one who's too good for Middleby, y'know.'

'It's not forever. There are some things in life you have to endure.'

Rippa leapt up. 'Time for a last dip?'

'Sure.'

He took her hand. 'And this time you're coming with me.'

'I really don't want to, Joey.'

'Just a paddle.'

'I'm only here to admire the scenery.'

'C'mon, why not?'

'How long have you got? It's cold, it's wet. I've not got my cozzie.'

'I have a spare wetsuit,' he said, beginning to remove his extra one.

'And I can't swim.'

'You can't what? Geezo, you Brits are becoming weirder by the day.'

'I'm not lying.'

'You've never been in the ocean before, have you?'

'I've never even been to the beach before.'

'You've never been to the whaaaat?' This was too much for him.

'This is the first time I've seen the coast.'

'Then that's settled. You are definitely coming in.' He grabbed her around the waist and hoisted her up as she squealed.

'Don't, Joey, don't you dare. These are my good cords.' But she was giggling so much the words wouldn't come.

'Roll them up then.'

She relented and reached down and did so. Then he lifted her to the shore and dropped her down.

'Fuck sake, it's freezing! Is it always this cold?'

'Not where I'm from.'

With her trousers up over her knees she began to relax, enjoying the cold water on her feet and legs,

'Does it compare at all?'

'Surprisingly so. Nothing like Merri Bay but I'll take it. We'll have to bring you back in the summer. Get you out there. Get you on a board.'

'I'd have to learn to swim first.'

'What on earth do you lot spend your childhood doing?'

'In Middleby, that is a very good question.'

They walked up and down the shoreline hopping over seaweed, Jane collecting shells along the way.

'What do you see yourself doing one day?' Rippa asked.

'What do you mean?'

'Career-wise, I guess. Where'd you wanna be?'

'Middleby's all I've really known.'

'There's more to life than there. There's here for starters.'

'It's not all bad. Once you get out of town towards the borders there's mountains, lakes, snow in winter.'

'Sure, but I mean the big wide world.'

'It's your time to do all that. It's not my time. Not just yet.'

They dried off. Flecked with dark grains of sand, they made their way back to the car.

'What size are you?' she asked when they were buckling up.

'Oooh, err, Missus,' he joked in his worst northern accent.

'Shoe size, you dirty boy.'

'Eight.'

'I've got something else for ya.'

'You've really done more than enough for me in this lifetime.'

'Look under your seat. I used to play in goal myself but gave up in my teens when the women's team folded. But they're good as new.'

Rippa looked and found a shoe box. He opened it to reveal a well-cared for pair of Umbros, complete with green and gold laces.

'You hate them, don't you,' she eventually said when he didn't react. It didn't even sound like a question.

But he was saying nothing because he was choked up. Having been deprived of just about all human kindness for months, this was too much.

'These are beauties.'

'You can change the laces.'

'I love the laces.'

'I thought that anything's got to be better than the clown shoes you've been rocking.'

'Thanks. I mean it. For everything.'

'It's nothing.'

'It's everything. Honestly. I'd be long gone if it wasn't for you.'

'Well now for the bad bit.'

'Which is?'

'Going back to Middleby.'

They waved goodbye to the ocean, Dylan's 'Blood on the Tracks' on the tape deck all the way. But heading back, as the darkness slowly swallowed them, was this time nowhere near as bad as Rippa had feared.

Chapter 26

Middleby United were disappointedly trailing one-nil at home to mid-table Runcorn. However, they'd enjoyed the bulk of possession and if it hadn't been for the visitor's seven-foot-tall keeper with the go-go-gadget arms, the scoreline could have been very different. The fans understood this and weren't too displeased.

And neither was Joey Rippa.

The reason for this was that he was sat comfortably on the sub's bench, a heavy wool rug over his legs, another draped over his shoulders, and had spent the first 45 minutes sipping Bovril and replaying those blissful moments of that Newquay surf over and over in his head. And that car ride, as he realised that he'd enjoyed the journey and the company just as much. Now, in the relative warmth of the home changing room (relative because, although they were out of the elements, Chapman Cole had yet again elected not to switch on the central heating), Rory was attempting to turn the game in their favour. He was stalking the tiles as he read from the cardboard cards in his palm — these ones cut from the back of a Frosties packet.

'Lads, the future belongs to those who believe in the beauty of their dreams.'

'Christ, here we go,' groaned Millsy with half an orange stuffed in his gob.

'You, Millsy. You have to dominate in the middle. C'mon you're built like a tank.'

'Yeah,' butted in Boonsy to big laughs. 'A sewage tank.'

'Fuck off.' Millsy pelted his midfield partner hard with the contents of his water bottle.

'Fellas, we've gotta pull together,' Rory told them. 'We're better than this lot. We gotta spread it wide more, to Giddsy in particular. He's been open. He's good for a goal every now and then. He could be the key to unlocking this lot. He's the ...' Rory looked around, 'Actually, where the bloody hell is he?'

They heard a high-pitched scream like that of a hysterical teenager who'd just been dumped by the head boy, screeching from the tunnel. Rory flew to the doorway and looked out. Giddsy was lying there, his white shorts covered in a sea of red.

'I've slipped,' he squealed again, even higher pitched this time.

'Well get up then, ya twit.'

'I can't. I've burst my stitches. My right bollock's dangling like a spider from its web.'

Jane came to help. 'C'mon Giddsy, back to A&E we go.'

'He'll be alright for the second half though, won't he?' Rory pleaded.

'You'll be lucky if you see him again before pre-season,' she said, helping him up, her hands now covered in blood.

Rory returned to his players.

'Giddsy okay, is he, boss?' asked Curtly.

Rory fumbled through his cards and read from another one. 'If you don't like the road you're walking on, start paving another one.'

'What's that mean?' asked Dawsy, growing worried.

Rory looked out at them blankly.

'Tell us what it fucking means.' Millsy knocked the cards out of Rory's grasp, and they fluttered around the room like confetti.

Rory came to, like he'd been slapped with a wet kipper. 'Okay? *Okay?* He is certainly not okay.'

'What does that mean though?' asked Millsy.

'Imagine the worst thing that could happen to a man and then multiply it by a hundred.'

Curtly thought. 'That would be to have your right bollock slip out of your scrotum and dangle like a spider from its web.'

Rory clicked his fingers. 'Got it in one. Right, Rippa, where are you?'

'Fucking hell,' the whole room now groaned.

The coach located the winger who'd been contentedly nodding off, behind the pillar, listening to the Divinyls on his headphones.

'Huh?' Rippa slipped them off.

'You know what to do,' Rory told him. 'Play like you did before we signed you. And nothing like what you have since we have done.'

Rippa popped back his shoulders, trying to look like he wanted to be here. He began lacing his new boots and applying fresh tape to his broken nose.

'Ooh, who's a pretty boy then?' Millsy lisped, noting his loud green and gold laces.

'Fuck that!' Dwayne threw his gloves down in disgust. 'It's beyond the pale. Beyond the fucking pale!'

'What's wrong with green and gold now?' asked Rory, really not needing this in his life.

'It's the colours of Australia. Aust—fucking—ralia. Might as well have swastika ones.'

'Keeper's right,' added Boonsy. 'That whole apartheid thing. It's awful what they're doing to that boy Mandela.'

'Hey, lay off,' Tilesy told them. 'It's a bloody lovely place. Best alps and schnitzel in the world.'

'Has anyone got any spare laces?' Rory asked. No one did. 'Well, there you go. We'll just have to put our likes and our gripes and all our politics aside for one afternoon and unite for the common cause of getting two goals and three points against ruddy Runcorn.'

The players got ready.

'If you lose us this,' Dwayne told Rippa, teeth grinding, as he took in the laces, 'I swear on the New Zealand flag that I will choke you in your sleep with those things.'

Rippa's peaceful vibes from the Newquay trip had already been choked from him as he lined up with his teammates. He'd always hated confrontation, and as much he'd never felt the need to be loved, he wasn't used to being this disliked. His father was a popular bloke back home on account of running the bar and being in a famous band back in the day. Then he thought of his mum's stories which were similarly far away from football, travelling the country following The Stones and The Who with all the friends she had before she became a hermit in Australia. He wondered as he sometimes did in moments of stress what the forty-something her would be like.

He was still in his haze and had barely realised he was out on the pitch when the whistle blew, and the game suddenly restarted. Almost from kick-off the ball rebounded to him on the edge of the opposition box. With the extra-tall keeper still pulling his gloves onto his extra-long fingers, Rippa thought he'd catch him off-guard and hit the ball first-time. Only the ball sliced off his new laces and smashed into the side-netting when it had looked easier to score.

'Stick to that eggball you lot play,' yelled one fan.

'You've got all the energy of a koala on smack,' yelled another.

'You're a dead man, Rippa!' This last insult came from Dwayne between the sticks as he sliced an index finger across his throat for added effect.

Rippa gulped hard in the knowledge that there were 44 long minutes still to go. If he could magically turn back the clock and deport himself back to The Bay at this very moment, he would in a second.

Even Beirut Bay would do right now.

But above the boos and death threats, he heard something soft, something ethereal, like the sweet siren call from a goddess, piercing through the void. 'Go on, Joey. You're way better than this.'

He turned and saw Jane giving him a tightly clenched fist of support. She was right. He didn't want to be here, no way. But if he had to, he was sure as heck gonna make the most of it and show them all or go down in flames trying.

His teammates were ignoring him, continually passing right or upfield even when all other Middleby players were marked. Rory was never going to sub a sub, especially as the remaining sub on the bench was Phil Finchley, a holding midfielder, but Rippa knew he had to do something — anything. So he threw caution to the wind and ignored the boss's instructions and started making runs inside to get the ball.

'What are you doing, Rippa?' Rory shouted. 'Stick to the plan. The plan!'

But Rippa's own plan was working as now he was able to break up play and get on the ball himself. It was also confusing his marker who was forced to operate more centrally, opening up a well of space on the left for The Schnozz to drift into and collect the odd long ball behind. When Millsy finally used his tank of a body to win a challenge, Rippa immediately switched back out left where there was yards of space.

'I'm open!' he yelled for the ball.

This time Millsy reluctantly passed to him, and Rippa was away from inside his own half. He ran thirty yards, the ball glued to his big toe. He looked up and there among the stew of players, lit up by the newly turned-on floodlights above and looking like the the Red Planet itself, there he stood.

The Schnozz.

This time Rippa gave a little glance back to make sure he wasn't about to have his own nose spread across his face by another late challenge. He saw he had yards to spare. He backed his once trusty left peg and pinged a sweet cross, true and straight. And it landed not on The Schnozz's nose but perfectly on his forehead — swishing off and sailing low and hard to the keeper's right, making it impossible for him to get down there in time.

And the crowd erupted as the ball hit the net.

The Schnozz ran to the stand, punching the air, as the Middleby players mobbed him, and the fans wished they could do the same.

'What a header.'

'Blinding finish.'

'Like Bobby bloody Charlton so The Schnozz was.'

For Rippa there was nothing except for a solitary 'bloody brilliant lad.' He looked into the stand and saw Nan on her feet, suddenly bouncing like a teenage hooligan.

Rippa waved back — that was plaudits enough.

But he wasn't finished yet and neither was Middleby. The side grew in confidence and were committing bodies in search of a winner. And at the heart of this was Rippa playing more left-wing-back than winger as he sailed up and down the byline while producing pivoting moves inside and making the Runcorn back four very nervous.

With a minute to go until full-time, the ball broke to him. He neatly turned his marker loving the lightness of his new well-fitting boots. He raced on, nutmegged another before running by him to collect. Now he faced the two centre-halves. However, The Schnozz was lurking, offering support.

Rippa drew the first defender and then slipped the ball lightning-quick inside to his striker. Then he ran clear, screaming for the return, holding the line to avoid being offside. The Schnozz thought about beating his man or even trying his luck from distance, but he knew Rippa was the best option and grudgingly reciprocated Rippa's assist by playing the return.

The winger now had only the keeper to beat. He thought about shooting for the corner but was wary of the keeper's obscenely long arms. Then he thought about his trademark scoop only to remember what happened last time. Instead, running at speed, he elected to use his momentum and round the big man which he did with ease. The crowd held its breath as Rippa prepared to stroke home the winner. Only Rippa hadn't factored in the right-back tracking back and, unable to get the ball himself, he barged into his back sending Rippa flying to the mud, the ball sticking there next to him, an inch from the line. The referee didn't hesitate to point to the spot and brandish the red card.

Rippa picked himself up, dusted himself down, and collected the ball. He managed to locate the spot among the sludge, placing the ball upon it.

'What the fuck you doing, Oz?' Millsy pushed him aside. Rippa had always taken penalties but now realised that the captain may have had a point. At this level there would be a designated taker and given his recent form he'd probably be the last one picked. Instead, The Schnozz stood up and, cool as you like, sent the keeper the wrong way, stealing the late win for the home side.

As the players made their way off the pitch to cheers, this time Rippa was recognised for his contribution as he heard fans near the touchline chatter.

'Always thought he'd be a player.'

'Imagine what he could do if that Kim Wilde thatch ever gets shorn.'

'Haven't seen a comeback like that since Aunty Sheila sent us that boomerang from Kakadu.'

And it was much the same in the dressing room.

'Top job, Rippa,' Rory said, giving him the mother of all bum slaps. 'I knew that getting you to cut inside would yield results.' He brought out one of his cards and read, 'Believe you can and you're halfway there.'

'Yeah, well, um, guess you were right.'

'Cheers, Oz,' The Schnozz called over, stark-bollock naked, his dangling balls looking even redder than his nose. 'Needed that brace like a ...' he trailed off. 'Dunno actually. Like someone who needs something rather than a lot. If that makes sense.'

'Total sense.'

'Fucking hell, maaaate.' Millsy thumped Rippa hard on the back. 'Who are you and what have you done with that shithouse Aussie winger they sent us?'

'Cheers, Cap.'

Rippa allowed himself a big breath and a slight smile as he took his seat. Yesterday had been a bigger thrill but today had really lifted a deadweight from around him. He poured himself a cup of hot black tea from the communal flask and tried to savour this moment. That special moment as a footballer when you know you've done your job and you've done it well.

'What a win, what a bloody win,' Chapman Cole sang, bounding in towards the semi-dressed bodies.

'Cheers, Chairman,' Rory said with some surprise as win, draw or crushing loss the chairman had never before bothered to venture into the players' domain.

'That were bloody great, so it was. Thank Christ we don't pay bonuses. I'll be skint as a tramp if you lot start playing like that every week.'

'Very nice of you to say, Mr Chairman,' said Rory.

'Anyway, pardon my intrusion but it's that Rippa of a winger I'm here to see. Young Joey, where are you?' Cole squinted round.

'Me?'

'Yes, you. You've a phone call in my office. An urgent one, apparently.'

'Really?'

'Yes, really. I do hope it's not that East London mob of bandits trying to pilfer you away so soon. Word travels very quickly in the world of Teletext and what not.'

Rippa followed him out wondering who it could be, hopeful it would be Sabrina finally telling him she couldn't live without him and that she was flying out here. Life in Middleby might just become manageable after all.

'There you go, my son,' Cole pointed to the desk once they'd ascended the creaky staircase. Then he put on his vintage British Rail train driver's cap and collected the controls. The Alaska Railroad on the tracks gave a whistle and was on its way, chugging over the bridge. 'Don't mind me.'

Rippa didn't.

'Hello,' he said happily down the receiver.

'Hey, Joey.'

Rippa punched the air. It was Sabrina after all. It was all working out. The plan was coming together. Nothing would stop him now.

'So good to hear your voice, babe. Guess what? I just made two goals and helped us get three points. Everything's coming up roses.'

'Joey.'

'And I'm gonna go back to West Ham and make a bundle and you can come here ASAP for a spell before we can get back there and maybe get a new shack with a roof that doesn't leak and —'

'Joey.'

'Oh, you're on your way here right now? I get it, you're already here. You're outside, aren't you?' Rippa peeked out the blinds.

'Joey, listen. I've been told to call you. Your friend Cal. He died yesterday.'

Rippa snorted, wrapping the cord tight around his fingers, not believing what he was hearing. 'Caaaaal? Nooooo, not at all.'

'I'm sorry.'

'Not Cal. Cal's coming here too. We're gonna make a demo. We're gonna gig on my days off.'

'The funeral's Tuesday.'

Rippa then began chuckling hysterically. 'Nooooo, that's not happening. Not for Cal. Noooo ...'

'Look after yourself, Joey. I know you were fond of him.' There were deep voices in the background. 'I gotta go.'

The line clicked dead. Dead as Cal, allegedly. Rippa remained standing, suddenly completely numb.

'Good news from the Antipodes?' came the other voice in the room.

Rippa stood motionless. 'Fine and dandy as always, Mr Cole.'

'Always seems to be the way down there from what I hear. If you need anything you just holler, young man.'

'Will do,' Rippa nodded his head quickly from side-to-side trying to put some feeling into his body. 'So here goes. I need to go back to Australia.'

'What? Now? There's six games of the season to go, lad. We must win them all. Promotion is in sight.'

'It's something I need to do.'

'Even with your fandangled new aircraft it would take days.'

'My best mate's gone.'

'Gone where? Australia?'

'He was already in Australia.'

'So why'd he go back to Australia.'

'He was from Australia. He died in Australia.'

'I am sorry. That's the thing about death, it's so final. Lost all the boys from squadron 516 in a two-year spurt in the early '80s. Pop, pop, pop. I'm the last man standing. When Mummy said eat all your greens, I'm sure as heck glad I listened.'

Rippa was alert now and heading for the door. 'I'll be back as soon as I can.'

Chapman Cole put down the controls and the Railroad ground to a halt. 'No, no, my boy. You made a commitment. A pledge. In sickness and in health.'

'I didn't really though.'

'Well, no you didn't as such. The solicitor wouldn't let me add in that clause. But the town needs you. Your friend, he's gone now. But Middleby lives on. And funerals are overrated. This coming from a gent who's been to 187 of them to be precise. Fifty-three of them last year alone.'

'I really need to go. For a lot of reasons. I'm hungry, Mr Cole.'

'Nothing wrong with being hungry for success.'

'No. Literally. I'm starving.' Rippa lifted up his dirty replica shirt, showing off his loose waistband and the sharp outline of his ribs. 'I haven't consumed anything edible for months. Also, I can't afford warm clothes. I couldn't even buy a pair of boots.'

'Get another job then, ya daft bugger. Millsy works as a prison guard some weeknights. Boonsy is a butcher. I've been told that Curtly is one of those male dancers that attend hen's do's but it's never been verified so please don't go around telling.'

'Don't worry. I won't.'

'How about some bar work? I could get you pulling Foster's at The Orient.'

'I had bar work back home. I could have just stayed there with my girlfriend and my band and my surfboard and been warm and content and had a meal every night like most people in the first world. And kept my best mate alive.'

'Well don't let me bloody stop you.'

'Great then, I'll send you a postcard.' Rippa opened the door.

'Hang on a bloody minute, it was just an expression.' Cole moved gently towards him. 'You go and I'll have Interpol straight on the case. You'll never play football again.'

'Wonderful.'

Cole could see this wasn't going to work and he had to try something different. 'Listen, you go into the Londis along the road and fill a basket and tell them it's on me. Same with Jessie's Menswear. Consider it my treat. But that, young man, is the limit. You get us promoted and we'll sort something else out. And you do well and with your ability, who knows how it could all turn out? The sky's the limit for you, which is more than I could say for most of those lazy buggers down there.' The chairman was up close to him now, awkwardly patting his shoulder. 'Do your duty, son. And then in the summer you'll go there.'

Rippa said nothing more. He retreated to the dressing room, head low, heart sinking lower as he thought of his best friend, the news so raw and unreal.

Dwayne was perched by the door of the change rooms, showered and changed, cup of tea and saucer in hand.

'Your card's still marked,' Dwayne told him.

'Excuse me?'

'I'm watching you like a kamikaze galah.'

'What the hell are you on about?' Rippa was most definitely not in the mood.

'You might have got lucky today, Mr Oz, but your days are numbered. And you can have that warning on the house.'

Rippa's body stiffened. 'You know what? You can shove your warning and your team and the whole of Middleby right up your fat Kiwi arse.' A loose ball was in front of him, and Rippa booted it at full force. It struck the saucer in the goalie's hands, shattering it, shards of ceramic and hot tea floating and landing on Dwayne's freshly laundered white Paul Smith polo as the entire squad watched and gasped.

Rippa didn't hang around to see if he was okay. He didn't hang around to bath and change.

Joey Rippa was out of there.

Chapter 27

He didn't know where he was going or what he was going to do. He wanted a smoke badly. He wanted a surf even more. And above both those all he really wanted was to see Cal, to jam with him, to joke with him and be there for him. But none of these outcomes were possible. Instead, he ended up back at his lodgings hoping he could at least sneak a quick bath and then border up his bedroom before the considerably bigger keeper came bounding home, thirsting for revenge.

When he put the key in the lock, he found Albert and Morag waiting.

'Here he is,' Albert announced.

'He is indeed,' tutted his wife.

'Too busy to sand the new parquetry in the basement but not too busy to go and hoof around that pig's bladder with the other shirtlifters.'

Rippa sighed. 'Honestly, I've had a bitch of an afternoon, and I really can't be doing with this.'

Morag gasped. 'He said a bad word, Daddy.'

Albert put his arm around her, holding her close as she whimpered. 'You brute. You caveman. You bloody son of a convict. I ought to sock you one in the bugle.'

'I didn't mean to swear.'

'You come over here to our town, taking our jobs, eating at our table with never a word of thanks. And staring, always staring at my peach strudel of a wife, undressing her with your devil eyes.'

'Yeah, only I'm really not.'

'Make him stop, Albert,' she shrieked, nuzzling her face in her husband's armpit. 'Make it all go away.'

'You're doing it right now,' Albert said.

Rippa snapped. 'Listen, baldy. I'd rather gouge out both my peepers and stick them up my backside than look at either of the pair of you. Ya couple of inbred creeps.' Then he left, slamming the front door so hard the windows rattled. The same windows he'd shined the other day. He felt better after the outburst but that feeling went quickly when he realised he was still in Middleby and he was without a friend in the world.

Then he remembered he did have the one — just the one — and that's exactly where he headed.

Lately in the town he hadn't been able to take a stroll for a pint of milk and a paper without being told to go back to where he came from or being taunted with 'Kim Wilde' this or 'Useless Australian fuckwit' that. But tonight, things were different as dog walkers nodded, van drivers tooted, and kids coming home from the match wearing Middleby colours hung out from car windows and shouted, 'You little Rippa!'

But Rippa was too glum to respond. He was hungry, he was thirsty, and above all he was heartbroken.

Luckily Jane's white Escort was in the driveway, and she answered on the first knock like he'd prayed she would.

'I'm so sorry,' Jane told him over a coffee and a chocolate digestive, Rippa for some reason not in the mood for a cup of tea when he saw her bring out the saucers. They sat in her kitchen as Nan watched reruns of *Wogan* which Jane taped for her — the only show the old woman liked.

'I said I'd write, and I never did. Cal wrote to me three times. And I said I'd call, and I never did that either. There was always something in the way here which is crap because how hard is it to pick up a phone and dial no matter where you are?'

'You were busy, love. With good reason. On the other side of the world starting a new job. And not just any job. A high-pressure, high-profile one. And if he was the true friend and as big a football fan as you say he was, then he'd understand.'

'True friends don't treat people like I did.'

'That's harsh.'

'And now I'm really stuck.'

'Why?'

'Because I can't go back.'

'You have to go. Is it the money?'

'Not that,' Rippa shook his head. 'I had ten grand set aside for Cal and me for recording which I'm never gonna use now.'

'There are some things in life you have to be at. What are you gonna do? Stay here and top yourself when you could be over there saying goodbye? Don't listen to Old King Cole. He once had the entire team wear black armbands for a month because his pet tortoise kicked the bucket.'

'I can't go though. He's got my passport.'

'Why's he have that?'

'West Ham sent it after I got here. It's a thing they do with international players apparently. Middleby got it as part of the deal.'

'When's the next flight?' Jane asked, her brain whirring.

'I know there's one from Manchester every Saturday night.'

'You gotta get on it.'

'But I can't fly without a passport.'

'I can get that.'

'You can?'

'I clean his office every Tuesday.'

'Is there any job you don't do at that club?'

'Not really. And because of that I know where the safe is and where everything's kept.'

'No way.'

'Yes way.'

'But we're not safe crackers.'

'We don't need to be. He doesn't know how to lock it.'

'Is it stealing?'

'You can't steal something that's already yours.'

Rippa didn't need convincing.

Chapter 28

Jane offered to drive him down but they both thought it would be more discreet if they walked. As it wasn't raining, they took the back trail to avoid the Saturday night madness which was getting into gear.

By the time they got there they found the stadium deserted apart from Chapman Cole's old silver Jaguar out the front, spread across three spaces.

'He'd have had a skinful of gin and called a cab,' said Jane. 'Just like every other Saturday, so don't worry.'

'I'm worrying.'

'The safe is under the desk. Right-hand side.' She removed a key and tried unlocking the front doors. It wasn't opening.

'What's wrong?' Rippa asked.

'It must be an old one.'

'There's another way.' He picked up a rock next to the flower bed and eyed the front window.

'Don't be daft. You don't want to go to prison, especially not the one here. You wouldn't see breakfast.'

'Prison? I feel like I'm already in one.'

Jane examined the drainpipe. It would involve a good 15-foot climb. Rippa started going up it.

'I was joking,' she said. 'You'll break your bloody neck.'

'Just keep the bottom still.'

She did so, not confident at all. Carefully Rippa edged up the copper piping like some drunk ferret, no longer caring if he was caught, knowing that prison would surely be a walk in the park compared to life with Albert, Morag and Dwayne.

He made it to the top ledge, grasping on. He peered through the venetian blinds and into the office. It was dark except for a lamp on the desk emitting a dull glow and red signal lights on the tracks which had been left on as The Scarborough Flyer idled in the station.

Rippa located the window lock. It was rusted and broken, and he managed to pry it open with ease. Using great dexterity, he twisted and bent his torso through the gap in the frame and away from the blinds. With all the bits of his wiry body now inside he rolled and pounced for the desk.

He was about to open the top drawer when he halted. A loud, monotonous droning sound was coming from the train set. He panicked. Then he heard a snore followed by the sleepy smacking of lips and a man's voice mutter, '£125? *A-hundred-and-twenty-five pounds?* You play like Dame Edna Everage in heels, and you want more than £125 a week?'

Without moving his feet Rippa peered under the track. He saw the folding bed set up with Chapman Cole passed out on it, cradling a half-empty bottle of gin.

Rippa thought quickly. He had two options. Retreat immediately or get what he needed and get the hell away. He thought of poor Cal, and he knew he had to choose the latter. He quickly located the safe. He went to open it and found it locked.

The snoring was getting louder and more random. He looked at the numbers on the black box. What could it be? He didn't know the chairman's date of birth or when the town was built. He turned to the wall and saw the Middleby United crest and the number 1892 on it. He spun the wheel to make the number.

He was in.

There was a stack of receipts to the local model shop for carriages, track and signals, along with one for a subscription to *Railway Modeller*. And then there was a wad of hundred-pound bills, reams and reams of the things which would have allowed Rippa to buy an entire street in

Middleby never mind give him the small raise he needed to buy a proper dinner and a warm coat. Underneath all these were two passports — one black with Dwayne's name and the navy blue one of his. He slipped his down his waistband and closed the safe with a too-loud click. He heard a movement and stopped dead.

'You thieving bastard.'

It was Chapman Cole, wearing a full-length nightgown, cap, and carrying a candle in a holder.

Rippa hauled his Middleby shirt over his head to provide some anonymity and leaped back to the window.

'I'll string you up by the ballsack, so help me God.'

Rippa wasn't hanging around to let him. He opened the window and gripped the pipe. From this vantage the 15-foot drop looked far more precarious than it had looking up. But the chairman was almost on him, wielding the front carriage of The Scarborough Flyer which he'd ripped from the tracks.

'Nobody steals from Chapman Cole. No—body!'

Rippa closed his eyes and wrapped his body around the pipe hoping to gracefully slide down. But it buckled the moment he let go of the ledge and there he was, hurtling forwards at a 90-degree angle and landing straight on the Jag, nearly going through its roof.

'I'll get you for this,' raged Cole from up high, fist shaking, his furious features lit up by the candlelight.

Rippa was somehow, miraculously, unscathed and scurried off out the car park and round the corner to where Jane was waiting in the darkness.

'All good?' she asked.

'Honestly, it couldn't have went any worse. But I got it.'

They jogged off down the back streets, past the glare of streetlights.

'That whole train thing with Cole is really weird, isn't it,' Rippa said, panting.

'How'd you mean?'

'There's no actual train line for miles.'

'If you started analysing all the weird things about Chapman Cole it would be a life's work.'

'Too true.'

'You're really going then?' Jane asked sadly.

'I'll be back before you know it.'

They heard a stray police siren in the distance.

'No, you won't.'

They cut onto Middleby high street now lit up by pubs and takeaway joints. They mingled in with the Saturday crowd. They tip-toed past the vomit and broken glass littering the pavement and sidestepped two groups of teenage girls battling, handbags swinging, nails scratching.

Jane turned to him. 'And if Australia is half as good as you say it is, I wouldn't either.'

Chapter 29

Rippa lifted his head from the side window and saw the familiar golden sea shimmering before him like forbidden treasure. It was the shoreline along the road to Merri Bay drifting past and it was the vision which he'd craved so much and that had filled his head and brought colours to his dreams over the dreary past few months.

His neck and joints were aching from his travels. He looked at the clock on the dash and saw he'd been asleep for almost the whole way from Perth Airport, realising that flying was not really his thing. The cramped space, the crap movies, and the ever-present fear of hurtling into the deep blue at top speed was not for him.

Rippa coughed. His uncle was at the wheel, fag wedged between his cracked lips, almost certainly on pack number two and looking as miserable as ever.

'Well, you know what I think,' he said, continuing the conversation he'd started before Rippa passed out.

'What's that?' Rippa asked, though he already knew.

'That you should never have come back to this shithole in a billion years. At least until you retire, a decade or so more if you move into coaching and management.'

'I know, Uncle Warren.' He certainly did as he'd heard him bang on and on about little else.

'But then again I never had any sort of talent for anything, never mind football.' He lit another fresh fag using the dying embers of the one already hanging out his mouth. 'And I've never been one for friends either.'

'Why are you still here?'

'What do you mean? I'm not. I'm in Perth.'

'You know what I mean. That's hardly the epicentre of the soccer world.'

'It's football. Not soccer.'

'They don't even have a team in the national comp.'

'I'm trying to branch out, ain't I. Establish myself in what is not a very crowded market and find these rough diamonds like yourself. The only trouble is that the players I punt on keep flushing back.'

Rippa said nothing.

'I'm sorry, boyo. I know you didn't want to go. I know the guts it took to do it, guts I don't have. Christ, East London's bad enough but to go to dreaded Middleby? That took kahunas of the Charles Bronson variety and I'm proud of you.'

When they arrived in Merri Bay, they found the beach lined with cars, Kombis and scooters. They drove into the packed car park and saw out on the sand that the funeral service had already commenced. As they walked down the dunes, Rippa caught sight of Voodoo, Muggs and Jacko in their usual spot not involved in the service and looking shabbier than ever before. They were skinnier and paler despite this being the tail-end of summer and looked like they hadn't slept or bathed in days. Voodoo was wearing a filthy LA Lakers cap and had puss-filled red sores circling his mouth.

'It's Mara-farkin-dona himself,' his old friend announced, not getting up. 'Or is it Madonna?'

Then Rippa noticed Sabrina there next to Voodoo. She was in a faded grey hoodie and he could've sworn she'd been holding his hand. 'Hey.' Rippa said. 'Why aren't you at the service?'

'Not our mate,' Voodoo answered for her.

'But he was mine. And he was from our town. He was one of us.'

'*One of us,*' Voodoo mimicked and laughed. Then he made his wrist into a rigid shape and did the same with his mouth, curling his tongue under his lip. Even Sabrina laughed at this.

Rippa saw the mountain of empty cans by the burnt-out fire and smelt something else. Something not from the fire but something else chemical-like, acrid and evil. He looked closer and saw there were numerous small baggies, the kind that weed didn't come in. Sabrina, looking gaunt and lifeless, hadn't met his eye.

Rippa left them to it. It wasn't about them today. It wasn't about anyone but Cal.

He went to the shore and found his old man and hugged him. He was holding a candle amongst the congregation, circled around a white-gowned minister saying a few words.

'It's good to see ya, son,' Stevie whispered.

'I couldn't miss this.'

The minister recounted the story of Cal's life and how he was never expected to see primary school, but on he went defying all the odds, getting to high school and beyond. They played some of his favourite songs on a ghetto blaster — The Byrds, Creedence, and the Beach Boys. Cal had never been much into newer '80s music. They played a demo from their band and Rippa cringed a little at how bad the home recording sounded. Cal's intricate melodies deserved so much better.

A row of surfboards were lined up, Rippa's Classic Malibu among them, and they all drifted out into the cooler autumnal waters, surprisingly calm for this time of year. Out there they joined hands, friends and family alike, and said a prayer of remembrance. It was broken by the noise of AC/DC coming from further up the beach. Rippa knew how much Cal hated Acca Dacca and he hated Voodoo even more for somehow making today about him.

The others swam back. In the clear day it was still warm enough that they didn't need towels. Rippa, though, stayed out on his board. The surf was flat, and he couldn't get high enough to get any traction going. But even if it had been rocking, he wasn't in the mood.

He eventually sailed in. The others had dispersed. It was quieter this time of year with holidaymakers having packed up and moved on. He saw Cal's mother waiting for him.

'I can't believe you made it.' She clutched his hand and held it tight and close to her wet cheeks.

'I had to, Mrs MacCallum.'

'We're honoured. Aren't you a big star over there now?'

'Don't believe everything you hear.'

The lady smiled. She'd been so good to him. She'd had a sad life and with her long brown locks now completely grey she looked old beyond her years. Cal was gone. Her husband had upped and fled long ago in the similar vein to Rippa's own mum, deeming parenthood too hard, particularly having a son with special needs. And her eldest, Cal's brother, had slipped off the cliff rocks shortly before Rippa arrived in the area. Death by misadventure they called it, though everyone knew it was something darker.

'Can I ask you something?' asked Rippa.

'Of course, love.'

'How did Cal pass?'

'In his sleep, like the angel he was. It's a miracle he made it this far. Every day was a blessing for me, and we were all truly blessed to know him.'

'We sure were.'

'He proved them all wrong.'

'He sure did.'

'He just got a bit tired fighting towards the end.'

'I'm sorry,' Rippa told her.

'What for?'

'I can't help thinking that it's my fault, y'know. For leaving.'

'You mustn't think that.'

'That if the band was still going, he might have hung on.'

'You have a long life ahead of you and I don't want you weighed down by something like that which just isn't true.'

'If you say so, Mrs Mac.'

'He loved you. He was so proud of you.' She held his hand and his head fell onto her shoulder.

He wept like someone who'd just lost their best friend and someone who hadn't been mothered in so very long. She had been like a surrogate mum to him at times. The woman with the Scouse twang had taken him under her wing when he moved to The Bay. Broken and lacking direction, he'd have dinner there most nights. She'd include him in family events, birthdays, picnics, and, a keen musician herself, she'd encourage them to play. Considering Stevie was rarely there due to the stress involved in establishing the surf club, Rippa didn't know what he'd be doing now if she hadn't put up her hand and helped raise him. Though looking over at the burnt out remains from Voodoo and his crew's latest party, he had a fair idea.

The world wasn't perfect. However, it had been close to that for Rippa and maybe only because he cut himself off from everything else and didn't dabble in reality. But with this, with Cal's death, he had to dive back in and it hurt like hell.

They looked out at the picture-perfect scenery and enjoyed a moment of calm.

'I'm leaving here,' Mrs MacCallum said suddenly.

'You're leaving? Why? You've been here forever.'

'And that's why. I have such wonderful memories of my Callum, of my Andrew too. I don't want to taint those by staying and becoming some crabbit old woman.'

'Where you going?

'No idea yet but I'm selling up and me and the dog are taking the campervan and hitting the road.'

'Good for you.'

'You only get one life and it's time to do something different with what I've got left of this one. You should think about that too.'

'I will.'

'Come and see me before you leave,' she told him.

'Sure.'

'You are leaving, aren't you?'

'I guess.'

'I've got a few things to give you.'

Rippa went back to his old shack. He spread out on his old hammock looking out at the ocean. He didn't feel like surfing. Instead, he had his first smoke since that time at the beach with Jane. It was leaf which he'd found in last year's boardies stuffed under his bed. He'd put a lemon rind in the foil to preserve it. It was a little dry but it smelled good. He couldn't be bothered finding Voodoo or Sabrina and getting anything fresh and wasn't sure if they even bothered with softer recreational drugs anymore. He packed the pipe and lit it. It made him feel a little weightless and dreamy but lacked the transformative effect he'd hoped for. Instead of making him euphoric and carefree it heightened his sadness and made him edgier with the haunting fear of just what the hell he was going to do with his life.

Chapter 30

On the surf club stage which Rippa knew so well, Cal's Everton-blue Pearl drum kit remained. Rippa sat on the stool and got a beat happening. Cal's drums had been everything to him. It was his escape from his disability because he became so good at playing them when most things in life were a challenge. He proved everyone wrong by mastering the most physical instrument going and, because of that, behind the drums he became untouchable.

Cal always hated it when Rippa attempted to play, and this made him laugh. He remembered the day when they had picked the kit up on one of their rare forays into the city. It was custom-made so the stands could sit in closer, and Cal's wheelchair could fit tight. It was Cal's 16th birthday and Rippa thought it might have been the happiest day of his friend's life. He remembered the smile on Cal's face when he first laid eyes on it and watched his frail body come alive when he tried them out in that warehouse in East Perth. And how he enjoyed playing with ease on a kit finally designed just for him, where he didn't have to sit on an old milk crate and stretch and strain for every beat.

'Surprised you came back,' Stevie said, pouring his son a ginger beer, in between setting up for the weekend crowd. It had only been two months, but his dad's hair looked thinner, the wrinkles around his tired eyes more pronounced.

'Told ya. I couldn't miss this.'

'You could have though. The English season's not over. Even I know that.'

'Thought you'd be glad to see me.'

'I am. Course I am.'

'What is it then?'

'Been doing a lot of thinking …'

Rippa took a big sip of his cherished drink. 'Here we go.'

'About back in the day.'

'And?'

'I feel bad about whisking you away from Perth. Away from your soccer. I mean, I knew you were good, but I didn't realise you were that good. I guess I didn't care enough.'

'Dad. You hate soccer.'

'Yes. But you didn't. And I'm not you. And I shouldn't have done it.'

'I learned to surf here. There's nothing better than that. And now I'm good at cricket and footy too.'

'But you were really, really good at wop-ball. Sorry, soccer. Even a crusty mutt like me should've seen that.'

'C'mon, The Bay's the greatest town in the world.'

'Is it?'

'Course it is. And now I know that for sure because I've seen a bit more of the world.'

'It's a dead town. Logging's long gone and all the jobs with it. Fishing as well.'

'Yeah but there's tourism.'

'No one comes here since the new highway opened.'

'It'll pick up. The bar will pick up too.'

'It's been two years.'

'And the bills are paid now.'

Stevie shook his head, wiping the sweat from his brow with his wrist. 'Those bills are only paid because of you. And there's another ten grand already mounted since and there'll be another ten grand owing after.'

'What are you saying?'

'I'm saying we're done, mate. It's all done.'

'No, it's not.'

'It is, son. All the smart ones that you were top of the class with have moved on.'

Rippa put his drink aside, suddenly not very thirsty. The front doors swung open and in dragged Voodoo and his crew. They were no longer laughing. Instead, they were looking menacing from a lack of sleep and what else.

Stevie whispered to his son, 'The only ones left are the dregs. And you, my boy, have way too much going on to be in that category.'

The group ordered Cokes from the young bar girl and then openly topped up their drinks from a half-bottle of Bundy. Stevie wasn't game enough to call them on it.

'What would you do if this place goes?' Rippa asked.

'*When* this place goes you mean. Dunno, mate. Can't see me moving away. Not now. I gave up everything to move back here. Your career. My marriage.'

'You can't think like that.'

'Maybe. Maybe not. A lot of people at the moment need a removal man. Could give that a bash.'

'I'm really sorry, Dad.'

'So am I, son. But nothing lasts forever and we had a good run. Anyway, it's still a work day and I have errands to run. You take care now.'

Rippa had watched Sabrina peel off to buy a Calippo, which had been her favourite since school.

'Hey stranger.' Rippa went for a hug, but she moved back, her eyes colder than the ice lolly in her fingers. 'I've been trailing you all day. Your mum's. Aunty's. The chip shop. Where've you been?'

'Just around.'

'Where around?' She'd lost a few kilos, and she didn't have the type of body which had it to lose. Her eyes looked bleary and lacked their sheen and Rippa could see the outline of her collarbone through her top.

'What are ya, my stalker?'

'No. But I thought I was, like, your boyfriend.'

'Boyfriends don't flee to the other side of the world.'

'You told me to go.'

'Did I?'

'I asked you to come.'

'Did ya?'

'And you told me no.'

'You were meant to be this big star. Now everyone says you lied. You're not a pro. You're playing for some pub team.'

'That's not true.'

'Is it a bit true?'

Rippa felt tongue-tied. 'Hmm, it's complicated.'

'Well, two months is a long time, Joey.'

'I know that. But it's all done with now and I'm back here and I'm staying.'

'So where's this fortune you made?'

'I'm getting it,' he fibbed.

She peeled the top off the Calippo. 'Yeah, yeah, heard all this shit before. Don't worry bout it, coz I'm with someone else now.' She glanced over at Voodoo, and he smiled back. Then he placed a v-sign over his lips and wagged his tongue at Rippa.

'Wow. Right. I see.' Rippa wanted to run over there and smack his old friend out. And yet he also wanted to break down and weep like a baby again as all the emotions of coming back and saying bye to Cal for the last time simmered.

But he did neither.

He steadied himself and headed for the exit keeping his head as high as he could. Only dignity wasn't something that Voodoo knew the meaning of.

'See you mob had a ride out,' Voodoo called over, unlit roll up between his lips.

'Yeah. What of it?'

'Why the fark you do that?'

'Cal was born by the sea.'

'Farkin retard had never been in the water. Spaz would have drowned in a minute.' Then he hit the floor and faked a seizure as his lackeys and even Sabrina laughed.

Rippa boiled inside yet stayed quiet. He waited until Voodoo's little act played out. He waited until he got up. And then when Voodoo was about to say something else smart-arsed Rippa did what he'd wanted to do for a long time.

He ran up and shaped to boot him as hard as he could right in the nuts.

Voodoo, though, was quick and twitched out of the way. And Rippa's left foot slammed into the heavy brick wall instead.

'Aaargh!' he yelled out, hearing a crack. And then he heard a louder one as the bigger boy was on him, blackening his jaw and sending him down and out.

Chapter 31

Rippa slumped at the front of the surf club on a plastic chair with his swollen foot in a bucket of ice. It didn't look as bad as his bruised face, but it felt a lot worse. Since first moving to Merri Bay, he'd either been smoking weed or surfing with a bit of music in between and not much else. But for the first time he didn't feel like doing any of those things.

He heard a yap and watched as Cal's mum approached, her old kelpie, Donovan, off its lead.

'What happened to you?' she asked.

'Busted foot.'

'You were fine a few hours back.' She was concerned and rightly so because if he'd lived in a bigger town he'd almost certainly have gone to A&E.

'Tripped.'

'Why don't I believe you?'

'It doesn't matter either way.'

She took the seat next to him. She opened her shoulder bag. 'He wrote you another postcard. He didn't get to send it.'

Mrs MacCallum handed it to him. This one didn't have Merri Bay on the front but a picture of a football instead. Rippa had no idea where Cal would have got something like that around here. He turned it over, its print so small he had to hold it up to his eyes to read:

Dear Rippa,

How you doing? I've been trying to follow your exploits but it's hard (bullshit Australian coverage) and since the newsagents here packed in, I can't get Soccer Week. *Anyways, haven't felt so crash hot lately. Weird because summer's gone, and you know this is my fav time of the year. I don't think I can make it over anytime soon. But promise me you won't come back. Sure, music and surfing are what you're good at (then again you're good at everything!). But you're a professional footballer, Rippa. Run, run and don't look back. The band, the surf, The Bay and all its beautiful girls will all be here waiting. I'm proud of you.*

Your bud, Cal.

PS. I haven't heard from you and don't worry at all. I know how busy you are. We'll make up for it someday.

Rippa had cried all his tears on the plane and earlier with the woman. And now that the penny dropped, he knew what he had to do.

'Thanks, Mrs Mac.'

'You did so much for him.'

'Not half as much as what he did for me.'

Rippa lobbed the stick into the waves for the dog to fetch and hugged her goodbye, not sure if he would ever see Mrs MacCallum again. Her house was already on the market. Her camper was packed. And somehow this was alright. He was realising that sands shift, and all things are meant to go this way at some point.

Rippa limped up to the car park where a group of younger guys were tooling around on a reconditioned moped. Rippa remembered them from school and surmised that they were two or three years behind him.

'Hey, mate,' Rippa called to the taller one with the long blonde hair and cut-off t-shirt. 'That your bike?'

'Yep,' he replied, chest puffed.

'I'll trade you my guitar and board for it.'

The kid looked at him to see if Rippa was high. 'Joey Rippa's Classic Malibu?'

'Sure thing.'

'And your Gretsch?'

'How do you know?'

'Dude, everyone knows you.'

'You can even have the bike back if you wanna pick it up from the airport.'

'That's all worth, like two k. This bike would be lucky if it cost me two hundred bucks.'

'Then it's your lucky day. Will it make it to the airport?'

'I reckon. Got two new tyres and a tankful.'

'That's all I need.'

'You want your stuff back?'

'I ain't coming back.'

Rippa told him the items were on his porch and to grab them before anyone else did. He squeezed on the kid's helmet. He kicked the bike pedal forgetting his sore foot and shuddered at the impact. He thought about stopping at a hospital along the way but knew that was far off the track and wanted no more delays.

'Good luck playing in England,' the kid shouted to him.

Rippa gently revved the engine, liking its purr. 'You know about me playing in England?'

'I reckon you're a bit out touch with how much of a legend you are in these parts.'

The wheels spun and Rippa was off. He drove along the coastal road no longer looking right towards the golden ocean and the crashing waves, which had brought him so much joy over the years. And definitely not left where his ex-girlfriend and mates and all those old demons might be lurking. He thought of his mother and knew that she loved him and yet understood, as painful as it was, why she left it all behind.

To save time he slipped onto the new highway, marvelling at its smoothness and how much more comfortable and quicker it was. As his surroundings faded into nothing, Rippa felt like a massive weight had lifted, a weight heavier than what his guitar and his surfboard had ever been.

Chapter 32

When Rippa arrived back in Middleby, things had changed. The once barren and lifeless trees were sprouting leaves flecked with green on their spindly branches. The sky which had usually been wallpapered by dark foreboding clouds was now showing pleasant cracks with etchings of bright blue creeping in. As the cab dropped him off at the front of the stadium, he realised he no longer had to watch his footing on the thawed out path, and that the breeze was now somewhat refreshing rather than leaving him struggling to breathe. It was April and well into spring, and winter in Middleby was becoming yesterday's news.

And it wasn't the only thing changing.

Rippa entered Clappers Lane with the new haircut he'd gotten while waiting for his connecting flight. A number three all over. Short enough to be edgy, just long enough to be socially acceptable and get the fans onside, the most important thing was that now he could see properly. He also had new clothes. Gone were the stubbies and thongs, replaced with 501s and Rollers, and a new Billabong corduroy jacket which made him warm. Still, he knew it wouldn't protect him from the storm that was lying in wait.

'Here you go, Mr Chairman.'

The older man hadn't heard him come in and nearly fainted when the passport was slid over the track towards him.

'Enjoy your sojourn in the sun, did you?' he seethed, gin and tonic in one hand, controller in the other. 'I hope you got lots of roller skating done over there, or whatever you mob call it.'

'Not exactly. But I'm here and ready to play.'

Cole's head leaned back as he assessed his star winger. Tanned and hair now cropped, he didn't hate what he saw. 'I have to grudgingly say that you look in rude health.'

'I told you that me going was for the benefit of all.'

'You don't think I'm going to forget, do you? We would have won this weekend if you'd played.'

'I'm here to play. Take me or leave me.'

'*Play*? This isn't the end of it. No one gets one over Chapman Cole. No one. I'll be on to the FA. UEFA. Scotland Yard. You'll never play again. You'll be in the clink facing 10 years down the salt mines.'

The door opened and Rory entered. 'Rippa! Thought it was you.'

'Hello, Rory.' The pair shook hands.

'How was The Sunburnt Country?'

'Very sad time actually. Still, it was something I needed to do. Sorry for the way it was done.'

'Needs must. Don't mention it.'

'*Don't bloody mention it?*' The chairman slammed down the controls, almost sending The Ghan jackknifing off the tracks. 'You're the reason we're not going up.'

'Not really, Mr Chairman,' Rory said. 'He missed two games. One was postponed due to flash flooding and the other abandoned after eighteen minutes because of high winds which lifted the corner flag and almost impaled Chorley's kit man. Thank heavens he was morbidly obese, that's all I can say.'

'Doesn't matter. We have no need for traitors like him here.'

'Actually, Mr Chairman, we really do. Giddsy's scrotum has become infected and Hardsy who's been filling in has spent the night in hospital.'

'What's the matter with him?'

'Let's just say, never cut your toenails whilst drunk. Nor clip your nose hair.'

'Help me Rhonda,' Cole tutted. 'This place is more like a convalescent home than a sporting club. Still, the players out there are men of substance and will never go for it.'

'Rippa, ya holidaymaking, new haircut, *Crocodile Dundee* wanker,' came a voice from afar. This was followed by a heavy clop-clop down the hallway as the players returned from the training ground. Then Millsy stuck his head in. 'It's not the end of the season yet. You gonna join us out there or what?'

They all looked to the chairman. After a beat he picked up the controls and blew out his jaws. 'What a piss-taking, spineless age we live in. I'd hate to see what it's like in the new millennium. No bloody scruples with you lot, nowadays. No bloody scruples. This is your get out of jail free card, lad.' He pointed to Rippa. 'This is your ninth life. And I want you on boot duty all week starting immediately after you've repaired the dent you made to my Jag. I want that car as good as new, and I want those boots so clean that I could eat my dinner out of them.'

Millsy guffawed. 'You gonna eat your pork pie out of a boot?'

'Get out of my office the lot of you.'

And they all did.

The treatment room was a small cupboard next to the boot one. Rippa peeked in to find Jane rubbing down Curtly's calf.

'Joey?' she hurried around the table, hugging him.

'Get a room the pair of you,' Curtly told them, his Walkman headphones in.

'Swore we'd seen the last of you,' she said, ignoring her patient.

'Didn't even think of not returning.'

'Yes, you did.'

'Hmm, yes, I did. I really did. Even when I touched down an hour ago, I was still thinking it.'

'Nice hair by the way.'

Rippa poked at it, not loving it. 'It's a bit square.'

'Folk round here will be happy.'

'That's all that matters at the moment.'

'What did Old King Cole say?'

'I've probably done myself out of an end-of-season bonus.'

'None of us get any type of bonus.'

'I forgot about that. What did I miss?'

'The usual horror. Club needs you for the run-in, I can tell you that much. You raring to go?'

'Sure am.' He leaned on his left foot and flinched. He moved in and whispered to her. 'Between you and me, though. I think I've hurt my foot.'

'You *think*?'

I know. I definitely know.'

'How'd you manage that?'

'Don't ask.'

'I'm the club physio. I'm asking.'

'A minor altercation with an old adversary.'

Jane's left brow arched in suspicion.

Rippa shrugged, sheepishly. 'Tried to give him a bit of kicking.'

'Didn't know you had it in you.'

'Turns out I don't. I missed and ended up giving the brick wall hell instead.'

'I'm leaving you love birds to it,' Curtly said, creaking up and taking his copy of the *Sunday Sport* with him. 'Get a room next time. A motel one. And leave the curtains open.'

'Show us the damage then,' Jane told Rippa once they were alone.

He removed his Roller and the flight sock covering his left foot. It had a bluey-grey shade all along the instep.

'Sorry about the smell. I haven't had a shower in 29 hours.'

'You oughta hear about the things I smell in here. And that's after the blokes have had a shower.' She touched his foot tenderly. 'That hurt?'

'Not so much.'

She applied more pressure this time at the base. 'That?'

Rippa gripped the table in agony.' Oh yeah, that'll do it.'

'Geez, Joey, I think that's a break. You need an x-ray.'

'Don't say that.'

'That's you done for the season.'

'Really don't say that. I'm fine to run on it. I just need some heavy strapping so I can wrap it round a ball.'

'I can't help you there.'

'The team needs me.' Rippa clasped his fingers together. 'You've said it, everyone's said it. And I need to make it up to them.'

'My professional opinion is that that would be a giant mistake.'

'And I respect that but, on my hands, and knees I'm begging you for the greater good.'

Jane shrugged. 'I'm very reluctant but I can lend you the materials and give you some instructions and then it's all up to you. You can give it a little go by all means. But I'm not having East London's finest suing me and putting me out the game.'

'Understood. And maybe don't tell Rory.'

'Tell him what?'

Rippa winked. 'That's the way.'

'He's not gonna mind. He had Tilesy play with a broken pelvis at the end of last season. Poor bloke had to stand to shit.'

'There are some things in life you just don't need to know and that is one of them.'

'At least you didn't have to help him do it.'

'Double gross. Anyway, don't worry. I'll kick with my right.'

Both her eyebrows shot up. 'You mean you have a right foot?'

'Hey, what does that mean?

'Thought you only use it for standing on?'

Rippa thought for a witty comeback but knew she probably had a point as he could never remember doing anything meaningful on a football pitch with it. 'Very funny. Tell you what, you got a sec?'

'Probably got sixty of them now that Curtly's skedaddled.'

'Is there a bag of balls anywhere?'

'This is Middleby United. You know the answer to that.'

'We had that scratch game. I think I saw the match ball lobbed up here.' Rippa climbed the lockers where he'd found his clown boots at the back of. He found a crusty sock, a pair of *Flat Stanley* boxers and a well-thumbed copy of the *The Book of Law* by Aleistar Crowley. And next to that was the old mud-covered Mitre size five, not quite flat.

'You used to be a goalie, yeah?' he asked her.

'Well, yeah, but why don't you ask one of your teammates to help?'

'This is Middleby United. I think you know the answer I'll get to that.'

They headed for the pitch.

'What the fuck you doing, Oz?' Millsy barked.

'Gonna do some ballwork.'

'Ooooh,' they all cooed like schoolboys.

'Save it for the bedroom,' joked Boonsy. 'Or the woods if you're feeling really frisky.'

'I mean to practise some skills, you perve,' Rippa said.

'Practise some *what*?' Boonsy asked, as the others stared at Rippa, mouths agape.

'Um,' continued Rippa, 'I meant nip out for a fag.'

'That's alright then,' winked Millsy as those in the room went back to what they were doing. 'I thought you were being even more of a massive weirdo than usual.'

Rippa walked into the muck and squalor which constituted Middleby's home ground, Jane being careful not to slip. She got in goal and rolled the ball out to Rippa on the edge of the box. His natural inclination was to touch it onto his left and then bend it into the near corner. Instead, he positioned his body the opposite way. It felt unnatural and he found it difficult to balance. He steadied himself as best as he could and swung at the ball with his right. The action sent him slipping to the surf and landing with a bump as the ball skied high over the goals, clearing the back wall.

'Ouch!'

And striking the post lady on her bike, sending her hurtling over a hedge.

'Sorry, Ethel,' Jane cringed.

The postie dragged herself out, pulling branches, twigs and a Robin's nest out of her hair. She gathered her letters. 'Surprised your fella made it back here with that sense of direction.'

Jane made sure she was okay and then threw the ball back to Rippa. He was up and ready and lining it up. This time he was being extra-careful not to go arse-over-tit or give it too much welly. Only it spun far right, trickling out for what would have been a throw-in.

Rippa was just thankful that there were no other fans watching to let him know exactly what they thought.

'At least power isn't a problem,' Jane said as cheerfully as she could muster.

'Yeah, but landing it in the right postcode is.'

'What about heading?' She tossed the ball up and he cowered and ducked low, instinctively throwing his arms over his head.

'Never tried it in my life.'

'I can tell.'

'Was always too worried about my hair. Also, something seems a bit unnatural about having a kilo of bull-hide land on your melon.'

'But hurtling over waves as tall as mountains on a plastic board in freezing water seems natural?'

'Hmm, now you mention it.'

She lobbed the ball skywards again. This time he stood there, shoulders hunched, eyes glued shut and let it glance off his head.

Rippa sighed. 'So much for expanding my repertoire.'

'You've just gotta practice.'

'Something I've never done. It's always come to me naturally.'

'Even the greats do it.'

'No one even knows the meaning of the word here.'

'Great and Middleby will never go together, sadly.'

'There's not even a wall I can use,' he said.

'Meant to ask. Where are you gonna live now?'

'Guess I'll go back and grovel to Mr and Mrs Munster. And then I'll let Dwayne volley a ball at my head or worse so that we're even. I really don't fancy another scrap.'

'You can't do that.'

'I have to do that.'

'Listen, I was speaking to my nan and we thought you could —'
'Yes,' Rippa interrupted her immediately.

' …take a look at our loft and see if —'

'My God, yes!' Rippa's mind was already made up, his arms aloft.

'It's cold and has no power or even windows.'

'And it already sounds like paradise.'

'It's really, really … like *really* not. Don't you wanna see it first?'

'I'm gonna sprint back to the House of Horrors this minute and get my things and be at yours within the hour.'

'We were thinking you could chip in a tenner here or there for bills.'

'Do you not hear?' He placed both hands gently on both her cheeks. 'I'll give you my entire wage. I'll cut off my good foot. I'll do anything. I don't think you understand how bad it is there.'

'I'm starting to get a pretty good picture.'

Chapter 33

Joey Rippa was going to face them all head on. He didn't care anymore. He was leaving the House of Horrors, and he had nothing to fear and even less to lose. What were they going to do? Drag him down to the half-renovated basement and chain him up, then castrate him and eat his manhood along with that poor excuse they had for potato mash?

Possibly.

And that is exactly why Rippa's knees were rattling like drum sticks because for all his fake bravado, he was shit scared. So instead of bounding right in there and telling them the score, he very quietly put his key in the lock, surprised that it still worked.

He heard Albert and Morag in the front room talking about something he couldn't decode and very carefully tiptoed up the stairs. He passed Dwayne's room and saw it was locked meaning he was probably still at the ground. With barely a breath he opened his own room door. His calendar had been removed along with his prized photograph of Sabrina. That was fine, he had no wish for either. It was so small, cold and dark in there, even in the middle of a bright spring day. No wonder he'd been depressed. He lifted his backpack and was preparing to make a quick exit when out of nowhere the hulking frame of Dwayne filled the doorway.

'It's you, you Van Diemen bastard.'

Rippa's eyes shot to the window as he wondered if there was another drainpipe he could slide down, not fancying another two-storey drop if there wasn't.

'Hi, Dwayne.'

'Didn't notice you back at the club. Not now that you've got a decent haircut for once and some sensible non-Australian clobber.' He looked closer, reaching over and feeling the material on Rippa's sleeve. 'Is that a New Zealand lambswool sweater?'

'No idea. Oh, wait, actually, of course it is,' Rippa pulled away and pretended to read the back label.

'Our clothes suddenly good enough for you?'

'Listen, Dwayne. About everything …'

'You nearly scolded me for life. If I wasn't wearing a thermal vest, winter warmer and my leaver's '79 jumper under my keeper's jersey, I'd have been in a bit of bother. And you'd have been a dead man.'

'I am sorry about all that.' Rippa went to go past and was blocked.

'Where do you think you're going?'

'I'm leaving.'

'For good?'

'For *good*, good.'

'You're not. Not yet. There's something I want to say to you.'

Rippa tensed, craning his neck to the glass to check if there really was an escape.

Dwayne extended one of his giant goalkeeper paws for Rippa to shake. 'I want to say I'm sorry for your loss.'

Rippa's eyes bulged in surprise. He took the hand. Dwayne's felt chilly and unwelcoming, like that of a dead man's.

'I know what it's like to lose someone close when you're living so far away.'

'You, um, do?'

'My mother passed shortly after I arrived in Middleby. I should have gone back for the funeral. I elected to stay here and fight for my spot instead. There's not a day that goes by that I don't think of her and regret my decision.'

'I'm sorry that happened.'

'So if you ever want to talk about it …'

'Thanks for that. Really.'

'And let's wipe the slate clean while we're at it. You might be a thieving, murdering, unwashed convict blood of an Australian. But you're Middleby now.'

Rippa realised they were still shaking hands, that they had been for some time, and that Dwayne wasn't for letting go.

'Lovely. This is all, um, lovely. I am, however, still leaving.'

'You mean leaving to the shop, right?'

'No, I mean, leaving, *leaving*. I have a new flat.'

'Why would you be leaving here?'

'Geez, you never think of doing the same? That pair down there need sectioned.'

'Beg your pardon. The Gristles are the kindest, warmest, most generous people I've ever known. Taken me under their wing into the warmth of their bosom. They've become like parents to me. I wouldn't have amounted to anything were it not for them.'

Rippa nodded along. 'Can I ask you a question?'

'Shoot.'

'Are you mental?'

'Are *you* mental more like? You'll never find a better home in the universe, never mind Middleby.'

'There you have it. Each to their own.'

'Indeed. Anyway, glad we cleared that up. I need to head into the town. Need new pruning scissors for the roses. Out of control they are.'

'Mind giving us a lift in, bud?'

'I'm still not your bud, Oz. You can bloody walk.'

Dwayne returned down the hallway. Rippa followed at a safe distance, only his quick exit was foiled by Albert and Morag.

'Here he is,' the woman exclaimed, her massive frame now blocking the front entrance after Dwayne had made it past. 'The prodigal son returneth.'

'What kind of establishment do you think this place is?' said Albert, joining her. 'Swanning back in here like nothing happened.'

'He thinks it's a hotel, doesn't he?'

'It kinda is,' Rippa said. 'I've been forking out to stay here. I'm paid up until Wednesday.'

Morag pulled back in horror, clutching at her abundant breast. 'All we do is give. All we do is help. And all he does is snatch from us and use us. And all the while he gives us these barbed remarks from the pit of his black stomach.'

'And you can get your vice-mad eyes away from my wife while we're talking to you,' Albert fumed.

'I am not looking at her.'

'Undressing me, so he is, Albert. Same as usual. Conjuring up evil and ungodly ways to defile me in his filthy mind.'

'Well your time is up because we are going to evict you.'

'That's fine,' said Rippa. 'I'm leaving now.'

Albert wasn't hearing. 'We've got a prospective new lodger who we're interviewing. He's in our good room right now as a matter of fact. A nice boy. A pure boy.'

'And the likes of you are no longer welcome,' nodded Morag.

'He's a better man, a rugger man. A gentleman from South Africa who's here to play.'

'He's a respectable Christian. Not some, some … heathen. Not some quaffer of the devil's juice.'

'That night really wasn't my fault,' Rippa protested.

'And he's a joiner on the side, so he can be proper useful around the house,' said Albert.

'It's almost impossible to find a fair and decent lodger these days, Albert, but by the grace of God we've found one.'

'I'm so happy for you both,' agreed Rippa. 'Now I'll just be on my way.'

Albert moved past him down the hall. 'I'm going to my desk right now so I can serve you the appropriate legal documentation in order to move you along from where you don't belong.'

'Are you even listening?' Rippa asked. 'All that really doesn't matter.'

'Come with me, Morag dear. He may try to act out one or two of his bestial fantasies in my absence.'

'Save my soul, Albert. Save my soul.' She desperately clung to her husband, and they went to the out-of-bounds nook under the stairs which was fashioned with a desk, typewriter and filing cabinet.

The exit was clear, and Rippa went for it. But out of sheer curiosity he couldn't resist sticking his head in the front room. A young African man was perched uneasily on the edge of the sofa. He wore his best tweed blazer, had a new suitcase by his polished shoes, and his eyes were popping at everything he'd just heard.

'Hey, mate, old lodger here.' The kid was about Rippa's age. He tried to smile but appeared too scared. 'I don't know you from a hole in the ground, but can I give you some advice?'

The kid nodded.

'See that case you have there. Pick it up and run out of here right now. Run as fast as you can and don't look back. If you insist on staying in Middleby, then take any other accommodation you can find, even if it means multiple bus and rail trips. Even if it means buying a car. Even if it means walking 20 miles. And if you can't find any, find a cardboard box and a back alley and sleep there. I promise it will be better.'

The kid shivered. He nodded again quickly. He lifted his suitcase and fled past Rippa onto the street and down the hill. Rippa followed, watching his back every step of the way until he, too, was in the clear.

Chapter 34

From the manager, to the Middleby players, and all the staff in between, everyone was most amiable to Rippa upon his return. Most of this was down to his previous appearance in a home shirt and how by some miracle he'd managed to fly around the world and not miss any matches. Everyone was realising that the club's other left-sided attacking options were missing in action and that should the Australian apply himself he had the ability to be a true standout in the league.

Rippa had enjoyed a fine week back and was loving the freedom and peace of his new abode. It was a rustic existence with home cooked food, no television, or distractions, and that was just how he liked it. The Texaco garage along the road had Old Jamaica Ginger Beer in its fridge — not a patch on Old Stoney but somewhere in the ballpark. It also sold Crunchies which weren't as good as his favourite Violet Crumbles either but were likewise not too dissimilar. This helped his homesickness no end, but he was careful to watch his fitness and limit himself to one of both per day. The garage also sold heavy plastic footballs for a pound. With his sleep getting somewhere back to normal due to a consistent diet and feeling safer and more secure away from the creepy confines of the Gristle's, Rippa began waking naturally once again at sunrise.

Not that there was much sun to see rise, nor to enjoy.

Instead, he'd cleared some space from the floorboards, flipped his mattress onto its side and lay it against the wall so he could practise striking the ball with his right foot against the single bed, over and over again for hours on end trying to make it useful.

And with those extra pounds in his pocket from the cheaper accommodation, he was enjoying the novelty of being able to eat out and go to the occasional movie (even if none of them were really to his liking) and spend each Tuesday night at the folk club. Middleby would never be Merri Bay, but at least it was becoming tolerable.

Today they were playing away at cellar-dwellers Weymouth in a lunchtime kick-off, and Middleby were expected to win and win comfortably to keep them firmly in the promotion hunt.

But for Rippa nothing was going right.

He couldn't blame the surface as it was easily the best he'd played on all season. The spring rain and subsequent sunshine created rich, green blades of grass which, when mowed, resembled something from centre-court at Wimbledon rather than a fifth-tier football ground. And luckily his teammates were up to the task. After much pleading from Rippa, Rory had allowed them some ballwork the day before and it was paying dividends. Their passes were crisper and their dribbles and turns sharper.

But this left Rippa with nowhere to hide. With his left foot feeling fragile despite being wrapped up like an Egyptian mummy, he was sluggish off the mark. And with the ball at his feet, his left-footed crosses were weak, failing to beat the first man. He then opted to cut inside instead onto his weaker right which he'd practised like hell on. But it was offering such little thrust and his marker soon caught onto this and was intercepting with ease.

In the dressing room at the break his teammates were letting him know all about it.

'Useless fucking convict,' moaned Millsy to Rippa about the stalemate.

'Playing like the barbaric African oppressor you are,' added Boonsy.

'You'll never get a game with the likes of Rapid Vienna playing like that,' quipped Tilesy. 'More like Slow Viennetta. Haha.'

'Come on lads,' Rory defended him. 'He's not the only one who's under-performing out there.'

'Are you for real?' spat Millsy.

'Let he who is without sin cast the first stone,' Rory continued, solemnly.

'Yes he fucking is,' said Boonsy, booting over the bin.

'I'll gladly cast a stone alright,' continued Millsy. 'Right between his eyes.'

'Sorry, Rippa, but he is kinda right,' conceded Rory. 'You've been so bad that I'm genuinely concerned that it's not actually you that's out there.'

'That's more like it, gaff,' Boonsy applauded.

'That you went back home and some Aboriginal skinwalker who's never even seen a round ball has taken your place. You laugh but I've heard it happen.'

'Bit much, gaff, but you're on the right track,' nodded Curtly.

'Is there anything you'd like to say?' Rory asked.

Rippa nodded. 'Can I see the physio, please? In private.'

The whole room grumbled in disgust as orange peels and cups of water were pinged in his direction.

'You already live with her,' pointed Millsy.

'Business and noshing should be kept well apart,' Boonsy agreed.

'*Can't you talk it over in be-eh-ed,*' sang Curtly, sounding like that one-hit wonder.

'He's a lodger,' Jane said at the doorway, hands on hips. 'Nothing more, nothing less.'

'I think there's a lot you two need to learn about the birds and bees,' said Millsy.

Rory thought about it as he stroked his chin. 'Just mulling over what Napoleon would do during such a conundrum. Or perhaps Kennedy. Or even Genghis Khan. Hmm ... in the interests of doing something, anything, to jolt you into action, you're permitted to go out into the tunnel where there's watchful eyes.'

The two of them did so.

'You have to tell him,' Jane whispered, examining his foot. 'You couldn't hit the barn, never mind the proverbial barn door out there.'

'Can you strap it tighter?'

'You can't fit any more strapping on. The boot's too small.'

'Shit.'

'You have to tell Rory. He'll just need to put on a right-sided player. It's rubbish but not half as rubbish as you've been out there. It's like playing with ten men.'

Rippa let his head despondently fall back onto the wall. 'Thanks a bunch.'

'You've got to know when to stop. There's always next season.'

'Is there?'

'Time, gentlemen,' called the ref, leading the officials back out.

'Wait. I've an idea.' Rippa rummaged through his backpack. He produced the left clown boot he first wore with Middleby.

'They're enormous,' Jane reminded him.

'Exactly. And if we strap my foot enough, I'll just about fill it.'

'If *you* strap it. I'm having nothing to do with it.'

'Whatever you want to call it. But please. Please help me.'

She reached for her bandages. 'I'm really not sure about this.'

'Neither am I. But I'm game for a go.'

'If this foot gets hit again you could be in serious bother.'

'I'll give it 10 minutes. If it's no good, I'll signal to the gaffer to come off.'

He bandaged it as Jane watched over, guiding him. It looked more like the end of a rowing oar than a foot but it made a neat fit, slotting tightly into the giant boot.

Out on the pitch anyone paying attention would have noticed the winger's left boot being twice the size of his right — and the smattering of Middleby fans by the touchline who'd made the five-hour journey were definitely paying attention.

'Did Coco the Clown transplant his trotter onto our star import at half-time?' asked one.

'Maybe it got hit by a mallet,' said another.

'I wish they'd hit his head with one,' agreed another. 'That would have been more useful than the clippers the barber used.'

'But maybe he's like Samson and he's turned shit without his hair,' said a balding fan.

'What do you mean *turned* shit. He's always been shit.'

The game restarted and Rippa felt better. Not great, nowhere near natural, but a bit better. He had more mobility and could at least trap a ball and give it straight back using his left foot with relative ease. The biggest test came five minutes in when a loose ball swerved left and the right-back and Rippa approached it at the same time. It was a standard 50-50 duel, but Rippa knew he had to make up for his forgettable first half and couldn't hold back. The foot rattled with the impact like he was Wile E. Coyote smashing into a stop sign, however the extra strapping had taken the load and Rippa was able to jog on.

After this he grew in confidence and his natural fitness meant he was getting the better of his older and heavier opponent as the match entered the latter stages. As the play whizzed by, Middleby were turning the screw and dominating, though they were lacking a killer punch in the final third. Then Dwayne played a long clearance over their right-back and Rippa was scurrying after it, outpacing him with ease. He had time to line it up on his unreliable right but knew that could send it anywhere. He looked over. The Schnozz had escaped his marker. Rippa braced his left and struck the ball. The connection was firm yet graceful and he felt minimal impact. But the ball was low, too low. The Schnozz had anticipated this, however, and sprinted to the front post. He dived head-first. It glanced off his head and evaded the keeper, firing into the bottom left corner. The away fans erupted and this time the players congratulated Rippa, though only after hugging and kissing The Schnozz whose nose was glowing redder than usual.

'Fucking knew you'd come good,' said Millsy ruffling Rippa's new do.

Facing relegation, Weymouth kicked-off immediately and pushed bodies forward in desperate search of an equaliser. Rippa filtered back to provide support. He saw one of Middleby's kids getting stripped and ready to come on. He saw a flash of a number 11 on the sub's board and knew his afternoon was coming to a close. He felt happier with his effort. Happy to have shown the players and travelling fans a little more of what he was capable of.

The ball was still in play as an overhit cross was struck from Tilesy on the right. Rippa was onto it. He skipped around his man in the tight pocket and nutmegged the onrushing midfielder and then he was really away. Weymouth had so many maroon jerseys forward that there was only the centre-half to beat. But his face was red, and sweaty and he was limping badly from cramp, and Rippa accelerated easily past him.

The Middleby fans were on their feet as the keeper rushed out. Rippa looked left and then right, searching for a way to squeeze it past him. The strapped foot was feeling good. Very good. He got his toes under the ball and up he scooped it. For a second he thought he'd given it too much welly and missed another sitter as a premonition of Weymouth going straight up the other end and stealing a late equaliser haunted him. But then the ball dipped at the last moment and bounced over the line.

Rippa ran to the Middleby fans who looked almost as shocked as he was. They'd never seen a goal quite like it and were elated by the contrast of his second half showing. And then it was Rippa's turn to be mobbed as Rory pole vaulted the touchline and leapt on his winger's back, punching the air.

'I knew you'd do it!' he yelled in his ear. 'Whatever that physio did to you, gimme some of that.'

Chapter 35

When the players got back from Dorset they hit The Orient. But despite this time receiving an invite, Rippa declined. Instead, he went to Saturday night bingo with Jane and Nan. The thought of hanging out with the pair was a million times better than hanging out with anyone else at the football club.

''Will you still need me, will you still feed me ...' began the caller.

'Bingo!' interrupted the same man in the beer-stained singlet, jumping up.

'You haven't heard me say the rest of the number.'

'But it's the song!'

'What song?' said the caller.

'The Beatles song. "When I'm 64". And I have it.'

'Have what?'

'64.'

'Can I continue?'

'You don't need to. I won.'

The caller ignored him. 'Will you still need me, will you still feed me - 19.'

'You're at the wind up, ya bastard!' A younger man hurried over, restraining him from the stage. 'You're sending me to early grave and you're coming with me!'

Jane had seen it all before. 'I can't believe you gave up a night with the lads for this.'

Rippa chortled at the scene. 'Have you met the lads?'

'Point taken.'

Being the weekend, the hall was busy. An old lady with oversized false teeth wheeled over in her wheelchair. 'Good showing today by all accounts, young Rippa.'

'Thank you very much.'

'Didn't know you had it in you.'

'I doubted it too.'

'Sign your autograph for me?'

'I'd love to.'

'Pick and mix — 26,' continued the caller.

The old woman unbuttoned her blouse, displaying her ample veiny and very saggy cleavage. She handed him a red marker. 'And make sure you do them both.'

Rippa blushed when he saw the whole hall was looking.

'Don't you leave the pair of them hanging now,' cooed the caller from the stage as he paused the game.

'What's the matter?' the old lady asked, enjoying the moment. 'First time you've signed a fine pair of breasts?'

'First time I've signed anything.' And it was the truth.

Nervously, he did so. The room applauded. The woman gave him a smooch on the lips for his trouble.

The game went on. 'Getting plenty — 20.'

'So much for a quiet night out,' giggled Jane as the game got back underway.

'I know, right.'

'I'm gonna get a drink. You want a Diet Coke?'

'After that ordeal, make it a real one. It is the weekend.'

'Oooh, look at you with your full-strength pop and your groupies. George Best, watch out.'

She left Rippa with Nan. He drank the rest of his tea and finished the last of his crisps as a man with buck teeth and a parrot perched on his shoulder called out that he had a full house.

'Heard you did well today in the early kick-off,' Nan said to Rippa, looking more lucid than she had since he'd met her.

'Second half yes. Scored one, made one.'

'That's more like it. Knew you'd come good.' She blotted a number on her card. 'You like the town yet?'

'I'm not going to answer that.'

'53 years I've been here, and I sometimes feel like that.'

'Why did you stay?'

'Life begins — 40,' came the call.

'You've gotta lay anchor somewhere.'

'There's no ocean anywhere near here to lay anchor anywhere.'

'My husband had work down this way. Teaching. I'm from Skye, Scotland. Right near the ocean. Fishing stock. It broke my heart being so far away from the sea as well as my family. But I stuck it out and I laid down roots and it got better. It became home.'

'I can't see that ever being me.'

'And that's fine too. But remember there's people like me here who call it home. And there's folk who've been here for generations. This town is everything and this football club symbolises that. When you're pulling on the shirt it might not mean much to you, but it means the world to them.'

'Top of the shop - 90.'

'I get it,' Rippa said. 'I really do. But there's no surf, no scenery. Just football.'

'Exactly. Just football. And that's what you're here to do. So, give it your all. West Ham and whoever's responsible are daft but they're not that daft. They wouldn't have signed you if you didn't have it in you.'

'You're right.'

'I'm old. I know I'm right.'

Jane was heading their way with a stacked tray of goodies.

'I think I really like your granddaughter.'

'I can help you understand Middleby but you're very much on your own there.'

'Droopy drawers — 44.'

Jane put down the drinks and a handful of fresh cards so her and Rippa could join in. Neither of the three had won anything tonight but Rippa knew the evening wasn't about that.

At around 10 p.m. Jane drove them home. Rippa was so glad he was heading back to hers and not Albert and Morag's place, even if he was essentially living in the eaves of her roof. Before retiring for the evening, Jane asked him if he wanted to head to her room and listen to records and jam.

He didn't need to be asked twice.

There, he strummed her Martin semi-acoustic as she put her nan to bed, politely declining his offer of help. Then they listened to Dylan and Nick Drake as they both strummed along, sipping tea for him and red wine for her and sharing a bowl of microwave popcorn.

She played the new singles coming out from the Madchester scene — Stone Roses, Happy Mondays and New Order. Rippa was into surf music, but he didn't hate what he was hearing. The bands held special significance for Jane as Manchester Uni was the place she got her degree, finishing just last year. And it represented the only years in her life where she was away from home and truly free, even if she had to come back each weekend to care for her grandmother.

'You've heard me play,' Jane said. 'Now I wanna hear you play. A song from your band.'

'I dunno,' hesitated Rippa. 'I think my days are over.'

'Just play. It doesn't matter what it sounds like … that's what you're always telling me.'

He did so, playing a stripped back version of one of Dune Landing's favourite songs, "Let Forever Fade". It was the first time he'd played it on acoustic and Rippa realised how good a song it was and that it was the drums which really brought it to life. And that he'd never ever hear them again. That thought was so sad that it had him choking up.

Jane put a comforting arm on his shoulder. 'That was so good.'

'Really?'

'*Really.* You should perform onstage again.'

'I can't. Or rather I won't. It was Cal's song.'

'But I'm sure he wouldn't want you to stop.'

'It was always more his thing. I liked it, I didn't love it. It was a way of hanging out with him. Of keeping out of trouble when I couldn't surf. With him gone, it doesn't have the same meaning for me. I'm thinking that it might be a chapter that's come to a natural end.'

'That's sad.'

'That's life. Anyway, your turn.'

'Sure. Only, wait. I got you something.'

'If it's half as good as your previous gifts to me then boy am I in for a treat.'

She reached into her bedroom drawer and handed him a small plastic zip bag. He unwrapped it, finding not a joint but what looked like a quarter ounce of hash. At the height of his smoking days this would have lasted him months. The way he'd been going in England, this could last years.

'Wow. Thanks.'

'What's wrong?' She noticed his slightly forced smile.

'Nothing. Nothing at all.' He looked at it closer. It was sticky and pleasantly stinky.

'I've known you long enough now to know that there is.'

'Would it offend you at all if I didn't accept this?'

'Not at all. Just thought you'd like it. For your foot and your head, y'know.'

'I mean, I love it. I love this almost as much as surfing, and boy do I love surfing. It's just … I'm trying to really focus right now on my football, and this here is tapping into a different me. The old me.'

'I think that's big of you. And I think that's right.' She lifted it from him and put it back in her drawer.

'It won't go to waste, will it?

'I told you, I'm part of a folk club.'

'Good' he reached over and fumbled with his backpack. 'I got you something too.'

'You didn't need to.'

'I did. Of course I did. Look what you've done for me. No way would I have played like that today if you didn't put me up in your home or strap my foot up.'

'If the courts ask, you did it yourself. Remember?'

'Course, course. You know what I mean.'

'Well what gal doesn't like a gift?'

He handed her a plain box with the word TEAC across it, about the size and dimensions of a shoe box. She opened it and examined the shiny electronic device within it featuring various knobs, faders and buttons.

'Thank you,' she gushed.

Rippa studied her expression. 'You have no idea what it is, do you?'

'Not a clue.'

He laughed. 'It's a four-track tape recorder.'

'I don't know how to use this.'

'I do. Well, kinda. We should have bought one for the band but never had the coin. For your stuff, it's perfect. You should get all your songs down.'

'They're really not that good.'

'I'm sure they are.'

'And they're not ready.'

'Who cares? Just record them. We can scrub them. It's to muck around with. It's to make them better.'

'Okay. But just the Dylan cover, yeah?'

'I love your covers. But they're not you. I wanna hear *you*. Loads will.'

She removed the machine from the box. 'What exactly do I do with it?'

'Nothing,' Rippa said, lifting it from her and plugging it in. 'Just you play.'

Jane sat there on the rug with her pink fluffy slippers on, and the glass of red next to her, and her nan down the hallway fast asleep. And all was quiet and peaceful on the sleepy back streets of Middleby. Rippa pressed record.

Jane cleared her throat. Then she loudly strummed and sang a widely out-of-tune version of "Agadoo" by Black Lace.

'Very funny,' said Rippa.

He found this nowhere near as funny as Jane who was struggling for breath. 'Oh my god, you should see your face.'

Rippa stopped recording.

'Sorry, sorry,' she wheezed. 'I'll take it seriously.'

Rippa pressed record. Jane composed herself and cleared her throat again. And this time she broke into an even louder and even more out-of-tune and obnoxious version of The B-52s "Rock Lobster".

She laughed even harder, and this time Rippa did too.

'Okay, okay. I'll do it. I can be serious.'

She wiped the tears from her eyes and cleared her throat. She fumbled with the sweet chords, and then stumbled over them again before she got going:

'Where'd the feeling go,
How I've wondered so.
I don't want somebody to love me,
The sky it weighs down on me because of you.
I don't want somebody to love me,
Just want somebody to hold me,
Just you.'
Rippa sat motionless, embarrassed by how much better this was than

what he'd played her. He sat there so long after she'd finished that he forgot to press stop or say a single word.

'You hated it,' she blushed.

'Wait, what? No, that was incredible. Honestly.'

'I need another verse.'

'Is it about anyone … in particular?' he asked hopefully.

'It's about Middleby. Mainly. It's about loving a place so much despite its endless faults and feeling trapped by it.'

Rippa nodded, trying not to look disappointed. 'You could actually do something here. With this. With your songs. This could be your ticket out.'

'Behave. I'm hardly Joni Mitchell. I don't know how you've done what you've done coming from over the other side of the world. You've balls of steel, not knowing a single soul. That isn't the life for the likes of us here.'

'It's not for me either. That's why I know that if I can do it then anyone can.'

'I don't think you understand Middleby. No one here gets out.'

'Myra Hindley did.'

Jane didn't laugh. 'We don't talk about that.'

'Sorry. I don't actually know who that is.'

'Trust me, you don't want to.'

'I just think with these songs you gotta take it at least beyond the local folk club. And not just music but your career too. You proved today how good you are with how you helped me.'

'You did that.'

'Sure, I did,' he lied.

'I'll think about it. Wanna watch a movie or something?'

'I want to hear you play. Could listen all night.'

'I'm a bit tired, Joey.'

'You'll never make it thinking like that.'

She put the guitar down. 'I don't wanna make it. I can't have everything like you can. You're here to play football and that's it. I have my job. I have my nan.'

'You're right. I'm sorry. What do you wanna watch?'

'I forgot. There's this program I've been meaning to show you.' Jane flicked through a stack of pre-recorded VHS tapes. 'Have you seen *Neighbours?*'

'Nope.'

'Apparently it's been airing in Australia for years.'

'I never had a telly.'

'It's probably too close to home for you but it's huge here. You've gotta take a look.'

And look they did. So this was who Kylie and Jason were? This was what everyone was going on about? The accents, the earthy decors, the cul-de-sac they lived in. It was Australia alright, but not his version. It was suburbia and not a jot like Merri Bay.

'Making you homesick yet?' Jane asked as she watched a scene where Henry Ramsay got locked out of his house in the nude.

'It's making me never want to return.'

'See. I told you it'd be worth it.'

Rippa relaxed. He took a handful of the popcorn and crammed it in his mouth, crunching the kernels, eyes glued to the screen. 'This is so bad that I'm gonna watch it every single day.'

Chapter 36

YOUNG AUSSIE LIGHTS UP THE NON-LEAGUE
AND HAS THE BIG GUNS IN HIS SIGHTS
By George Kostas
Soccer Week
May 3, 1989

After a disastrous start to his professional career, Australian winger Joey Rippa is finally taking England's GM Vauxhall Conference by storm.

The teenager has now scored in five of his last five appearances and laid on another six assists to lead Middleby United to maximum points and third spot on the table, requiring a victory on the final day to ensure a return to the Football League.

Rippa famously shot to fame after a whirlwind friendly performance for a WA state select side against West Ham, which saw the English outfit nab him on a two-and-half-year deal, allegedly offering him a contract at half-time. However, West Ham manager Bobby Noll was dismissed shortly afterwards, and Rippa was farmed out to the struggling Northern English yo-yo club, Middleby United, playing in the fifth tier. He failed to make an early impact and fled back home only to return and show his worth.

Middleby boss Rory Brady praised the on-loan player's commitment. 'To be honest, I wasn't sure if it was really for him for a while there. I mean, I thought it was a wind up, that they'd sent us some imposter. Now, I respect Bobby Noll as much as the next footy aficionado but even I was thinking he'd lost his mind. The kid didn't look lost, he looked like he'd never seen a ball before, never mind kicked one. But fair play to him, he's stuck in and turned it round.'

It was chairman Chapman Cole who brokered the short-term move back in January through his model train connections with a West Ham director. Cole maintained it was Rippa's trip back to Australia following a bereavement which has seen the move eventually pay off.

'The lad came to see me about losing this pal of his, a month or so ago,' Cole said. 'He wanted to stay here but I said no, no, no, you go. Football isn't more important than life or death, what dinosaur would think that? I said, you go over and do what you need to do and windsurf or skateboard or whatever it is you Down Under buggers get up to and then you come back and worry about us. I even offered to pay for the whole trip. And I'm glad I did all that because he's come back here and played like the bloody Duracell bunny.'

Third-place Middleby face second-place Barnet at home on Saturday with a point separating the pair. With Maidstone having already won the league, a win will earn the home side the other promotion spot while a draw will be enough for The Bees. Either way it looks to be Rippa's final game in the grey and white stripes as his loan deal expires and he is due to return to East London. But Cole said this was too early to confirm.

'It's all about the points. The Mighty Clappers can't afford another season in this vortex of a league. Some never get out. And if that happens my solicitor says I'll have to downgrade my plans for my new model village in order to fund the divorce. That's why I rolled the dice and picked up Rippa. It's all on this one.'

Editor's note: Joey Rippa was unavailable for comment. Our journalist went to his official residence but was chased from the premises by a bald, thin man brandishing garden shears and ranting about 'shirtlifters'. Local police are investigating.

Chapter 37

It was matchday on the final day of the season and Rippa wandered to the ground with a spring in his step. He'd had a full and hearty breakfast, which for him now consisted of cornflakes and banana with lots of milk, followed by French toast and a couple of cups of coffee. Then he'd practised for two hours with the plastic ball against his turned-over mattress — right foot, right foot, right foot, over and over with a little of the left thrown in for good measure. The right one would never compare to the other one but at least he could now control a ball with it and spring an occasional pass.

Rippa also caught up on yesterday's episode from Ramsay Street where Bouncer knocked Mrs Mangel off a ladder, and she lost her memory. Rippa found the stories wafer-thin, the characters likewise, the sets beige and dreary compared to the colour and natural vibrancy of the Australia he knew. But there was something about the accents and the laid-back vibe of the show which filled a void within. And he was strangely drawn to the story arcs of the older kooky characters such as Harold, Madge and Helen Daniels rather than the hipper younger ones who graced magazine covers.

He wondered if Martin Vasey did get that meeting with Kylie and Jason after all?

And anyway, *Neighbours* for its myriad of faults was still ten times better than watching *Saint and Greavsie* or *Grandstand*. He couldn't understand why any footballer would watch anything football-related when the sport already consumed their lives.

Rippa strolled to the stadium. As the RAF planes darted through the sky loudly completing their latest mock sortie, he could see the sun peeking through the clouds bringing colour to the familiar grey. There were lush and thick green leaves now sprouting on the trees. And without his jacket for the first time, the breeze, usually icy and sharp, had a hint of something warm and welcoming.

A bus tooted its horn as it passed. The driver in the grey and white beanie gave him a thumbs up and the destination above him was changed to the words 'BEST OF LUCK MIDDLEBY UNITED'.

Rippa paused at the fruit and veg stand for an apple to munch on. Connie the fruiterer wouldn't hear of him dipping into his own pocket.

'Here, take a bag, ya daft bugger. You want a cabbage as well? How about a fat turnip?' She held the misshaped pieces of veg up to him.

'I'm fine, really.'

'I couldn't bear the thought of us blowing it today and it being my fault because I wouldn't give you what you wanted.'

'That's very kind.'

'For my dog's sake, just make sure you bring home that promotion.' She suddenly winced. 'There's no way he wants another booting from my old fella.'

The whole town was a brighter and sunnier place. Even the players had started to warm to him over the last few weeks and he'd warmed to them.

Well, most of them.

He waited to cross at the traffic lights. A black Cortina he knew stopped at the red light and rolled down its window.

'Alright, Rippa?'

'Alright, Dwayne.'

'You want a lift there?'

'Um, sure.' He didn't really. The ground was in sight, and he'd told Jane he preferred to walk on game days. He'd always liked a stroll before any sort of sport, even as a kid, finding that it limbered him up and cleared his head.

'Well go and buy a car then, you tight Australian wanker.'

Dwayne cackled and screeched off in a plume of fumes leaving Rippa spluttering. Of all the people in the town he'd won over, Dwayne was not one of them. But they had forged a slight mutual respect based on each other's talents.

At least Rippa liked to think so.

At the ground he got stripped and changed and went to see Jane about his foot.

'How's it feel?' she asked.

'About as good as it ever has.'

'Ooooh,' Millsy lisped, walking past, completely naked. 'Getting your pre-match nosh, Rippa?'

'Not really, Millsy.'

'Well Little Miss Massage Therapist, would you mind giving me and all the lads one because whatever you're doing to him it's sure as all fuck working.'

'Looking at the state of your beer gut,' Jane told him looking at his bulging stomach, 'It's time you lay off the real nosh altogether.'

Rippa never had to stick up for Jane because she could do so herself in a way he could only dream.

'You want more strapping for this week?' she asked him.

'You know what, I was thinking none for today. I walked here and it feels great.'

'It wouldn't have healed yet.'

'It feels like it has. I want to give it a go with your old boots instead.' Rippa rotated the foot with ease. The colour had returned to normal. In fact, his whole body felt better than it ever had. Jane's shepherd's pies and homestyle dumplings were building him up nicely. And Rory's training, now with a bit of added ball work, had him looking fitter than a butcher's dog. Though he desperately missed surfing, the weed that usually went along with it — and the subsequent munchy cravings that were filled by meat pies, Violet Crumbles and Masters Choc — were not missed at all.

The players were changed and ready and bouncing off the walls, waiting to tear into the opposition. But Rory still felt it his duty to take out a fresh stack of palm cards he'd carefully compiled, these from the back of a box of Shredded Wheat.

'Nine score and seven years ago our forefathers brought forth league football to the town, conceived in quality and dedication to the proposition that all men are created equal, except for us.' The players looked at him blankly, as usual, with no idea what he was on about or why he was using an American accent. But Rory seized the moment and pulled it together at the end roaring, 'Because — we — are — Middleby!'

The boys might not have needed it, but they lapped it up with a cry so loud they could have heard it back on the not-so mean streets of Barnet.

And with that, they were out and at them. Clappers Lane was a sea of grey and white and closer in size to the WACA crowd when Rippa played there, instead of what Middleby usually pulled. He gave his now customary nod and wave to Nan in the crowd who sometimes responded and sometimes didn't depending on how she was faring. But today she gave a hearty wave in return and Rippa had an inkling in the pit of his stomach that this would be Middleby's day, and he wanted to do it for her and the town.

Feeling pumped by the speech and the sell-out crowd, United immediately hounded down their opposition and then were breaking at speed. Rippa was feeling near his best. His foot was holding together nicely and giving him a level of dexterity that he hadn't enjoyed since arriving back in the country. While the clown shoe had functioned well, this boot clung tighter and felt more natural. However, his marker was young, fit and agile. Rippa had heard from Rory that he'd been scouted by Division Three clubs and, the way he was sticking to him, Rippa was finding it difficult to conjure up anything substantial. The home side were struggling to create the chances they needed to score the goal they desperately required to take the points and earn promotion.

As their frustration grew, the visitors were growing in confidence — a confidence fuelled by the agitation around the ground. And against the run of play, Millsy was dispossessed in the centre-circle and Barnet broke, getting their own midfielders forward. Rippa was snapping at his heels as he raced towards goal. He swung out a leg. It was his left leg. Had he had on the bigger boot which provided him with an extra inch or so, his toe would have nicked the ball. But he forgot he had the smaller pair on and instead of getting the ball, he clipped his opponent's heel and sent him tumbling. The ref looked to the linesman for confirmation and saw that he was waving for the infringement. The ref pointed to the spot and gave Rippa a yellow card for his troubles. Rippa lay there wanting the ground to swallow him up. He could barely watch as the spot-kick was easily dispatched, and the home fans groaned.

Dwayne picked the ball out of the net and made a beeline for the wideman who primed himself for the rollicking of all rollickings. The keeper plunged the ball deep into Rippa's chest, hard. 'You got us into this mess, now you get us out.'

'Yeah, yeah,' said Rippa, trying hard not to appear winded.

'No. I'm serious. Do it. You're the only one who can. We're relying on you and you fucking owe us.'

Rippa knew he was right. From kick-off the ball trickled out his way and he switched to his right side. With Dwayne's words ringing in his ears he ran at his marker. He feigned left, then right, and then left again and sped past. He slipped a ball inside, low and hard across the box to Millsy. The captain struck it first-time, low and sweet. The keeper dived and reached it but the ball had been hit too hard for him to hold and the ball spilled away from his grasp. Rippa had been continuing his run towards the goal and was waiting to pounce. But so was the big opposition number five as well as the keeper. It wasn't a 50/50 duel. It was 33.333/33.333/33.333 duel and it was on Rippa's left. With no strapping he knew this would hurt and he knew it could put him out of not just this game but any game for the foreseeable future. But he also knew that with the goal gaping before him that this was a real chance. He steadied himself, and steamed right in. The pain exploded up through his leg and then his back and into his brain and for a split second he blacked out. It was like a speeding train had passed and took his leg clean off as the impact threw him high and wide and straight off the pitch. Rippa couldn't even open his eyes.

He couldn't move.

When he came to, Jane was gently trying to lift him onto a stretcher. Rippa looked up to see the outcome and saw the players of both teams leaving the pitch.

'Full time?' he croaked, his mouth like dry ice. His vision was blurry and he couldn't feel anything at all on his left side, and not just his foot.

'Half-time,' she told him, carefully unlacing his boot.

'Did I score?'

'You scored, hon. Ages ago. It bobbled over the line.'

Rippa struggled up, attempting to follow the players.

'Slow down,' she told him.

'Gotta get ready for the second half.'

'You're getting ready for no such thing. Your foot — if it wasn't broken before, then it sure as hell is now.'

'We'll bandage it again. Use the old clown shoe.'

'No way. You could really hurt it if you haven't already. I've told Rory to warm up a sub.'

They abandoned the stretcher. She put an arm around him and helped limp to the tunnel. On the way he received a warm round of applause from the Middleby faithful.

'Well done, Rippa.'

'Hope we haven't seen the last of you.'

'Proved us all wrong, lad,' said his old neighbour with the bobble hat.

Rippa forced a smile but had never felt more downbeat.

'You've done so well, Joey,' Jane told him as they hobbled along together. 'No matter what happens, just remember that.'

Chapter 38

Rippa slumped against the cool and muddy grey tiles which ran along the dressing room wall. Rory was giving another speech, this one based around the words of Martin Luther King. This time Rippa wasn't listening. As he removed his dirty shin guards, he realised his day, his season, was done.

'Rippa,' Jane called over. 'There's someone here to see you.'

Rippa didn't look up. He couldn't.

'Tell them I'll come out once I've had a bath. If I haven't slit my wrists in there first.'

'That won't wash. C'mon.'

'Go on, Oz,' Millsy ordered. 'Your missus has spoken and in these parts what our missus says, goes.'

Rippa was too despondent to fight them. He dragged himself up, his bones stiff, his left foot now blown up to the size of a mini football.

'Who is it?' he asked her.

'Dunno. Some Cockney who won't take no for an answer.'

Rippa saw it was Uncle Warren. He was looking good in a fresh grey Lacoste shirt, with his hair neatly trimmed. He'd even had a shave.

'What you doing here?' Rippa was so glad to see a familiar face that he hugged him, and Uncle Warren was someone he'd never hugged.

Warren reciprocated for a second before pulling back and re-engaging with his prickly English demeanour.

'Got asked over. This Ethiopian refugee in the WA state squad had a trial with Oxford.'

'The uni?'

'The football club, you giraffe.'

'Of course.'

'They're keen. Now Norwich are too so we're checking them out as well.'

'Sounds hopeful.'

'Maybe. If he can put on a few pounds and stop crying for his mummy every night before he goes to sleep.'

'Tough gig.'

'I had to sell my van to make it happen. Hope you don't mind.'

'It's yours. But where will you live when you go back?'

'That was only temporary, ya plonker. Life will be very different when I go back. Or rather, *if* I go back. I'm starting to think this might be the place for me after all. And this kid's really something. Quicker than a rash off an East End hooker. And if you can continue this form that I've been hearing about then I might get a few extra bob from you.'

'I'm trying.'

'If I can represent you that is. Officially.'

It took Rippa just half a second to respond. 'Course you can.'

'I think you need someone.'

'I was about to ask you myself.'

'Good then. Great even.'

'I'm trying my best over here.'

'You certainly are, boyo. Honestly thought that last time I saw you, that was it. That you'd be stuck in Moonshine Bay forever.'

'If I had my way, I would be there forever, but life doesn't always pan out how you plan.'

'Telling me. Been following you in the paper. Turned it right round, so you have. How are you going today?'

'Didn't you see it?'

'Just got here. I mean, I knew Middleby was far, but fuck me. This took a whole day. It's all bog tracks and sheep crossings. And it isn't half depressing.'

'Try being here for winter.'

'What's it like living here?'

'You wouldn't last a week.'

'Surprised you have. What's the score anyway?'

'One-all.'

'You get the goal?'

'That I did.'

'That's my boyo,' his uncle thumped him on the back. 'Now get out there and get the winner.'

'Nah, my day's done.' Rippa looked down to his bare foot, blue and sore and now resembling a basketball. 'Think it's broken.'

Uncle Warren scoffed. 'Turn it up, Princess.'

'I'm toast. Burnt toast.'

'I'll toast your backside. 45 minutes left of the season. You got three months to sit and nurse that. You get it strapped up. Dave Mackay once played an entire cup game with a shattered knee cap for Spurs at Doncaster. And three days later he was fit for the replay.'

'I don't think so.' Even Rippa knew he was spent.

'I come all this way to this mediaeval cow patch. Y'know I had stand tickets at Carrow Road and that chef off the telly has been giving me the eye all week.'

'I really can't.'

'You really can. You didn't give up your paradise in Minging Bay or whatever you call it to sit in the stands and mope during one of the most talked about games in the country. There's more cameras than Dixons out there. I'm presuming this bunch of hicks have bothered to hire a physio?'

Rippa pointed to the opposite room where Jane was delicately applying a single stitch above Dawsy's eye.

'Jesus Christ, they didn't half. What I wouldn't do to get stitched up by that. You get it sorted, boyo, and I'll see you out there. You got a title to win.' And with that he was off back to his seat.

Jane had heard the whole thing. 'I'm not doing it, Joey.'

'Listen, you said yourself what the club means to the town. It's too important not to go up.'

'I'll never forgive myself if you get properly hurt.'

'We tried it before and it worked. And there's one half to go.'

'I can't. You know I can't.'

'Rory,' Rippa called into the dressing room. 'Hold that sub. I'm giving it another ten.'

'Attaboy!' The coach punched the air. 'Rippa the Great. That's what they'll call you in the annals of history.'

'Joey, don't do this,' Jane begged.

'I'm doing it. So you can either guide me and make sure I strap it right and safely. Or, well, that's up to you.'

She sighed. She sent Dawsy on his way and got out her medical bag. 'You must promise me no 50/50s. Not even any 60/40s. No, make that no 75/25s.'

'No duels with any loose balls whatsoever. You have my word.'

And this time she bit her tongue and bandaged it for him.

Chapter 39

If the first half had been a feisty affair, the second ramped this up to eleven. With so much at stake, the ball rebounded around the dry pitch like a pinball as bodies clashed and crunched, and tackles flew and tempers frayed. But Rippa — with his foot feeling as fragile as antique stained glass, and that promise to Jane — was hugging the touchline trying to avoid any skirmishes. While at the same time making himself useful and available and limiting himself to sideways return passes so Middleby could retain possession. This was the safe option, but with ten minutes gone and the clock ticking that wasn't what was going to get Middleby the goal they needed to clinch promotion.

And the home fans were letting him know it.

'Skin him, Rippa!'

'Whip it in.'

'Fucking do something, you Aussie twat.'

But Rippa was way off the pace in a way he hadn't been since first arriving. And it was evident when the ball was worked to him and, unable to cross with his left, he switched it to his right and the ball drifted into the side netting. The fans were now howling for a change to be made.

Rory left the safety of the dugout and ventured over. 'I'm gonna pull you, Rippa. Put one of the kids on. We got the under-18's striker here who's hot to trot, especially since he got his first ever snog at The Orient on Tuesday night.'

The under-18 striker was 5' 2" and had scored one goal all season for the youths which was a rebound from a spot-kick which he'd missed.

'Give me a bit longer. Please.'

'I'm not sure.'

'I *am* sure.' Rippa didn't know where this newfound stubbornness had come from but he had a feeling that he could make something happen.

'Don't be the Brutus to my Caesar. The Judas to my Jesus. Please don't let me down.'

Rory took the bold step of dragging Millsy instead for the thimble-sized debutant. The crowd were livid and the captain himself was ropeable.

'Are you fucking joking?' he raged as he stomped his feet towards the bench. 'Biggest game in history and you drag the skipper? That corner flag's moved more than our left winger. Sub him.'

And Millsy, for once, had a point.

The next time the ball came Rippa's way he controlled it, and this time went to skin the full-back. But the promising Barnet kid was far quicker and more agile at this late stage and easily dispossessed him.

The next time the opportunity arose, Rippa played it inside to the young forward who played it back to him. Rippa gritted his teeth and ran on to it, collecting it before it went over the byline. The Schnozz had run into the box along with another four grey and white jerseys. This time he knew he had no choice but to strike it with his left as there was no room to hit it with his right. He gritted everything he had and wrapped his throbbing foot around the ball. This time he got the ball off the ground and into play.

But the keeper was there, and it was easily caught. The groans of pent-up disappointment echoed loud and all-too clear, most coming from the captain, huffing away in the dugout. Though not from Rory, who, having now used both his subs, had slumped to the turf with his head in his hands.

Rippa knew he'd messed up. The foot was cooked. He could jog on it — just — and that was it. The clock above the stand told him it was quarter-to-five. The busload of Barnet fans in the away section were letting them all know about it as they were in party mode and singing loudly with the result enough for them to secure promotion to Division Four.

'In the Middleby slums,

You hunt through the dustbins for something to eat,

You find dead rat and you think it's a treat,

In the Middleby slums.'

Rippa peeked into the crowd. Shoulders were slumped, some were looking away. Others were making an early exit. Then Rippa spotted his uncle. He was peeking though his fingers like Rory unable to watch. He saw Nan and she was doing the same. And then he noticed Jane. She gave him a warm smile and her now customary fist salute.

'One minute left, Joey. One minute,' she mouthed.

Rippa steeled himself and ventured inside to where the two Barnet midfielders were stroking the ball back and forth between their exhausted Middleby opponents, happy to keep the possession. They hadn't counted on the left-winger making a challenge because he hadn't all half. Yet here he was steaming in and pinching the ball from the number eight with his bulbous left boot. Then he rounded the number four, only the ball ran away a bit further than he would have liked, and the bulky centre-half was on the scene.

It was a ball Rippa could win, that Rippa normally would win, but it was on his left side. It was probably a 65/35 in his favour though not what he and Jane had agreed. Then Rippa thought of his Nan and his uncle and the whole of Middleby and that ticking clock hanging above him.

And he went all in for it — crunch.

And, oh, did it hurt as a pain 10-times worse than the pain at the end of the first half surged right up through his leg, and shot up his spine and into his brain and on and on and growing and growing and not stopping. Only this time he didn't fall into unconsciousness and miraculously he was still standing, still moving, still stumbling. And still he had the ball.

He was on the edge of the box and saw that the ref had the whistle at his lips primed to blow for full-time. Rippa looked to the goal and saw a gap at the bottom right corner which the keeper hadn't covered. If his left-foot was working, it would be a sure goal. But as it was, he couldn't knock it more than two yards never mind stand on it. His teammates were all marked or behind him. He heard the stamping of opposition feet coming faster. He had just enough time to stab it with his right foot.

He arched back his boot and closed his eyes tight and tried to shut out the bad memories of that afternoon practising with Jane in goals. Instead, he remembered the tens of thousands of reps he'd done against that mattress with the ball in that loft morning, noon and night, albeit with mixed results. And he visualised that his right was in fact his left foot which they all raved about, and he swung with everything he had. The ball spun off his laces. It didn't run true. He didn't get the height, never mind the direction, which he craved. He did get the power though, and it looked like the ball was about to go out for a throw in and through the gap in the wall and take out another passerby.

But luckily at the last moment it struck the left full-back's knee and spun up. Rippa kept running on and the keeper ran out. But Rippa was quicker. Still, there was no time to let it fall to his feet, be it left or right. Instead, he closed his eyes and leapt for it. He got there first and struck the ball cleanly with his forehead. But not before the keeper struck him in the chest with his full weight. Rippa's body collapsed. Just before he hit the turf, he managed to arch his neck up and watch the ball loop up and up and over the keeper this time trickling slowly, slowly into the net.

If Rippa's foot hurt before, now he was in tears as all nine outfield players, even the keeper, along with Rory and Millsy from the bench, swamped him.

Middleby had scored and Middleby were back in the football league.

When the mayhem settled, Rippa crawled back to his half. Barnet kicked off and the ref blew immediately. Rippa collapsed again as memories of Cal filtered back and the harsh realisation he wasn't around anymore for

Rippa to tell him about it. And he also felt a volley sadness about Sabrina and how she broke his heart and how Merri Bay was no longer home.

But the tears were mostly about his shattered foot and the fears that he might never walk again, never mind kick a ball. Still, he had no chance to dwell upon this as the fans swarmed the pitch, the green patchy surface now a sea of grey and white as they celebrated promotion. Rippa was hoisted up onto the shoulders of a stout and overexcited fan. He looked out to the crowd and saw Uncle Warren with his new grey Lacoste shirt off, twirling it in the air like he'd been a Middleby fan all his life, as he sang along to Chas & Dave's 'Mustn't Grumble' playing over the Tannoy. A larger, sweatier businessman with a wilting quiff was sitting in the stands with his laptop on and a rum and cola by his side. He made a hand motion for Rippa to call him. And through his exhaustion Rippa saw a woman a few rows along, in her 40s with luminescent grey eyes and shaggy long blond hair not unlike himself. She was smiling proudly and waving. Rippa waved back and was about to move closer when Dwayne reached up and grabbed his arm. This time he shook it with such force that it was nearly going the same way as his foot.

'I'll never forgive what you thieving convict bastards did to my nation. But you're okay with me, Rippa. Not great, not good, but you're okay.'

When Rippa looked back up to the stand where the woman had been, there was no one there.

Chapter 40

The captain shook and then popped the cork of the bottle but there was no foam. Instead, he found himself shooting a sticky drab yellow substance around at his fellow players.

'What's this, Mr Cole?' Millsy asked. 'This is flatter than my first girlfriend's funbags.'

'Apple juice, my dear boy,' Chapman Cole said, lighting another Cuban. Despite the sweaty chaos of the dressing room, he somehow still looked pristine in his top hat and suit.

'Where's the fucking champers?' added Curtly. 'I didn't pack up my home in Peterborough and take the kids out of school and the wife away from her sisters for fucking apple juice. We're back in the Football League.'

'Well I didn't know you were going to do that, now did I? I got this for a bargain. 12 bottles for a tenner in Tesco.'

'But we're the next best thing to champions,' said Millsy. 'I wanted to do a Nigel Mansell and spray it everywhere.'

'Yes, though for eight-and-a-half months you were absolute diddies.'

Rippa clutched a bottle and took a thirsty glug. His body was starting to unwind, and some feeling had come back into his foot as the swelling subsided.

'Fuck this for a game of soldiers,' said Millsy. 'Get scrubbed, get clean and then let's get to The Orient and paint the town grey and white. And Mr Chairman is covering the tab.'

'Like hell I am. I'm not made of money.'

'Yes you are. Compared to everyone else in the town you certainly are. So yes — you fucking will. Or I'm going out there and telling all those cameras that I've been injecting steroids into my arse all season.'

'Have you really?'

'No, of course not. I've been injecting them into my tadger.'

'You'd want a bigger one than that for your bother,' Jane quipped and the whole team creased up.

'I don't know what you're laughing at,' Millsy told Rippa. 'At least my one's not dead centre of my head. Or up Rory's backside.'

'Leave me well out of this,' Rory replied, sticking his neck back in as he spoke to reporters.

'Let's fucking get out of here for some real bubbles,' Millsy ordered them all. 'You too, Rippa.'

Rippa looked to Jane as she finished taping up the youth striker's finger from when he was leapt on by an over-zealous fan at full-time and broke a nail. 'Nah, mate, got somewhere to be.'

'The bingo?' taunted the captain. 'You're gonna blow off the lads and say no to one of the biggest Saturday night's the town's seen since 1966 for the fucking bingo?'

'How'd you know?' Rippa asked.

'It's a small town. Everyone knows everyone's business.'

'You should come along.'

'Fuck off. You Aussies are one dull bunch.'

'You go,' Jane told him quietly. 'It's a special night. Maybe once in a lifetime. Bingo will always be there.'

'No, it won't.'

And just as he said that Rory swung his head back in. 'Rippa. Popular boy today, you are. There's someone up in the stand waiting to talk to you.'

Rippa wondered why his uncle was in such a rush to chat and why he wasn't coming down to see him like he did at half-time. With the weather now warmer, he threw on his t-shirt and thongs and limped out down the tunnel and up the steps of the stand. He dodged the empty drink cartons and chip wrappers and saw that it wasn't his uncle after all.

It was Ron Burke, manager of West Ham.

'Good game out there, son,' His gold tooth was shining as he smiled, something that, judging by their last meeting, Rippa wasn't sure he ever did.

'You came to watch me?'

'Course I did.' He placed an over-familiar arm around Rippa. 'We're not playing until tomorrow away at Boro, so I thought I'd do a bit of a scouting mission. Not that I'm scouting you. You are our player after all.'

'I am?'

Rippa heard '*championees*' ring out from the bowels of the stadium beneath their feet and felt the foundations vibrate. He looked across and saw the Middleby fans who were still here join in, scarves aloft, refusing to leave. He saw his uncle was now among them.

'Course you are, sunshine. Special day this is for you and you're gonna have a lot more of them in the famous claret and blue, let me tell you.'

'I'm not so sure of that. You cut my wages.'

'We'll have to field you in a few reserve matches first …'

'You left me up here to starve. Literally.'

'… Just to ease back into life at a big club …'

'The digs were unspeakable. The food, the landlords, all of it.'

' … And then we'll have you raring to go.'

'You haven't called me once to check that I wasn't floating in Clapper Lake.'

'Son, son, son.' Burke brought him in closer. 'I hear everything you're saying and more. But read your contract. It was all above board. It was all to build character. Which as I saw out there, you have done so in spades. So pack your bags and I'll see you in the car park.'

'What about my summer holidays?'

'You've been on holiday up here. You'll be working through them to make sure you're ready for August.'

'Is that even legal?'

'Joseph, my boy. What do you want, a kiss and a cuddle? This is football. British football. It's grim at the best of times and absolute hell at the worst. And you are one of the very lucky few who have chosen to be part of it.'

'You reneged on my Newquay agreement.'

'Too fucking right I did.' Burke's smile died. 'Like I said, Noll must have had far too many Foster's in the sun to agree to that bollocks. Imagine the other lads if they knew you had a day off each week to visit the seaside?'

'Doesn't matter. It was a deal.'

'It does matter. This isn't some fantasy Ramsay Street shit. Welcome to the real world.'

'It's not fair.'

'Life ain't fair, and this game sure as shit ain't. Now I didn't drive five hours to Chernobyl to hear this bleeding heart bollocks. So grab whatever crap you need out of this steaming dive and meet me out front. I'm giving you a lift.'

Chapter 41

'Still here?' Rory asked as the winger returned to the dressing room. The room showed all the tell-tale signs that it had just hosted a group of lads who had done their job and done it well and who'd celebrated in style. Aside from the usual mud, tape and dirty kit strewn around the concrete flooring, there was sticky apple juice sprayed across the tiles, shaving foam smeared on the mirrors, an inch of water from the overflowing bath, and the radiant stench of Old Spice. All topped off by the anticipation of a great night or three ahead.

'I was about to say the same to you.' Rippa replied as Rory was always the first to get away from the ground once he'd done a brief post-match talk to the players and said a few words to reporters.

'Hmm, created a bit of a media frenzy as I think they call it down in the metropolis,' Rory said.

'How come?'

'I went and quit.'

'No way.'

'No way, indeed. Because I immediately rescinded it.'

'Wait. Why did you quit? You just won promotion. You *are* Middleby.'

'And that's just it. Isn't there more to life than here?'

'There most certainly is. What was your plan?'

'To walk the earth.'

'And what exactly does that entail?'

Rory scratched his stubble and stared off into the distance. 'If I'm honest, that's where the plan fell apart. I was just going to get up and go on foot. Walk across to France.'

'Think you might need a boat for that.'

'And then hit the mainland and go where the road takes me. Wander to where all the great thinkers lived and worked and see where I ended up.'

'I see. Kinda.'

'I told the wife out of the blue just then and she quite rightly reminded me that the kids are in school, that we have a 30-year mortgage, and that her sister's coming down from Morecambe for Sunday lunch. Then I told the chairman and he told me I had a contract and he'd take my house along with my car if I pulled a stunt like that.'

'That's a shame. What about a holiday instead?'

'That's what the wife said. So we booked two nights in Bournemouth.'

'Nice.'

'There'll be a time and a place for me to go and seek my destiny. My work is here for now. I've got Division Four football to look forward to. And a revolutionary new plan which will put us firmly on the front-foot.'

'Which is?'

'Putting the phrenology aside for a little while and training with the ball. Not all the time, mind you. Must keep some element of novelty and hunger within the ranks. But that is really some concept, Rippa. How you came up with that I'll never know.'

'Nor will I.'

'Anyway, you don't look like a fella who scored two goals and won the town promotion.'

'I know. Ron Burke is waiting outside.'

'Who?'

'The manager of West Ham.'

'Was he just? That's great, isn't it?'

'He wants me back at Upton Park.'

'That *is* great.' Rory offered a small round of applause. 'Sad for us, of course. You're really settling in here nicely. But you're too good for Middleby, so it's good news for you.'

'I don't want to go there. They treated me like trash and they'll do it again.'

'But it's football with one of the main boys.'

'There are other boys. Boys that aren't in London and are nearer the coast. If I have to go with those boys, I'd rather quit and go home.'

'And did you tell him this?'

'More or less.'

'What did he say?'

'He says I've no choice.'

Rory rubbed at this chin again, like the philosopher he wanted to be, as he eyed a toilet roll dangling precariously from the lighting. 'There's always a choice.'

'He says it's in my contract in black and white with no shades of grey.'

'What if I told you there was a splash of grey in between?'

'How'd you mean?'

'What if I told you there was a way around it?'

'I don't think there is?'

'Like Churchill showed us back in '42. There always is.'

'There is?'

'We'll buy you.'

'Buy me?'

'There's an option in our agreement with The Hammers to purchase you at the end of your loan deal for a hundred grand.'

Rippa waved the idea away. 'Chapman Cole wouldn't sanction a new tin of boot polish, never mind a hundred K.'

'He would, y'know.'

'He would?'

'He would if he knew he could double his money the very next day.'

Chapter 42

JOEY RIPS UP WEST HAM DEAL AND HEADS TO PLYMOUTH
IN WHIRLWIND £200K MOVE

By George Kostas

Soccer Week

May 10, 1989

Joey Rippa topped off a frantic weekend — which started by scoring the two goals that took Middleby United back into the football league and lifting the GM Vauxhall Conference Player of the Month award — by signing for the club and then immediately departing for Plymouth Argyle.

Middleby exercised their option to pick up the winger after his impressive form in the run-in, much to the frustration of his parent club West Ham United who offered a new deal and double his money to stay.

But with the ink barely dry on the Middleby deal, second-tier Plymouth, who last week announced the appointment of ex-West Ham manager Bobby Noll as their new boss, swooped in and doubled Middleby's record transfer fee to make Rippa their first buy of the summer.

Rippa spoke of his delight after agreeing a three-year deal with the Devonshire side.

'I was about to give the game away in all honesty. But finally getting the chance to work with Mr Noll and relocating nearer the coast has got me raring to go.'

As part of the deal surf-mad Rippa will be allowed to reside in Newquay, 40 miles away from Plymouth, and make the most of Britain's premiere surfing destination while commuting to the Pilgrims' home ground for training and matches.

'Listen,' Rippa continued. 'I like my football. I really do. But surfing is

everything to me and being near the ocean will make me happier in the long-term and really improve my game.'

New Plymouth boss Noll famously discovered Rippa while West Ham toured Australia back in January and signed him on the spot only to be sacked a week later, with pundits believing the shock signing led to his removal. But the new manager had no hesitation about moving for the player again, despite the weighty transfer fee.

Noll said: 'I think a few fans and pundits were scratching their loaves of bread and thinking, what has Bobby Noll done here nabbing this long-haired surfer kid who looks a lot like Kim Wilde and believing I'd had far too many XXXX's Down Under. Which I have to admit had a hint of truth in it. But I'll tell you what, anyone who's watched this Rippa lad in the last few games of the season ain't laughing now. The Hammers were desperate to keep in the end. I even had to chase off a few Kray associates who were found mucking about underneath my car. But they all ain't saying I should be sectioned now, are they? I had a night on the turps with George Graham and even he was having a sniff around the kid. And let's not forget Rippa's had a broken foot too. Imagine him when that heals and he can hunt crabs or build sandcastles or whatever it is he wants to do by the seaside.'

Middleby were delighted with the piece of business with chairman Chapman Cole promising his players real champagne the next time they achieve something, before cryptically adding that the unexpected windfall meant that competitors in the 1990 Great Model Railways Challenge had better watch out.

'I've had my eye on a vintage Flying Scotsman,' he cryptically claimed.

And this has got tongues wagging that he may be about to attempt an audacious move to lure Gordon Strachan from Leeds United.

West Ham's management declined to comment on the deal. It is understood that their plans to tour Australia have now been shelved and a pre-season trip to the Shetland Islands has been booked instead.

Chapter 43

Rippa rode to Jane's house on his brand-new Vespa. It was deep green and white — the colours of Plymouth Argyle. The sun was now high and shining bright, the orchards and irises in full bloom, and it looked like the man upstairs had flicked on a switch as all the gloom had been scrubbed away from Middleby and the place was awash with colour and the anticipation of the summer to come.

Jane heard the soft hum of the new engine and came outside. She was dressed in a Kate Bush t-shirt and a pair of shorts, her cheeks flushed with warmth. The pair hugged before she admired Rippa's new wheels.

'So this is what two signing-on fees in 24 hours gets you?'

'Apparently so,' said Rippa, who's blonde locks were slowly growing back.

'Thought you were heading back to Oz for a break?'

'So did I. I thought hard about it. Sent some cash my dad's way instead. The bar's saved. But I'm thinking maybe there isn't a whole lot there for me anymore.'

'And in Newquay there is?'

'There might be, but first I'm taking my backpack and this baby across the channel,' Rippa pointed to the Vespa. 'Want to see the waves in Spain, Portugal, maybe even Italy and Greece too depending on time.'

She looked down to Rippa's moon boot. 'And what about the foot?'

'It's on the mend. The doc says I can swim but no surfing this summer. This time I'm listening.'

'Damn, boy. Was all that pain worth it?'

Rippa smiled. 'You know what, I reckon it was. Though only just.'

Jane smiled back. 'Looks like it all worked out. I'm happy for you, Joey.

You really deserve it.'

'I couldn't have done it without you.'

'Don't kid yourself. Will you miss Middleby?'

'Like a hole in the head. But I know I'll miss you.' He noticed Nan peel back the net curtains. He waved at her warmly. She didn't wave back, looking at him plainly.

'She's not great today,' said Jane.

'I'm sorry to hear that. I couldn't have done it without her either.'

The pair's eyes met, and for the first time they were short of words.

Rippa broke the silence. 'Come with me.'

'I can't,' Jane said.

'I know you can't. Not for good. But the club shuts up shop for the break. You have a month of holidays.'

'You know I can't.'

'Yeah, I know you still can't. Not right this minute. But listen, there's a folk festival coming in Holland. And you're playing.'

'You what?'

'I sent them the demos you did.'

Jane really reddened. 'You should have told me.'

'If I did you wouldn't have let me. They like your stuff a lot. You're flying there. Your Nan too. They're paying. I'll meet you there. I'll take care of her. You just play.'

He handed her a flyer for the weekend fest in Amsterdam. The Pogues and Little River Band were headlining. And Jane's name was near the bottom of the bill among 30 or so other acts.

But she was there alright, in bold.

She clutched her mouth to hold in her gasp and the conflicting emotions. 'You did all this?'

'Say you'll see me there.'

'I don't know if my Nan can.'

'Then I'll get someone, someone good to fill in just for a night or two.'

'I don't know.'

'Please. It's my way of saying thanks.'

'Okay, then. I'll think about it. Thank you, Joey.'

'And say you'll visit me in Newquay.'

'That I will do.'

She hugged him close.

He pulled back and looked at her closer, mere inches from her face. 'And please say you'll give me and you a go.'

He lunged in, lips first. She lurched her head back quicker.

'That is something I can't do.'

'Ah, damn,' Rippa's heart broke again, and he turned away. 'I'm … sorry.'

'Did you not know?'

'Know what?'

'I'm not into you.'

'Oh.'

'I mean, it's not you. You're the best. But boys, full stop. I'm just not. At all. I've tried. Lasses are more my thing. Not that I see much action around here, but in Manchester it's off the chart. You have no idea.'

'No, but I'm getting a pretty good idea.' Rippa tried to smile. 'I'm happy for you. I mean that.'

'And one day when I break out of here … well, you get the picture.'

'It's great. Really.'

She thought for a moment. 'Geez, Joey, did you not know? I thought it was pretty obvious. Clothes, short hair, single earring. Don't you Aussie surfer dudes know much about girls?'

Rippa took it all in and it started to make sense. 'I'm thinking we really don't.'

'But I do like you, Joey. I really like you. Is the fest still on for us now you know I'm not gonna bone you?'

'Certainly not.'

'What?'

He laughed. 'Course it is.'

'And can I still visit you in Cornwall?'

'Heck, if you and your nan want to come down and make my place your own then please do.'

'I'm not sure the bingo scene could handle us.'

'We could find out.'

'See you in The Dam first, Joey.'

They hugged again, this time firmly as friends. He gave another wave to Nan and hopped on the Vespa and was out of there. He was keen to squeeze out every bit of summer until the English winter predictably and all-too-quickly rolled back in. But in a weird way, Rippa was no longer dreading it.

As he roared out of Middleby, backpack on, plastic ball poking from its top, he passed Dwayne scrubbing his Cortina with a bucket and a soapy sponge. Rippa tooted and waved but all he got was a mopey V-sign in return. Further along the street Albert and Morag were struggling up the road with shopping bags in a trolley. They saw him. Morag winked and blew him a kiss while Albert clenched his fists in fury. Rippa sped on and spotted Rory getting in his Volvo, a woman around his age in the passenger seat in sunglasses, and two screaming kids and a bloodhound were in the back. And Rippa saw Rory was happy. He gave a bigger toot and a wave as he followed the exit and left Middleby for dust.

THE END

ABOUT THE AUTHOR

P.J. Laverty is a Scottish-Australian writer specialising in historical football fiction (with a comedic spin) with a PhD in Creative Writing from Curtin University.

Under the moniker Paul J Laverty, he is the host of 94.9 Main FM literary book show, *The Quiet Carriage*, which also airs nationally on the Community Radio Network. He has written two novellas, *Man Overbored* and *Cider Country* (RoadHouse Media). He also wrote the first biography on Grammy award winners Arcade Fire and another on Beck (Artnik / Schwarzkopf & Schwarzkopf Verlag).

He is a football tragic who will never tire of telling anyone within earshot all about his adventures in Germany during World Cup 2006. He lives in Castlemaine, Victoria, with his wife and two children.

MORE REALLY GOOD FICTION FROM POPCORN PRESS

High Heels
and Low Blows

The End
of the Game

Anna Black – this
girl can play

Jarrod Black
Chasing Pack

Game

The Yawning Giant